P9-CLS-988

IT'S A WHOLE SPIEL

LOVE, LATKES, AND OTHER JEWISH STORIES

KATHERINE LOCKE

&

LAURA SILVERMAN

THIS IS A BORZOI BOOK PUBLISHED BY ALFRED A. KNOPF

Visit us on the Web! GetUnderlined.com

Educators and librarians, for a variety of teaching tools, visit us at RHTeachersLibrarians.com

Library of Congress Cataloging-in-Publication Data is available upon request.

ISBN 978-0-525-64616-7 (trade) — ISBN 978-0-525-64617-4 (lib. bdg.) — ISBN 978-0-525-64618-1 (ebook)

Printed in the United States of America
September 2019
10 9 8 7 6 5 4 3 2 1

First Edition

CONTENTS

FOREWORD

BY MAYIM BIALIK

Being Jewish and young in the twenty-first century is a spectacular thing. Jews have become a part of the cultural vernacular since I was a young woman in ways I never would have dreamed of. Judaism is more widely discussed and more prominent in the arts, media, and politics. Jewish-themed TV shows and films have witnessed an explosion. International attention is being given to aspects of Jewish life previously unexplored. Gal Gadot is everyone's sweetheart. *Fauda* and *The Band's Visit* have captivated a global media market. This is a new Golden Age.

But being Jewish and young at this time is not without complexity and tension. An emphasis on distancing oneself from traditional Judaism in many circles and even on detaching from the politics of our historical homeland has made for a potentially fractured sense of community among young people. Racism still rears its ugly head. Bigotry abounds. And in a country deeply divided by politics, Jewish identity is up for grabs.

The collection of stories you hold in your hands is an antidote to this divisiveness. A girl wrestles with being *Jewish enough* when she joins her more observant boyfriend's family for Shabbat dinner. At space camp, two boys search for God among the stars. An Orthodox girl navigates unfamiliar territory at college orientation. These varied stories of faith and love and youth are a solution to a problem we may not yet fully understand. The notion that young Jews feel a need to attach to a Judaism that is fractured is important. The feelings many young Jews may be having about where they fit in are real. Jews of all backgrounds need to find a common ground where we all can stand together. This anthology is that common ground.

Judaism is not about choosing things you always agree with in your religion and clinging to them. Judaism is about seeing the world for what it is and being part of a community that is greater than the sum of its parts. The beauty of the Jewish experience is in its ability to adapt, and its enduring principles of faith, understanding, and acceptance.

There are so many ways to live a Jewish life and to feel Jewish. Growing up Jewish was, for me, a wonderful thing. I loved my cultural identity, I embraced the structures of Jewish learning, and I resonated deeply with the connection I felt to Israel and to my fellow Jews. I was raised in a climate aware of the uniqueness of Jews and simultaneously supportive of Jews fitting into the world in ways that allowed us the freedoms many of our parents and grandparents did not have the privilege of enjoying.

This book speaks to a larger vision of a Judaism that is engaging, open, and wise. Young people, especially, should take note of their awareness shifting as they explore the stories here.

There is no "right" way to live, think, or be. What unites us all is our desire to fit in, to stand out, and to lean in to what has sustained the Jewish people for thousands of years.

Read on and find your place among those of us who are proudly and undeniably lost as wanderers of a nation that was once a stranger—and simultaneously find your place among those of us who have put in the hard work and discovered new ways to be found.

INDOOR KIDS

BY ALEX LONDON

It happened somewhere over Canada, although it had probably been happening since Australia. No one even knew anything had gone wrong until the International Space Station was over the Atlantic, a tiny dot of light heading toward the west coast of Africa, not a single earthly eye on it, and we only found out at camp because Jackson Kimmel had an aunt who worked at NASA.

She was not an astronaut.

She was in human resources, so she didn't actually do anything with the space program, but she texted her nephew, because space was his "thing," and her nephew told me, because he knew space was also my "thing," and that's how summer camp works: find someone whose thing is your thing and geek out together.

It would've been nice if I'd had someone to geek out with who wasn't a ten-year-old.

"They think it was an impact with space junk," Jackson said, waving his arms around while he circled me. He was one of those kids in constant, exhausting motion. "Did you know that NASA tracks over *half a million* pieces of space debris that orbit the earth? It travels at seventeen thousand five hundred miles per hour, so, like, that could cut through a space station. Usually they have all kinds of warnings and ways to maneuver around space junk. They call it the 'pizza box' because it's an imaginary box that's a mile deep and thirty miles wide around the vehicle, and if anything looks like it's gonna get too close to the 'box,' they take steps to keep the astronauts and the equipment safe, but not all the debris is tracked, so maybe they missed something? My aunt doesn't know; she just does paperwork for people's travel to conferences. She got to meet Leland Melvin once. Do you know who he is? He's spent over five hundred sixty-five hours in space during his career, but you probably know him as the astronaut who took his official NASA portrait with his dogs? You ever see it? The dogs' names are Jack and Scout. Or Jake? I can't remember. Do you have a dog? I named my dog Elon, after Elon Musk, but now I think that—"

"Okay, Jackson." I interrupted his monologue. He had actually made air quotes with his fingers around the words "pizza box." What ten-year-old makes air quotes? "Take a breath and change for basketball."

His smile vanished, his face a crash landing, no survivors.

"Do I *haaaave* to?" he whined. I wanted to tell him, *No, of course not! Who sends their ten-year-old space nerd to a sports camp when there is an actual place called Space Camp! Your parents should be punished for this!* But sports were required at Camp Winatoo, and Jackson had to go play basketball before he could come back for afternoon science club in Craft Cabin.

It was my unfortunate duty to make him go play basketball, just as it had been some other seventeen-year-old counselor-in-training's job to force *me* to go play basketball when I was a ten-year-old space nerd here. That's the curse of the indoor kids. People are always trying to make us go outside and play. The bastards.

Now I was one of them.

"Yes, you have to," I told him.

I would have much rather spent the morning talking about the merits of the Falcon 9 rocket in commercial applications, but that wasn't an option, not if I wanted to keep my job. The silver lining of this job was that I, personally, did not have to go to basketball. I had the entire early afternoon to do what I pleased. I was extremely lucky today, because I didn't even have to supervise the aftermath of basketball, which was one of the worst jobs you could have. Those kids smelled *ripe*. Old enough for BO, not quite old enough to have figured out deodorant. And the ones that *had* figured it out? Axe Body Spray might be the worst thing to have happened in the history of mankind. It's chemical warfare marketed to tweens.

After Jackson skulked off in his too-big basketball jersey, I pulled out my phone, trying to see if there was any news about the space station. Nothing had hit the mainstream media yet, but @GeekHeadNebula on Twitter had posted about a possible catastrophic hull breach impacting all ISS life-support systems.

That seemed a bit dramatic, in the way of breaking news, and I knew the reality would end up more mundane. Not that the mundane couldn't be deadly in the void of space. It was usually the mundane that turned deadly up there.

Kind of like my life on Earth.

The Deadly Mundane could've been the title of my autobiography. Nothing dramatic ever happened to me. I was a junior counselor at the same summer camp I'd gone to as a kid, where I'd known most of the other junior counselors since forever. Back home, I lived in the suburbs and went to the kind of school where teenagers on the Disney Channel would go: everything was well lit and oversaturated, every adult was caring and concerned and a bit clueless, and every family was more affluent than the national average, but not so affluent that we'd be the bad guys in a dystopian novel.

I'd had my bar mitzvah and come out of the closet the same year, and both went . . . fine. I almost cried when my voice cracked during the haftorah recitation, and I also almost cried when my dad told me he was proud I was "living my truth." The bar mitzvah involved me getting envelopes with eighteen-dollar checks in them, and coming out involved my mom putting a pride flag on our car. Neither was earth-shattering.

The bar mitzvah money went into a savings account I couldn't touch, and just because I was out and "living my truth" didn't mean I could get a date. Four years later and I'd never had a boyfriend, and not because I was the only gay kid. That would've at least been a good reason, but there were, like, five other cis gay boys in my class by the time we got to junior year, and a trans gay boy, and three other genderqueer kids, all of whom might've been dating material, except not a single one of them had any interest in a science geek with acne, no muscle tone, no taste in music, and more than one T-shirt with Carl Sagan on it. None of them were mean about not dating me—my life wasn't even that dramatic. They just didn't express any interest. So I mostly hung out in my room, read, and fantasized about being trapped in a Mars simulator for six months with Troye Sivan.

In his Instastory, Troye teased a new video while standing shirtless in the rain—seriously, I didn't think Jewish boys could look like *that*—and NASA had an update in their Insta with a video of Japanese flight engineer Isao Tatsuta and American flight commander Anne Frisch explaining that they had sealed off damaged sections of the structure and were working with their international partners to prepare for a space walk to assess the best course of action. They reassured everyone watching that they had protocols in place. Commander Frisch ended the story with a view down at Earth through the window and then back up to herself giving a thumbs-up.

When, in the history of thumbs, was that ever a comforting gesture?

I put my phone away and thought about hitting the showers while I might manage some actual privacy. Being at summer camp was a lot like being on the International Space Station: privacy was nearly impossible to find, and sometimes it meant putting on a space suit and walking into the void.

In this case, "the void" was the boys' showers, and the danger was more about what you took off than what you put on. My younger years at camp had been spent largely in dread of the showers, less for fear of a wet towel whipping across my butt than for fear of being noticed by anyone or being caught noticing anyone.

My fellow campers and I had matured since middle school; the shower stalls themselves had gained privacy curtains, and my showering was no longer ruled by terror and shame, but I still wasn't going to miss an opportunity for quiet and privacy.

"You ever think about the golem?"

Apparently, I wasn't the only one who'd been seduced by the idea of having the showers to myself.

Levi Klein-Behar was standing at the wide mirror in the changing area, wrapped in a towel and studying a bunch of symbols he'd written in the mirror mist. I recognized the symbols as Hebrew, but that's as far as my Jewish knowledge went. After my bar mitzvah, my parents didn't make me go to Hebrew school anymore, and I'd worked pretty hard to forget everything I'd learned.

"Uh" was the brilliant reply I mustered, as befuddled by the question as by his lean back and broad shoulders and the way that towel hung off his hips as if balanced on a breath. He was not one of the Winatoo Lifers and had only started this summer . . . which wasn't to say I didn't know anything about him.

I knew he was from Philadelphia by way of Havana, Kampala, Buenos Aires, and Yangon. I knew that he was the son of a pair of traveling rabbis who supported Jewish communities in far-flung corners of the Diaspora; that he wore clicking Buddhist prayer beads around his wrist, which definitely deserved the eye rolls they got; but also that he didn't care about the eye rolls. He was one of the few kids at camp who wore a yarmulke; his was a small black knit one with a rainbow border he said he got from an LGBTQ synagogue in New York. He was also an "indoor kid," but not like me. He too did his best to avoid sports, even though he looked like the kind of guy who would be good at them, but he worked with the artsy kids, doing drama and painting and music. He was especially good at music and could play at least three instruments.

Why did I know so much about Levi Klein-Behar? Did I mention the towel hanging off his hips? My romantic life might've been as empty as the vacuum of space, but you didn't have to be an astronomer to admire Orion's Belt.

"Like, really think about it?" Levi turned around to look at me, leaning back on the sink in a pose that could only be described as insouciant, forcing me to fix my face into an expression that could only be described as awkward.

I mean, I didn't know rabbis' sons could look like *that*.

He didn't seem to notice my total lack of chill, because he just kept going. "Like, why hasn't there been a superhero movie about the golem? Ferocious and holy, inhuman but lonely, called forth to protect the innocent?" He folded his arms across his chest, and my throat went dry. Also, I thought he'd been talking about Gollum from *Lord of the Rings*. That was not who he meant. I just nodded. This was the most we'd talked in three weeks. "He's brought to life in times of need, activated by a word pressed into his forehead. Emet." He pointed at the word behind him. I nodded like I knew that's what it said. "I mean, how cool is that mythology? Someone at this camp has got to be related to a producer, right?"

"We *do* control the media," I told him. "Or the banks? Or we're all communists. I can never remember."

He smiled and shook his head, and his braces caught the fluorescent light, and I wondered what it must be like to be a seventeen-year-old with braces and what it would feel like to kiss someone with braces.

"The golem is, like, a guaranteed hit! The Jews need our own Black Panther!"

"I think we've got Superman."

"But imagine if it wasn't some metaphor, but, like, an actual Jewish myth kicking ass on screen. It's specific, but universal, right? Did you know that *Fiddler on the Roof* was one of the biggest *international* hit musicals ever made? They were worried it was 'too Jewish,' and it ended up being huge in India, and it is Jewish AF. We need the twenty-first century's version, which would absolutely be a superhero franchise and— Sorry." Levi stopped himself. His cheeks had flushed. The Hebrew words behind him on the mirror misted over. "I have this, like, mission to make Jewish stuff mainstream. Why do you keep looking at your phone?"

I hadn't noticed that I was, but I was. It was something I did when I got nervous, which I also was. Easier to look down than up sometimes, especially when up meant Levi's dark brown eyes with their Venus-flytrap lashes.

"Oh, well . . . I was just . . . uh . . . checking on the space station." I glanced down and saw the updates. Space walk aborted. Egress not optimal. Possible ammonia leak. People were talking about the *Challenger* explosion and the *Columbia* explosion and the Apollo 1 fire. Warning of the worst space disaster in decades. Official statement from mission control to come.

"What's going on with it?"

"Just, um, like . . ." I didn't want to geek out too much. "Kind of a crisis? They got hit by space debris? It's pretty serious? Four different countries have astronauts up there?" Why *was* everything coming out of my mouth like a question?

"Damn," Levi said. "It's like our own Tower of Babel. They keep falling, and we keep building them."

"Huh?"

"Nothing." He fidgeted with his prayer beads. "I don't mean to be all theological; I just get like that sometimes. I'll let you take your shower."

Now I had a problem. How could I take my shower with Levi, of all people, right there?

When astronauts are faced with a tough situation, they "work the problem" with a decision tree, spelling out each choice in a given scenario and its probable consequences. Right now, on the International Space Station, the multinational crew was likely working through their decision tree, solving one problem at a time until the crisis was over or until they ran out of oxygen.

I found the certainty of decision trees comforting. One formed in my head almost instantly.

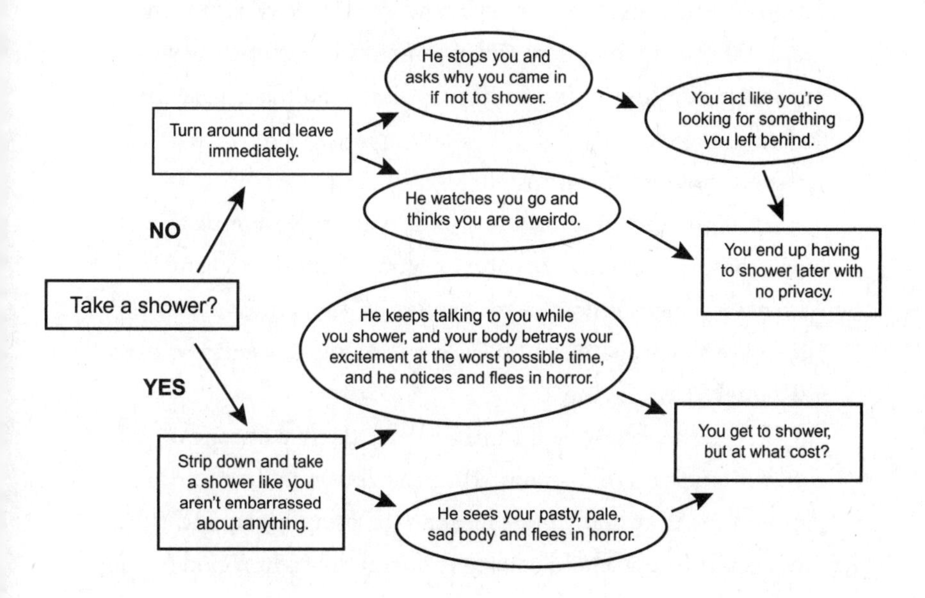

No good outcomes, but waiting to wash was definitely the wiser choice.

"Oh man." I furrowed my brow at my phone. "I forgot I have to get ready for D block science club. No shower for me!"

I was a terrible actor, but it didn't matter. He'd already turned around to change into his shorts, and I risked one nervous glance as his towel dropped, and I stepped out in the sunlight, sweating more than when I'd gone in.

* * *

"Catastrophic failure!" Jackson wailed, or something like that, through his snotty tears. I handed him a Kleenex, told him we didn't know what was happening and we shouldn't assume the worst. Although assuming the worst was kind of a Jewish tradition. Assuming the worst was how we'd survived for millennia. I didn't actually know why we shouldn't assume the worst, but it felt like something someone wiser would say to a child, so I said it.

It did not comfort him.

"If their life-support system is suffering complete collapse, how is that *not* a catastrophic failure?" He sniffled. "They've sealed almost every section of the station! Can you check the news again? Is SpaceX preparing a rescue? What's @RogueNASA saying?"

"I just checked," I told him. "Why don't we work on our rubber-band sonar?" I pointed at the cool science project I'd planned for that hour, but Jackson had no interest, and three other science kids who'd chosen to spend their afternoon inside with me had more interest in Jackson's meltdown than my perfectly planned project.

"What if it crashes? What if radioactive compounds explode in the atmosphere?" Jackson's voice was like a siren, and his tears started the other kids crying, and I wanted to shake the kid and yell at him to get it together. I was the closest thing to an adult in the room, and I needed to either calm him down or get one of the actual adult counselors to help.

"Do you want to call your moms?" I asked him.

"They're lawyers! How can they help?" he yelled in my face, then collapsed back in his chair, weeping.

"Uh . . ." I needed to think of something. I hated the uncertainty as much as he did. I pictured Commander Frisch from her Instastory, betraying no worry. What did her face look like now, trapped in a tiny part of the International Space Station with her crew, knowing that millions of people were looking up from the planet below, counting down the minutes until the ISS became her tomb and one of the greatest feats of human engineering, scientific endeavor, and international cooperation died with her. It wasn't the Tower of Babel; it was a statistically improbable catastrophe that was, nevertheless, not impossible. A problem of physics, not God. Why would Levi have even brought some Torah story into it? And why was I thinking about him right now?

"They're working the problem like they've been trained," I told Jackson. "If there's a solution, they'll find it."

He looked up at me with big, wet eyes and offered this nugget of tween nihilism: "The astronauts are all going to die!"

"Uh . . . ," I said again. I was really not great at this, but what did I know about counseling a ten-year-old through the possible death of his heroes?

"Isn't it great?" A too-cheery voice cut through the room, surprising Jackson out of his meltdown. All our heads snapped to the doorway, where Levi Klein-Behar stood in sunlit silhouette, a six-foot shadow bursting into full color as he charged into the room. His metal smile beamed at us. "*Everyone* is going to die! You! Me! Our parents! The astronauts!"

"Levi?" I wanted to stop him from making this situation worse. Also, to ask him what he was doing in the Craft Cabin.

"Death is one thing that everyone on Earth has in common," he said. "It is nothing to be afraid of. It happens to every single person in the world, and no one's ever come back to complain about it, right? We *all* do it sometime, and how lucky would these astronauts be if they got to die doing what they loved? If it was *my* time, I'd want to die while dancing naked in the desert!" The kids giggled nervously, their eyes puffy, but they were curious about this sudden change in the mood of the room. I still gaped at him. He turned to me and winked. "How 'bout you, Josh? How would you want to die?"

"I . . . um . . ." They all looked at me, expectant. Jackson's lip was still quivering, but he was breathing normally again, sniffling and waiting for my answer. Levi wore a smirk now, and I had to meet it. I forced a smile and drenched my voice in cheer, trying to think of something kids liked. "I guess I'd want to die in an explosion at my cotton-candy factory on Mars?"

"How about you, Jackson?" Levi asked, leaning toward him like a co-conspirator.

"I'd want to—" Jackson wiped his nose on his arm, his brow furrowed in thought. Then his face lit up. "I'd want to die because I ate all the pizza in the world and then farted so much it opened a black hole and I fell in!"

The other kids cackled.

"I'd poop a nuclear explosion!" Marie, a quiet eleven-year-old girl, added. "And blow up my sisters, too!"

More laughter. More fart and poop deaths. Levi pulled out some chart paper and decided we'd rank our ways to die, coolest to dullest, and no one brought up the disaster on the ISS again, and pretty soon the hour was over, and it was time for them to go to free swim. They groaned because they wanted to stay and learn about embalming, which Levi promised they could do another day, and when we were alone in the room, I collapsed into a too-small chair, relieved and exhausted and in absolute awe of Levi Klein-Behar.

"That was amazing."

He shrugged. "Distracting ten-year-olds is my one talent."

"Oh, you have more talents than that," I blurted way too quickly and way too loudly. "I mean, like, music and stuff, right?"

Why did I sound like such an idiot when I talked to him? I had fives in AP Physics and Bio, was going to get a five in Chemistry, too. I was so much smarter than "music and stuff."

"I guess," he said, which was an understatement. The first Friday night of camp, he had played an original acoustic "The Room Where It Happens" parody—"The Shul Where It Happens"—that had every *Hamilton* fan at camp, which was basically everyone, rolling in the dirt laughing so hard. An eighth-grade girl peed herself from laughing, and she wasn't even embarrassed.

"So was Jackson right?" he asked me. "Is it bad up there?" He looked at the ceiling, but he meant "in space."

"It's not good," I said. He waited for me to go on, and I went . . . and went . . . and went . . . "The outside of the space station is covered in pipes to keep the solar panels cool, and they're filled with ammonia gas, which, if it leaks into space, is harmless, but if the leak is *inside* the space station, high concentrations of ammonia gas can kill everyone on board in just a few minutes. It seems like some space debris flying at seventeen thousand five hundred miles per hour made multiple impacts with the hull of the station, breaching it and the coolant pipes, which forced the crew to seal most of the ship. Normally, they'd put on the space suits and perform a depressurization for controlled breach egress into a shuttle or pod, but they've been cut off from their space suits by the breaches, and the atmospheric ammonia levels are rising. SpaceX is prepping Falcon rockets for a rescue, but the mission window isn't for at least twelve hours, and the crew might not survive that long. Hull breaches and ammonia leaks are two of the 'big three' scenarios that are considered the most catastrophic in space. The third is fire, and, because of the system damage, they can't confirm there *isn't* a fire burning somewhere on the station. Fire on Earth is predictable, but combustion events in space burn in every direction. They can't even place smoke detectors with one hundred percent accuracy. The air could literally catch fire anywhere and burn up and down and sideways. Also, the CO_2 levels in the pod where they're sealed are going up fast, and they're trying to fix that system, too, while the NH_3 levels are rising, and their venting process risks cutting short their breathable air supply. Managing the chemical composition of the crew environment is one of the most challenging aspects of life in space under optimal circumstances, but in the event of catastrophic system failure, managing O_2, CO_2, and about a dozen other potential hazards under a severe time limit is the kind of challenge that— Sorry."

I noticed his eyes had glazed over. That happened to people when I got excited about atmospheric chemical management. "I—I know . . . it's nerdy. I just—it's really important, actually. Or, like, I think it is? Most people think it's just weird. . . ."

"No." He shook his head. "People with passions are cool."

"Literally no one thinks this stuff is cool."

"You do."

I shrugged. I wasn't sure "cool" was how I'd describe it.

"Anyway, cool is overrated," he added.

"I wouldn't know."

"Yeah, neither would I." He leaned on the edge of the wooden table in the middle of the room, one leg crossed over his knee, and I saw his thigh vanish into the shadow of his shorts, which made my eyes dart up to his face like nervous carp avoiding a predator.

"We move around so much, I'm always the new kid," he said. "And this doesn't help." He pointed to his rainbow yarmulke. "I'm not Jewish enough for the Jewish kids, too religious for the other queer kids, and too Jewish for everyone else. Also, I genuinely like spending time with my parents."

The other queer kids, he'd said. There was a combustion

event in my heart. It burned in every direction, sideways and up and down. And down farther. I suddenly hated the treasonous shorts I was wearing.

"So what are you doing here?" I blurted as I adjusted my legs and leaned forward.

"Beatrice sent me over," he said. "Told me she didn't need me at play rehearsal, and I could either help out in the science club or senior-camper flag football."

"Oof, anything to avoid football, right?"

"Something like that." He flashed his metal-mouth grin, and until then I never thought braces could glimmer. That was the only word I could think of, though. When his lips parted, his mouth *glimmered*.

"What?" I asked, because he was just staring at me.

"I'm thinking." He stood and went to the chart paper, tapped my martian-cotton-candy-explosion answer at the absolute bottom of the "cool" list. "What's your *real* answer?"

"About death?" Why did he want to talk about death? Was he some kind of undercover goth? "I don't know. I try not to think about it. What's yours?"

"This *was* mine," he said, tapping his answer just below David Sussman's *crushed inside my mecha by the falling corpse of a Kaiju*. "I'd want to die dancing naked in the desert."

"Why the desert?" I really wanted to ask *Why naked?* but if I said the word "naked" to him, I felt like I would die then and there in probably the least cool way possible.

"When my parents were living in Uganda, where there are, like, only a few hundred Jews in this cluster of tiny coffee-farmer towns, we needed a break from all that small-town life, and we went over to Kenya to go on a safari. One night, I had to pee, and I slipped out of the tent and wandered off. The guides had told us to stay close to camp because of lions and stuff, but I wandered farther off anyway—I was fifteen and figured nothing could hurt me—and when I got far enough away, there was nothing but me and the noises of the desert and endless stars."

I was tempted to correct him that he was probably in a savanna, not a desert, but I didn't want to ruin the story.

"The stars were everywhere, all around me from horizon to horizon. It was like I was bathing in them! So I decided to strip down, like I was in the bath. I stood there, in the desert, totally naked, dancing in circles and waving my arms like I was splashing the stars all around me, and I'd never felt happier in my life. I thought I finally understood what my parents talked about when they talked about God. I even said the Shehecheyanu! You know it?"

"It's, like, a prayer . . . uh . . . for saying thanks?"

"Especially whenever we do something amazing for the first time," he said, then laughed at himself. "Yeah, so I'm saying the Shehecheyanu, and then there's this noise in the brush right in front of me. I froze. I couldn't see anything. It could've been a lion. I didn't know what to do, but the stars were still there and so was I, and if it was a lion, there was no way I could escape . . . so I just started dancing and singing the Shehecheyanu again. I just danced and chanted until the tiny bird that was in the tall grass flew away. Then I put my clothes on and ran back to camp, laughing the whole way."

"You could've gotten eaten!"

"But I didn't! And *that* moment of not knowing was the most in touch with God I've ever felt. I think that's what faith is, you know? Living with the tension of not knowing what happens next. I'd be totally happy to die dancing in that tension, because I think God is actually *in* that tension. It's like dancing *with* God. Like, God is in a lion as much as he's in the stars, you know?"

I nodded, but I didn't know. I just didn't want him to stop talking. I had fallen in love with Levi Klein-Behar at some point while he was talking about how he wanted to die.

"Maybe those astronauts are feeling the same," he said. "Maybe they're up there, doing what they love, bathing in the stars, and knowing that they've never been closer to God than they are right now, whether they survive or not."

Someone who was slicker than me might've told him that he didn't believe in God, but did believe in the laws of attraction. Someone who was more clever than me might've come up with a poetic story about death of his own. Someone who was braver might've stood up and kissed him right then.

But I am who I am, so instead, I said, "I have to get ready for tabletop games," and stood up so fast I nearly passed out.

"E block doesn't start for another five minutes," Levi told me with a puzzled glance at the old-fashioned wall clock.

I leaned on the table while the blood came back to my head. "I need to make sure all the Settlers pieces are sorted. A few of the kids freak out if they're not." I started pulling out random boxes, even though none of them were the Settlers of Catan box, just to avoid making eye contact with Levi.

"Got it." His voice was kind of quiet, and I knew I'd done something wrong, but I didn't know what. Was saying "freak out" about the gamer kids ableist? Did I offend him? Or did he think I was running away from his God talk? Was I afraid of God or afraid of him?

"I guess I could hang out a minute longer," I tried. "Those kids can live within the tension of a few missing Settlers pieces, right?" I laughed in what I thought was a polite chortle, but which came out more like a snort and which got no reaction from him. I'd totally ruined our thing, and now he thought I was making fun of him. Crap.

Why couldn't we just go back to talking about death?

"I should get to the music hut," he declared, and I felt like an air lock had just closed between us. "It's free drumming time, which is exactly as horrific as it sounds."

As he brushed past me through the screen door without looking, I felt all the air rush from my lungs. Should I stop him? Should I say something? Decision-tree time.

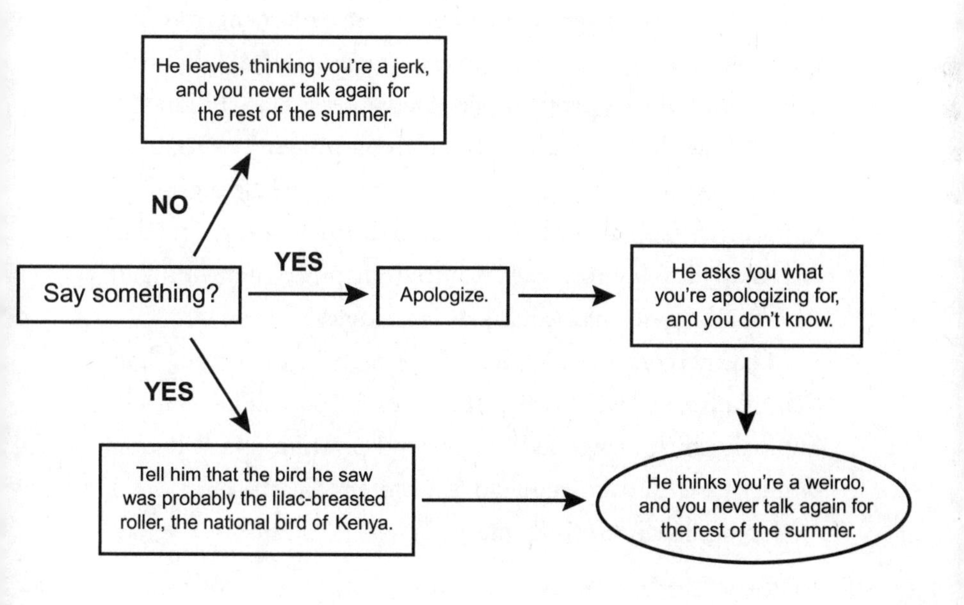

No good outcomes.

I stood frozen on the inside of the screen door, staring after him as I tried to work the problem another way, but he turned back and shouted up the steps, "Hey, find me at the dining hall at dinner? I need to know what happens with the astronauts."

"Oh, okay, yeah." I tried not to cheer like mission control after a successful splashdown. When he'd gone, I sat in the tiny plastic chair again and dropped my head into my hands, wondering what had just happened. Maybe I *hadn't* ruined everything by not being spiritual enough for him. Or maybe he was just being polite? Was he curious about the crisis on the International Space Station . . . or had I just been asked on my first-ever date? Could it be a date if you had to go to the camp dining hall anyway, whether he asked you there or not?

I didn't even know what I didn't know. I would've made a decision tree, but the kids burst in for gaming, and I had to scramble to get everything out for them. The hour and a half was a blur. Two of my regulars got in an argument over how many wheats one of them needed to trade in if she didn't have a dedicated wheat port, and two boys whose names I didn't remember nearly got into a fistfight over a contentious round of Uno. I was so distracted I completely failed to help a group of kids learn a new game where you tried to grow a forest, and they ended up just playing checkers until the dinner bugle sounded.

Yes, Camp Winatoo has a dinner bugle.

The moment the kids left, I sprinted to the dining hall, then realized I hadn't checked my phone, so I didn't actually know anything new to tell Levi when I saw him. I pulled it out of my shorts, and sure enough, the battery had died.

Oh no. Decision-tree time.

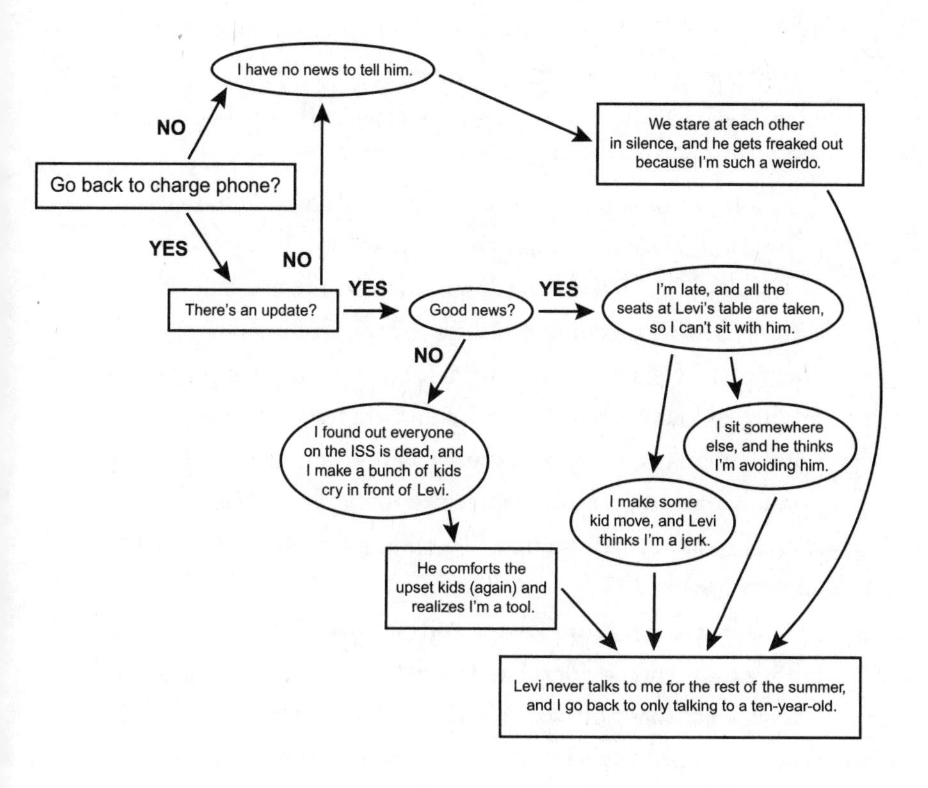

Okay, so going back to the bunk was not an option, but I couldn't stand there outside the dining hall, muttering through a catastrophic decision tree while kids streamed in, all red-faced and loudmouthed from their afternoon activities.

My salvation appeared in Jackson Kimmel, like a rescue launched from Kennedy Space Center. He scuttled up from the lake, mysteriously dry, and I wondered for a moment what deceit he'd come up with to avoid swimming. (I'd always used the journeyman lie "My stomach hurts.")

"Jackson!" I called him over. "Any news?"

He shook his head. Campers weren't allowed to use their phones during activities, so of course he didn't have any news, which meant I didn't have any news, which left me exactly where I'd been. But I was a counselor! Sort of! I could give him permission to use his phone!

"Sorry," he said. "I left it in my bunk when I changed for swimming. I was gonna ask you for news."

"But—" I realized it was as stupid to point out that he hadn't actually *gone* swimming as it was to argue with a ten-year-old about how he should have information about a catastrophe unfolding in low Earth orbit so I could flirt with another counselor, who may or may not actually care about said catastrophe or know that when I said *depressurization for controlled breach egress,* I was actually saying *Please let me taste the ChapStick on your lips.*

I sighed a little too loudly and promised Jackson I'd find out for him, and decided I had to risk going back to charge my phone, regardless of the probable outcomes. It was the only possible choice that might give me something to say to Levi Klein-Behar. This would be my Hail Mary pass, which was a terrible metaphor for the moment, being so overtly Catholic and so aggressively sportsy. But desperate times called for desperate metaphors.

No one was in the bunk when I got there, thankfully, so no one saw my mad scramble for the one outlet. I plugged the phone in and sat on the edge of Jeff's bed, which was next to the outlet. Jeff was a college junior, which made him the senior counselor in this bunk, and he hated when campers sat on his bed while they charged their phones, and he considered me nothing more than a glorified camper. He also coached tennis and liked to make snarky comments about me and my "indoor kids," so I didn't really care about ruffling his sheets.

It took forever before I had enough power to restart and then a second forever until I got onto Twitter. @GeekHeadNebula had the same message that everyone else seemed to have: media blackout.

No one was allowed to talk to the press, which meant either they didn't know what was happening, or the worst had happened and they were preparing a grim press conference.

@RogueNASA's last tweet confirmed that all combustion events were safely contained, but there was no news about the ammonia situation. For all anyone knew, the ISS could be orbiting the globe at 17,150 miles per hour with five dead bodies on board.

"Shit," I said, and I looked at the crew's Instagram account again. The most recent post was a still from their last story, Commander Frisch giving the thumbs-up. What if they were already dead? What if they were in the process of dying while I looked at their picture? I hated not knowing. I hated this tension! This wasn't some beautiful moment of connection to God! This was a bunch of disasters cascading on top of each other, and why did Levi care anyway, and why'd he have to act so interested and screw up my totally mundane day?

I threw the phone down onto Jeff's bed and cursed again. "Shit shit shit."

I knew it made no sense to be mad at Levi, but I didn't know where else to hurl my anger. I didn't want to go back to the dining hall to eat too-dry mashed potatoes and too-wet mac 'n' cheese while the astronauts might be dying and killing my chances of kissing Levi with them—and what kind of jerk conflates those two things anyway?—so I just sat there on the edge of Jeff's bed, listening to the crickets start their chirping while I ground my teeth, hated myself, and regretted that I'd let my first maybe sort-of date hinge on the worst tragedy in modern spaceflight.

I'm not sure how long I sat there bathed in self-loathing. The bunk was my own sealed capsule, hurtling through my own void of a life, where the odds of anything ever happening were even less than the odds of a catastrophic impact with space debris. Nothing ever leaked in or broke out. I was a lonely astronaut, but as long as I stayed in my capsule, I was safe.

"You didn't come to dinner."

I sat bolt upright on Jeff's bed, and there was Levi, clicking his stupid beads while he leaned against the doorframe. He loved leaning on things. He looked so damn good leaning on things. Somehow, night had fallen. Gnats buzzed around him in the puddle of light in the doorway.

I held up my phone on the end of its cord and wiggled it. "Charging," I said.

"You shouldn't nourish your technology before you nourish yourself," he told me, like he was quoting something. Most of what he said sounded like he was quoting something. It was cute before. Now it annoyed me.

"Not sure how nourishing canned green bean casserole is," I replied. I was proud of myself for how cool I was playing it.

He came into the bunk and bent down in front of me. "You okay?"

"Yeah? What? Why?" I said too fast, and realized by his expression that my eyes were puffy. I'd been crying. So . . . not playing it *that* cool.

"Worried about the astronauts?" he asked, and I was ashamed to tell him that that wasn't exactly it. That I was worried about myself and about how badly I wanted to kiss him and how not badly he wanted to kiss me and how every time I spoke, I'd just make it even less likely. So I just nodded.

He put his hand on my shoulder, and the heat of it nearly ignited me.

"There's a new plan," he said, and before he could go further, Jackson burst into the bunk, shouting, a horde of kids following him like a comet's tail, kids who didn't normally pay any attention to him.

"They're coming down!" he yelled. "They're coming down! They're coming down!" He repeated it, bouncing, and the quiet bunk was transformed into absolute mayhem as boys shouted over each other. Jackson, in his element for probably the first time in his life, shushed them all, and they actually, shockingly, shushed. "Camp Director Cheryl made an announcement. NASA said that they rigged the crew's module into a kind of ILV—improvised landing vehicle—and they are going to use that piece of the space station to attempt reentry and splashdown. They think it'll hold, but they have never tested this scenario. They could suffer complete hull collapse or burn up in the atmosphere, but they decided the risk was worth it because they had no other choices. Their air levels were at critical—"

"Okay, okay, slow down," I told Jackson. "Breathe."

"We're going to be able to see it from the Northern Hemisphere!" he shouted.

"What? The reentry?"

"That's what Cheryl said," Levi clarified. "Everyone's going to the Big Green to watch. We'll be able to see the lights cross the sky in, like, twenty minutes."

"If it burns up, it'll be like the brightest shooting star ever." Jackson bounced, then remembered he was talking about human beings who might die, and he looked down at his sneakers, ashamed he'd only been thinking about himself. I knew the feeling. "Not that I want that. I didn't mean—"

"It's okay," I told him. "I know what you meant. Let's go out to the green, then?"

He nodded and bounded off. The other kids followed him, the sciencey ones in the lead for once.

"I hope I didn't freak you out with all that God and death stuff," Levi said when we had the bunk to ourselves again. "I can be . . . intense."

What was he saying? Had he been worried about *me* judging *him* this whole time? "How would you have freaked me out? I'm the one who—"

"Hey! Sheldon!" Jeff crashed into the bunk like a meteor. "Get the hell off my bed or you can't use my outlet anymore!"

Jeff always called me Sheldon, like from that TV show.

Jeff was a prick.

I grabbed my phone at thirty-eight percent and stood up. Levi and I rolled our eyes in unison.

"Follow me," Levi said as he led me outside, where we slipped around to the back of the cabin. He grabbed the window frame and started to climb the wooden lattice to the cabin's roof. "Come on. We won't have to smell all the Axe on the Big Green."

"But won't they wonder where we are?" I kept both feet on the ground.

"We're indoor kids at a sports camp," Levi answered. "No one *ever* wonders where we are."

He was right about that, but the cabin was not made for climbing, and he was already halfway up. I wanted to follow him, and I was terrified to follow him.

Time to work the problem.

Decision-tree ti—

"Come on!" He thrust his hand down to help me.

There was no decision to be made.

I climbed.

When I reached the top, I sat down on the sloped roof, my feet tingling even though we weren't really that high up. I pressed my hands against the wooden shingles, as if my palms could hold me if I fell.

"Relax," Levi said, standing with arms open. "Look up."

"I am relaxed," I told him, keeping my butt firmly against the shingles. "It's just, sometimes relaxing means keeping a low center of gravity to keep myself from plummeting to my death and— *Whoa.*"

I'd looked up.

I loved looking at the stars and always had. That was nothing new. I could name the constellations and explain why the planets burned in different colors, and, if he wanted, I could tell Levi all about the Doppler effect and the expansion of space, the nature of black holes and the firewall paradox and on and on like a wannabe Carl Sagan. The stars were *not* why I'd *whoa*'d.

I'd *whoa*'d because I'd looked up at *him*. It really did look like he was bathing in the stars.

"Stand up," he urged me, extending his hand one more time. I took it and let him help me to stand and keep me steady, and I looked at the stars surrounding us.

"I am not dancing up here," I told him.

"We're *all* dancing up here," he said, which meant nothing, but he still hadn't let go of my hand, and he was smiling and his braces glimmered like a mouthful of stars, so it didn't matter that half of what he said was nonsense. It was beautiful nonsense. "Is that it?" He pointed at a dot of light moving fast toward the horizon.

"No, that's a satellite," I said.

"How about that?"

"That's Venus," I laughed. "It's not moving."

"Where is it, then?"

"Well . . ." I tried to focus on the sky, even though every part of my brain was in the space where our fingers had intertwined, and I was sure he could feel my pulse racing in my hand, but if he could, he didn't seem to mind, because he hadn't let go, and when my weight shifted, he held my hand tighter. "I don't think we'll be able to miss it."

"How'll we know if they'll make it without burning up?"

"We won't, I guess," I said, scanning the night sky for movement. "We'll just have to live within that tension."

He squeezed my hand when I quoted him back at himself, and I don't know if God lived in between the stars and the astronauts or the lion and its prey, like he said, but I felt like there was a supernova in the spot where our palms pressed together, and I'll probably never know what a space station careening through the atmosphere looks like, because I wasn't looking up anymore. I was looking at him and smiling, and he was smiling back at me, and his braces were gleaming like starlight, and he whispered, "Shehecheyanu," and I leaned forward, and I pressed my lips against his stars.

TWO TRUTHS AND AN OY

BY DAHLIA ADLER

Three dresses. Two pairs of jeans. Five—no, six—shirts. I have no idea what people wear to college, but this has gotta cover two days of it, right?

I add two cardigans, just in case. Yeah, it's June, but New York City gets chilly at night, and what if I go out?

I'm gonna go out, right?

It's college orientation, Amalia. Of course you're going to go out. With your new friends. That you will make immediately. Because how can they not realize how funny and brilliant you are?

Thank you, brain.

Satisfied, I zip up my little rolling suitcase just as Mom calls, "Mali, you ready?"

Ha ha, no.

"Yep!" Ironed into submission, my hair looks as good as it's gonna get, and I went for the natural look with makeup, which means I'm wearing fourteen products on my milk-pale skin to make it look like I'm wearing two. Eyebrows have been waxed, teeth have undergone bleaching, and . . . that's it, because I know shockingly little about putting myself together for a soon-to-be college freshman. But I do know if I stand here trying to figure any more out, I will drive myself up the wall and probably scare myself out of going, so.

I've never even seen NYU. That didn't seem weird to me when I was applying early, or even when I sent in my deposit. But now, as I get on the Metro-North to get from Westchester to the city, it strikes me as a little weird that I don't really know what awaits me on the other end.

But I do know what doesn't, and that was so much of the point.

There's no dress code forcing me to wear tank tops under my shirts in case the neckline is too low or make sure my skirt hits my knees. I can wear jeans to class. Flip-flops too. Tank tops, if I'm feeling truly daring, but I haven't decided whether College Me wears sleeveless yet.

There won't be an absurd network of literally everyone knowing everyone else's business. I might actually get to introduce myself without hearing "Oh, I've heard of you" in response.

There won't be a stupidly expensive unofficial school uniform I'll feel compelled to buy because it's easier than figuring out how to dress myself.

And most of all, there won't be a whole second curriculum of Tanakh, Talmud, Hebrew, and other Judaic studies—not unless *I* want to supplement my education with those things. And let's be real, after thirteen years of it, including a year of learning in Israel, it isn't bloody likely that I will.

I am finally done with yeshiva life, and then I have one

last super-Jewish summer at camp before I become a Normal Person.

And the next two days are going to be the perfect preview.

My mind is whirling as I stare out the windows of the train, then switch to take the 6 down to Astor. I know where I'm going, but I also don't at all. I grew up right outside of New York City, but I've never actually been below Thirty-Fourth Street. It's the fastest and slowest trip in the world, and then I'm looking at the map to find my way to the dorm where I'm staying and then I'm there and I'm checking in and I'm upstairs and a girl I've never seen before in my life is going to be sleeping on a bed a few feet away from me and she holds out her hand and says, "Hey, I'm Marie."

I look at her hand a few seconds too long before I realize I'm supposed to shake it. I've never really been in a shaking-hands situation; my people are not the physically touchy kind. I recover too slowly and say "Amalia" while wrapping my fingers around hers, unsure whether my grip is too tight or too loose. "Are you from New York originally?" I ask, because it's something to say.

"Indiana, actually."

"Oh! I've never met anyone from Indiana."

"Insert some joke about flyover country," she says with a smile, sweeping up her thick, dark hair into a ponytail.

Oh God, was I being offensive? Stereotypical New Yorker? "No, no," I rush to explain. "Indiana is totally cool and exotic to me. It's just, I'm Orthodox Jewish, there aren't so many Orthodox Jews in Indiana, I've only really known Orthodox Jews, so."

I hate myself for the explanation the minute it comes out

of my mouth, especially because I promptly see her give me a once-over, her eyebrows drawing into a question as she takes in my short sleeves, my jeans, my shoulder-length hair. The words "Orthodox Jewish" always conjure up men in black hats and payos, women in long skirts and snoods. "Modern Orthodox," I clarify, though I don't know why I had to say anything about being Jewish at all. "I wear pants and don't, like, *have* to cover my elbows or collarbone or whatever." As if she knows the rules of tznius.

She smiles, a little lopsided this time. "I guess we're even, because I've never met an Orthodox Jew before."

Of course you haven't, I wanna say, but don't. She didn't have to know she'd met one now, but I couldn't seem to keep my mouth shut about it. My tongue sticks to my palate as I try to figure out what to say next, but then she speaks. "I'm gonna take a shower—do you need the bathroom first?"

I shake my head, and a second later, she's gone.

I'm torn about waiting around for her—partly because I feel like I should and partly so I won't have to go to orientation by myself—but my suspicion that she doesn't *want* me to be there when she gets out wins. I throw on a shirt that might be point-six percent more flattering than the one I was already wearing and head downstairs. "Okay," I mumble to myself, grateful to be alone in the elevator. "You got your weird out of your system with Marie. You only get one."

The elevator opens then, and I promptly press my lips into a thin, awkward smile as two hysterically laughing girls pile in, dressed in cute tank tops and jean shorts. They both have tattoos visible on their skinny golden arms, and it rocks my world a little to see the verboten designs in the flesh, especially on people my own age. Once again, I'm staring like a weirdo, grateful that they're too busy cracking up to notice.

Why the hell am I so culture-shocked? I live in New York. I watch movies. There's nothing I haven't seen before. And I'm not *judging* any of it. I should not be this much of a mess.

I will stop being this much of a mess.

When I reach the room in which everyone's meeting up, I stand around awkwardly, doing the thing where I play with my phone as if I'm texting friends who simply cannot wait to hear from me, but I'm actually checking the weather in New York City, in Jerusalem, in Miami for no good reason. Then we're split up into groups of ten, and my group seems nice enough and not too scary. Half of them are from states I've never met anyone from before, states whose names bring up images of cornfields and huge, starry skies, and people who've never met a Goldstein or Berkowitz in their lives. There's a guy and a girl from California, both enviably tanned, and the last two are locals like me—a kid from Jersey, whose gender is unclear (by design, I'm pretty sure), and a guy from Dobbs Ferry, who breaks into a big smile when I say I'm from Yonkers.

"Did you go to Yonkers High? Do you know Darius Chivers? Or Martina Gardner?"

"I didn't, no. I went to private school in the city, actually." And then I worry that sounds snobby, so I add, "Jewish school."

Of course I drop the J-bomb again. So much for only playing a single Awkward Card today. I brace myself for an onslaught of questions, but he just nods and says, "Ah, cool, cool."

Literally the opposite of cool. I give myself a point for not saying that out loud and just letting the conversation move on.

Names fly around the circle: Lee, Anthony, Nicole, Riley—names that don't constantly make people ask what they mean or force them to just say "Amelia" at Starbucks because it's easier than having people stumble over the second vowel sound. I think about introducing myself as Mali, but it bothers me to know that everyone will assume it's Molly, and I go with Amalia instead.

When an Indian kid from Nebraska introduces himself as Akshay, I try to exchange a *high five for unusual names* glance, but he's not having it.

I sink farther into my chair.

"Okay!" The group leader—"Charlotte, but call me Charlie"—claps her hands enthusiastically. "Now we're gonna do a little icebreaker. How many of you are familiar with Two Truths and a Lie?"

Everyone raises their hands and is polite enough not to groan, but oh man, I really wanna groan. I don't know why this is the leading game of Icebreakers Across America, but I have played this game at every single Shabbaton, new camp season, and orientation of my life, and I hate it. You spend your whole life learning about how honesty is the best policy, and then suddenly you're supposed to be a good liar for other people's amusement.

This is all to say, I suck at Two Truths and a Lie.

Akshay kicks us off, and I want to guess his lie is about having helped deliver a baby, but it's actually the much more mundane "I've never gotten a speeding ticket." Devin from Montana lies about having had mono twice, and Julio from Tarzana designs his set around making sure we all know he drives a really nice car. For some reason, it only hits as Lee is lying next to me that I'm about to go, and I have no idea what to say.

My standard "truths you're supposed to think are lies" are that I know how to lein all five megillahs (the things I did for extra credit in high school) and that I was captain of my school's Torah Bowl team (which is hilarious if you know me and what Torah Bowl is, but none of these people know either). My lie is that I've never been to the Kotel (which was already a lie before I spent the year in Israel, but now it's *really* a lie). I don't think those things will translate terribly well here.

I try to fill in the blanks, come up with a different weird thing from my knowledge base or another place I haven't been, but all my brain's roads seem to point to awkward Jewishness. I swear it takes me five minutes to cycle through things like that I memorized a whole chapter of *Pirkei Avot* on a bet or the fact that the only time my Torah Bowl team ever won was when a team from a Syrian school had to forfeit because their captain had gotten engaged. Finally, I reach deep into my nerdery and come up with that I can name all the US presidents in order. I try to think of something to replace the word "Kotel" for my lie, and all I can come up with is "Disney World." (It's Disney*land* I've never been to. Oh, I am so clever.) And finally, I come to needing a second truth, and . . .

"I just came back from a year in seminary in Jerusalem," I blurt because, so help me God, I can't think of anything else.

And then I freeze. Because now of *course* I'm the weird girl.

Why did I have to mention something so Jewish again? Part of me wants to pretend that seminary is the lie, but it's a stupidly specific thing to make up, and now it's out there, making me sound stiff and spiritual and maybe judgmental and definitely different and all of these things I'm not.

People start guessing, and my skin heats and prickles with

the feeling that I've turned myself into a sideshow. The seminary girl. The rule follower. The kind of girl you don't want at your parties or as your roommate. Seminary sounds like a choice you make when you plan to remain abstinent your whole life and devote your existence to God; there's no explaining now that it's the thing most Modern Orthodox people just *do,* even if you barely learn a thing all year and spend every night shopping at Malcha Mall or getting dinner at Makhane Yehuda.

"So, which is it?" Charlie asks.

"Oh, um, it's Disney World. I've actually been there a bunch of times. It's—" My tongue trips as the word "davka" almost spills off it. It's not even a word I use that often, but now I can't think of any other way to express my intention: *It's davka Disney*land *I haven't been to.* Only no one here knows what "davka" means, and what the hell English word am I supposed to use in its place? There has to be one. There has to be one, and I have to know it, because English is my first freaking language.

Mercifully, the word "specifically" pops into my head, and I realize that'll work in this case. I finish my sentence with what I hope is only a slight stammer.

"They're pretty similar," says Christina from Montana, who lied about roping steers, and it occurs to me that I've never met someone with the name Christina in my entire life. For some reason, it feels like seeing a tattoo, and I just nod. No one asks about seminary. No one asks why I stumbled on my sentence. No one notices that I just had to *search* for an English word to replace the Aramaic one that came to my lips. No one cares about anything else I've said at all.

We move on to Anthony, and with the pressure of taking my turn behind me, I let myself really look around the circle. These kids don't look like anyone I've ever gone to school or camp with; they don't look like kids at all, really. No guy I've ever known has muscles like Lee or Anthony, whose polo shirts strain against their biceps. Only the Sephardi kids at Hebrew Academy of Westchester had scruff to rival Akshay's or Brian's. Looking at Nicole reminds me that there were exactly two Asian kids in my entire school (Jen and Dave Greenberg, who'd been adopted from Vietnam as babies), and Julio makes me think of the kid who was technically Latino—his mother's Cuban and had converted—but whom I'd never heard identify as such in any of our four years together. There's real sun-streaked blond hair and hair streaked with blue and, in Riley's case, an immaculately shaved head, and all of it screams, *You are not in Jew World anymore!*

That was exactly what I wanted. That was supposed to feel awesome.

Instead, it feels terrifying.

These people are so much more . . . everything than I am.

I bet they've all had sex, I think as I look around at the easy, comfortable way they slouch, drape their arms over the backs of each other's chairs, show off taut abs and sculpted biceps—and, good Lord, is *everyone* here thin? It feels like everyone is thin. Or if not, they somehow seem to carry their weight with more confidence, make it look beautiful, like it fits, in ways the padding on my arms and belly and thighs never seems to. I think of all the things they haven't had to make sure they don't do, all the ways they can be less careful about silly things like what foods they mix together and who they touch, and it isn't envy that I'm filled with but just complete and total panic that they can all tell I am a *child.*

I have no idea how much of my fear shows on the outside. It feels like probably all of it, but no one seems to be looking at me sideways. No one seems to be looking at me at all, this average brunette nothing with untamable hair who spent way too long picking the world's most boring outfit.

"So what's everyone thinking about majoring in?" Charlie's question breaks through the rushing sound in my ears, and I breathe. This one I have an answer to, and it's a normal answer, just like everybody else's. I feel calmer as we discuss journalism and English, history and French, and the different possibilities of premed classes. I sidestep the conversation about studying abroad—I don't know yet what locations are doable for me from a kashrut/shul/general Jewish perspective, and that's the last thing I wanna talk about right now—and before I know it, the meeting is breaking up for lunch.

"The food court at the Kimmel Center is open, if anyone wants to eat on campus," Charlie instructs as people start pulling out their phones, texting, making plans with I can't even imagine who as I have no one downtown to contact. "Otherwise, there are a whole bunch of places right nearby."

"We're gonna go to Galaxy," Lee says authoritatively, and it's clear "we" is somehow half the group, who managed to make plans when I wasn't looking, I guess. (When wasn't I looking?) "If anyone wants to come," he adds as the after-est of afterthoughts.

"What's Galaxy?" I ask, because I seem to be the only one who doesn't know. Restaurants don't really register to me as anything more than neon signs on the street; no point internalizing more than that when you can't eat at any of them.

Thankfully, no one looks at me like a moron, but I feel like one anyway, for being a New Yorker who doesn't know this New York restaurant they all do. "It's a pizza place on the next block," says Nicole, dabbing on hot-pink lip gloss, and my stomach sinks a little more.

"Oh. Thanks. I keep kosher, so . . ." I contemplate whether I can go anyway, just sit with a bottle of water, but I don't feel like looking weird, and now I've just said I can't, and how do I take that back?

"Pizza's not kosher?" Riley asks, pulling on a thin jacket.

"Well, there *is* kosher pizza, but it's at kosher pizza stores, and there aren't any of those down here," I explain. "Because cheese has to be kosher, and we can't have it with meat, and . . ." Everyone's eyes seem to be glazing over as they edge to the door. "Anyway, no worries. I'll just go to the cafeteria. They probably have packaged stuff."

"And you can eat that?" Akshay asks.

"Depends," I say, and oh God, I'm holding up their lunch now while I explain this absurdity. "But packaged stuff says on it if it's kosher, so it's easy to know." I debate explaining the different kinds of marks of supervision, but Lee's already out the door, and I don't think anyone's really interested. "I'll be fine. I'll see you guys later." And I will, because we have another gathering in a few hours, this one to go on an evening tour of the Village.

I have no choice but to see them again, no matter how stupid I just let myself sound.

And they have no choice but to see the weird girl who can't eat pizza with them again.

I watch as they all file out, including Charlie, leaving me alone to wander toward the Kimmel Center.

I'd been bluffing about the packaged food in the cafeteria, but I'm relieved to see that I'm right—a benefit of going to school in a massively Jewish city, no doubt. There's kosher yogurt and fruit and packaged sandwiches, wraps, and muffins, all with either OUs or Kof-Ks. I fill up my tray with more than I'm likely to eat, just in case they don't have the same options come dinner, and after paying, stuff wrapped baked goods into my bag like a grandma at a buffet.

I eat while scrolling through Instagram without really focusing on anything I'm seeing, wondering if everyone's bonding over pepperoni, and thinking how miserable tonight's gonna be when they've all become best friends without me. Not that I was ever gonna click with effortlessly cool Nicole or Christina, who look like they should be babysitting me. And oh God, after I finish eating, I'm supposed to go back to the room I share with *Marie*?

How was I *ever* so excited to go to college? College is horrible. College is terrifying. College is for grown-ups, and I am so, so far away from that, sitting in a cafeteria by myself with my head in my hands and clenching my jaw while trying not to cry in public.

The beep of a text message coming from my phone makes me lift my head, and for a second, I feel slightly less loser-y for getting a text.

Then I see it's from my mom, asking how the day is going and if I've checked out the Hillel yet.

Of course.

I can't even bring myself to answer her, not after how many times I fought with her over her forcing me to go to Israel for seminary instead of straight to college, yelling that I wanted to start real life *now*. I put my phone on silent and go to rest my head back on my folded arms, and that's when I spot it.

A kippah.

It's big and blue and flecked with colors like a little universe perched on thick, dark hair, and I have to blink twice to make sure it's real. But it is. The guy wearing it hasn't noticed me staring at him yet; he's reading something on his phone and eating a falafel wrap. There's a tiny smear of hummus just above his lip, and he doesn't seem to care that little diced bits of cucumber and tomato have fallen all over his brown plastic tray, but he could not be a more welcome sight to me if he tried.

Before I can even think of all the reasons this is awkward and stupid, I'm out of my seat and standing over his mess of Israeli salad. "Hi!" I say brightly, and I don't care that I'm disrupting his lunch. "I just wanted to introduce myself because you're the only other Jew I've seen here today, and also I'm used to knowing every Jew I see from either living here or going to Camp Sharsheret for basically my entire life—I'm a staff kid—but I don't know you, so, I'm Amalia. Mali. Reichman."

He smiles, and there's a little *you're weird* in it, but I don't even care. Because I know he's weird too. And we're gonna be weird here together for the next four years, whether we're friends or not, whether we hang out again when we both actually go here or not. "Akiva Lipman. I'm not a New Yorker, so I'm usually a couple of degrees away in Jewish geography. But you go to Sharsheret? Do you know Dov Savitsky? Or Nava Block?"

"I'm friends with both of them! I actually had Nava at my house for Simchat Torah last year." Two truths. No lies. "Does that mean you're from Dallas?"

"Born and raised," he says, and I don't know when I sat down or at what point in his story about going hiking with Dov he offered me from his bag of chips or when we started talking about how we both love to read and write, but it's the first conversation all day where I feel like I can breathe, and the irony is that we aren't even talking about anything Jewish at all.

So where was this comfortable, conversational Mali when I was surrounded by my group? Why did it take a kippah to unlock her?

The alarm I set on my phone to remind me not to be late to the next part of orientation rings before I can dig up an answer, and I'm forced to get up and collect my things. "It was great to meet you," I offer. "I guess I'll see you in the fall?"

"Are you not going to the barbecue at the Hillel tomorrow?"

The barbecue. I'd completely forgotten about it. Not that I didn't plan to make the Hillel part of my college experience—of course I did—but orientation just felt so early to do it. Like I was already penning myself off into the Jewish corner before I ever got to be anything else. But now I ache at the idea of finding a comfortable spot where I can eat hot food that didn't come wrapped in plastic and use the word "davka" to my heart's content. I long for another conversation at college in which I manage to talk about my fondness for baking without explaining that I can't use lard or most gelatin, or about movies without feeling inexplicably compelled to explain why I never see them on Friday nights. Akiva and everyone else who'll be at Hillel already know the context in which my entire life is couched; they don't need footnotes for the asterisks in my bio.

All because they're exactly the people I thought I needed a breather from.

Plus, I guess going to the barbecue would make my mom happy, so whatever.

"Oh, right! Forgot about that." Technically still a truth. "I guess I'll see you tomorrow, then."

"I guess you will," he says with one last brief smile as he looks back down at his phone, and I turn and head out. I'm still dreading joining back up with my group, and I'm dreading the meal conversation happening again about dinner, and I know that whatever I wear and however I look, I'll feel wrong. I know that if they talk about going "out," all I'll be able to think about is how I don't know how to dance, which doesn't matter because I also don't have a fake ID.

But there's only one more day of orientation, and then there are two months of camp—two months of singing "Hatikvah" together in the mornings alongside "The Star-Spangled Banner," and two months of zemirot and Shabbos walks and snacks from the canteen, whose kashrut I never have to think twice about.

I only get two months left in Jew World, and I am going to live it all the way up.

THE HOLD

BY DAVID LEVITHAN

1.

To me, Jewish isn't matzoh ball soup; it's lighting the candles. My grandmothers lighting the candles. My mother lighting the candles, ushering in the flames. My grandfather joined the New York Police Department as soon as they let Jews take the entrance exam. Jewish is changing the course of your life to prove that particular point. Jewish is being the exception to Christmas. My best friend (for a time) in high school had a Hanukkah bush. I told him, "That's a Christmas tree." He said, "No, it's a Hanukkah bush." I told him that in order to be a Hanukkah bush, it would have to be burning, the fire started and exclusively fueled by a single drop of oil. Jewish is both having a Hanukkah bush *and* making fun of Hanukkah bushes. It's also spelling Chanukkah any damn way you please. I like a *C* in there, but not when referencing Hanukkah bushes, because they don't exist. This is, I understand, a possibly wicked son thing to say. Jewish is knowing once a year your family will rate your behavior and slot you into one of four sons at the seder. I never wanted to be the one unable to speak, because he didn't have any good lines. The wise one seemed holier than thou, and while I often felt holier than thou, it was never in an actual *God Loves Me More* context. So basically, I campaigned for the wicked son. Let me be the doubter. Jewish is doubting, because Jewish is being screwed over by authority time and time again. (Dayenu.) I've never asked my brother if he wanted to be the wicked son. I feel my biggest competition was my cousins. We were all oldest sons. We all wanted to be the wicked doubter. I wonder what Rabbi Akiva would make of that. Jewish is knowing all the names but not remembering exactly who they were or what they did. (I know Elijah comes to the door. BUT WHY?) Jewish is six years of Hebrew school, six years of half-hearted attempts at learning the language and children's Shabbat services where the cantor would strum his guitar. For a while, I thought all prayers were Soft Rock. Hebrew school created an alternate universe from real school, and in this alternate universe all the other kids were Jewish and knew the difference between a brei pre hagafin and a motzi lechem min ha'aretz. Later I'd go to camp with kids from Hebrew school and go to college with kids from Hebrew school and bump into kids from Hebrew school on the sidewalks of New York City; we don't remember the names of all of Jacob's sons, but we do remember each other. I can still read Hebrew. As long as there are vowels. As long as you don't ask me what it means. As a writer, I respect that God's name is unpronounceable. That makes sense. Jewish is giving words their worth. I don't particularly believe in God, but I believe in saying Kaddish. I believe in it because it's what my great-great-grandparents said when someone died, and it's what my parents said when my grandparents died, and one day when I die, it's what will be said for me. Jewish is choosing our traditions and choosing what they mean. I fast on Yom Kippur not because I care what God thinks of me, but because I've been offered a vocabulary for introspection and repentance, and I choose to use it in solidarity with all the others who have used or are using it. I don't spend the day in synagogue; I spend it at my parents' house, with my family, because that time is holier to me. My parents' friends and their children come over to our house to break the fast, or we go over to one of their houses. The rabbi sometimes drops by. A nice guy, but when gay couples couldn't get married at our temple, I went out of my way to avoid talking to him. For me, Jewish has always been about acceptance and social justice and saying we are all slaves until everyone is freed. So Jewish and gay have never been incompatible. But we're liberal. Just after college I saw a documentary called *Trembling Before G-d* about gay Orthodox Jews and their struggle, and I realized My People can be as blind and intolerant as any other People. To me, Jewish is understanding this and fighting this. Jewish is tikkun olam, and knowing the world is broken, and wanting to fix it through love and kindness. My family taught me this. Jewish is when we gather together. It is hiding the afikomen where the youngest cousin can find it. It's the joyful cacophony of a family that can't sing well still singing the blessings. It's latkes and maror and marshmallows melted on sweet potatoes and—okay, so maybe Jewish *is* matzoh ball soup to me. I'm vegetarian, so I can't have it with chicken stock. My mom makes a separate vegetable stock for me and puts two matzoh balls in. That's Jewish too, to me.

2.

If you were young and gay and Jewish in the early 1980s, you edified your desire however you could. Even if it involved a book called *Great Jews in Sports.*

I am sure there are kids who would have chosen to read *Great Jews in Sports.* But mostly it was a book given as a gift. It was a hagiography of Sandy-Koufax-Who-Wouldn't-Play-On-High-Holy-Days and Hank Greenberg and others I can't remember. And if you were young and gay and Jewish in the early 1980s, the centerfold of your attention was always Mark Spitz.

Oh, Mark Spitz.

Nine-time gold medalist at the Olympics. Perhaps the greatest Jewish sports hero of all Jewish sports heroes. Swam himself into the history books.

The iconic shot (look it up) is him wearing a number of his gold medals.

But if you're young and gay and Jewish in the early 1980s, the gold medals are mere jewelry. Because what you see isn't just a sports hero. No, what you see is a strong, sexy, confident Jewish man proudly parading in a very short, very tight swimsuit.

This goes against all the iconography you've thus far been given about what it is to be a Jewish male. This isn't Tevye. Or Billy Crystal. Or Sandy Koufax. The cultural models for your maleness: the rebbe, the comic, or the Noble Great. All worthy models. But none of them have anything to do with desire.

Mark Spitz is hot.

This is not a word you would use, or necessarily acknowledge. But you turn to this picture of him so many times the book starts to open of its own accord to his spread. The book is telling you something, and it has nothing to do with sports.

3.

When the most popular Jewish dating site decided to finally match same-sex couples, I gave it a try. This was many years ago now.

One of my first dates was with a guy named Akiva.

We were both in our twenties. Both from the New York area. Both Jewish. Both incredibly awkward on a first date.

I asked him where he'd gone to school. He mentioned a yeshiva that sounded vaguely familiar. Which made sense, because they all sounded the same to me.

He told me it had been a challenge.

I said, "Wait—you're Orthodox?"

"Was," he told me.

"So you jumped off the God bandwagon?" I joked.

And he looked at me seriously and said, "No. I just changed the road that the bandwagon was driving on."

It became one of those conversations where the other person shows you his scars, and you have to decide whether or not to tell him that, actually, they're still bleeding. He was telling me about making his own life, about making his own relationship to God, but at the same time it was obvious (to me) that he was still defining himself entirely in opposition to where he was coming from.

"It's hard," he said after he'd taken about ten minutes to tell me how okay he was. "When you're raised one way and then try to raise yourself another way. You're given this absolute and then, wham, it's no longer an absolute. All along you thought God was closed to interpretation, and then you realize it's *all* interpretation. It's like being told there's no physics or chemistry, or that the dictionary isn't real."

I had a sense that I wasn't the first person with whom he'd shared these analogies. But I nodded. I asked him what it was like growing up gay and Orthodox. This led, naturally, to us sharing our coming-out stories—in gay dating, this is what separates a frivolous first date from a substantial one, the willingness to take this particular story down from the shelf where it sits next to the moment you first knew, and your first kiss, and the first time you had sex.

So I told him, and he told me, and his story was more interesting than mine. But I might not have remembered it if, at the end, he hadn't said, "There was this one boy at my school—he was a year older than me. One of those redheaded Jews. Copper, really. I had the biggest crush on him. Only, I wasn't sure what his story was. Then—get this—one day he runs away to San Francisco! Like, completely out of the blue. Says, 'Mom, Dad, I'm gay and you're never going to accept that, so I have to get the hell out of here, goodbye.' And then he calls a few of his friends and tells them why he's leaving. Of course, the next day, it's all anyone could talk about. The school doesn't know whether to have an assembly or order vaccinations. And I have to tell you—it gave me hope. Even though I had to live through two years of hearing his name used synonymously with every gay slur you can imagine, Hebrew or English, I would daydream about him being out there in the world, and knew that while I didn't have the guts to run away, I would get there eventually."

"Which you have," I pointed out.

This got the first smile of the date. "Which I have."

Aware of a tingle spreading from my heartbeat, I asked him, "What was that boy's name?"

"Moshe. Although I think he changed it when he left."

I asked his last name. Akiva answered with a very common Jewish last name.

I asked him what town in Long Island he was from. He named the town.

It was all falling into place.

"What happened to him?" I asked. "What happened to Moshe?"

"He's doing great. My mom sees his mom every now and then, and because my mom has so few gay sons to report back about, she always makes a point of telling me he's doing great. Still in San Francisco. Going to grad school at Stanford for some science thing. I couldn't tell you if he's, like, partnered or anything—I think his mom only tells my mom about his academic achievements. Why do you ask? Did you know him?"

"I'm not sure," I lied.

4.

We met at my cousin's bat mitzvah. Of course.

(To be Jewish is to know the full meaning of that *Of course.*)

My cousins weren't Orthodox, but most of my uncle's business partners were. (I'd tell you his occupation, but it's such a Jewish cliché that I'd rather not.) We were sixteen years old, and we were still at the kids' table. We weren't sitting next to each other, but we were the only people at the table old enough to see over the centerpiece, so we made eye contact immediately. When I wasn't trying to help one younger cousin find a Transformer under the table or another younger cousin get the exact same size slice of challah as her sister, I tried to make conversation. It was all pretty generic until we acknowledged the centerpiece itself—a blowup of the Playbill for *The Phantom of the Opera.* (Because my cousin's bat mitzvah theme was Broadway. *Of course.*)

Now I was intrigued. This copper-haired Orthodox boy knew his musicals. (While I avoid Jewish clichés, I clearly don't mind sharing a gay one.) Only . . . he knew most of them through cast albums taken out from the library, while I had already seen plenty onstage. Most crucially, I had just seen *Into the Woods* for the first time—my grandparents, thinking *fairy tales = safe fun for the grandchildren!* had taken me and a couple of my cousins to see it; the rest of the children didn't listen, but I did. And now I was switching seats with my seven-year-old cousin so I could sit next to Moshe and recount it to him, scene by scene, as the salad plates were lifted from our table and the dancing began.

I had kissed boys before. I had felt that extra electricity between me and another boy—at first not understanding what it was, then understanding exactly what it was. While I still hadn't sewn the word "gay" into my identity, I was definitely keeping the space open for it. I was not innocent to what I was feeling as I was talking to him, as I was trying to explain what happened in the woods between the Baker's Wife and the Prince. But I couldn't tell if Moshe was having the same kind of conversation I was having.

The band launched into the hora, and before I fully knew what I was doing, I was taking Moshe by the hand and pulling him to the dance floor. Even with my family and his family and everyone else around, we could hold hands this way. He smiled at me, and I read everything I wanted and needed into that smile. Once we started dancing, I wouldn't let go. As we kicked and swirled, I wouldn't let go. As my grandmother tried to cut in to dance next to me, I wouldn't let go. As my uncle tried to pull me to the center to help lift my newly adult cousin on a flimsy folding chair, I wouldn't let go. And neither would Moshe. By the end of the dance, we both knew something had happened, and neither of us said a thing about it.

The younger cousins at our table sometimes demanded my attention, but the rest of the afternoon I devoted to talking to Moshe, and he devoted it to talking to me, right until his father showed up behind his chair and told him it was time to make the drive home. Once his dad was gone, Moshe wrote his phone number on his place card and gave it to me. Then I did the same for him.

This was before cell phones. Before the Internet. This was a time when if you had a phone number, it was your family's phone number. What you said might be private, but the fact that you were talking to a boy on the phone was not.

I hatched a plan. Michael Feinstein, a singer I admired for reasons I didn't fully fathom, was about to do a limited run on Broadway. Using the money I'd earned from working at my high school library, the next time I was in Manhattan, I went to the box office and purchased two tickets for the following Sunday. Then I found a pay phone and called Moshe to ask him to join me. He asked his parents if he could. They said yes. (No doubt, all they had to hear was "Feinstein" to know he'd be in good hands.)

He took the train in from Long Island. I took the train in from New Jersey. We met at a kosher pizza place for lunch beforehand. I had never had kosher pizza before, and while I'm sure culinary science has improved kosher pizza significantly in the intervening years, the pizza that day tasted like someone had taken a frozen pizza out of its box, and then served us the box. Worse, because we were surrounded by so many other Obvious Jews, our conversation was guarded, afraid of the very Jewish geography that had brought us together.

It was only when we got to the theater that we relaxed into being ourselves. It was a concert of jazz standards, and we were the youngest people there by a good two decades. In walking from the kosher pizza place to the Broadway theater, we had stepped from Moshe's world into my world, and my world was far more welcoming. Even if we were the only teenagers there, we were far from the only gay couple. We noticed them. We took their existence as permission to exist in the way we wanted to exist.

Where do you start? Michael Feinstein sang.

I took Moshe's hand in mine.

Isn't it romantic?

He leaned into me. We watched other men lean into one another.

How about you?

Some of the songs were new to us. But you don't have to know a song to feel it run through your nervous system. You don't have to have the words on your lips to understand their meaning.

They can't take that away from me. . . .

It was still daylight when we left the theater. We each knew the trains we were supposed to catch. As we walked to Penn Station, we talked about the show, mostly because it was too scary to talk about anything else. The distance from the Lyceum Theatre to Penn Station was not a long one. When we got to the escalator leading down to the tracks, I started to formulate a goodbye—but all that came out was how much I was enjoying myself, enjoying his company, enjoying us.

Then he surprised me. More than any boy had surprised me up to that point, and more, I would guess, than any man has surprised me since.

"Let's go," he said. And I genuinely didn't know what he meant. But then he was grabbing my hand just like I had grabbed his for the hora, and he was pulling me across the street to the Hotel Pennsylvania.

I might not have understood what was going on, but the guy behind the front desk did, and he loved it. Absolutely loved it. One of our kind, I realize now. He made sure to ask us if we were getting the room while our parents "parked the car." He didn't look at all surprised when Moshe paid in cash.

"I was planning to pay you back for my ticket," Moshe said, "and I wasn't sure how much it cost. But this is better, right?"

I nodded. This was better.

The Hotel Pennsylvania was about half a century past its prime, but we didn't care. That ramshackle room was the most magical place either of us had ever been. The minute we got inside, Moshe kissed me like a soldier who'd just come home from the war. He gave me everything in that kiss, and I tried to give him everything in return. Somewhere in the back of our minds, we knew our parents would be waiting for us at two different train stations, but that part of our minds no longer mattered to us. What mattered was the inextricable velocity drawing us toward each other. What mattered was that we were free to touch each other the way we wanted to touch, free to be touched the way we wanted to be touched. I took his sweater off, took his pants off, and only hesitated at the tallis that had been under his sweater the whole time; he folded it neatly and put it on a chair. We were the wise sons, the wicked sons, the simple sons, the sons who didn't have the words for what we were doing, but knew nonetheless that what we were doing was larger than our lives. This, to us, was sacred. We learned: For some things, enlightenment does not come from above or even from within. It comes from beside. From being beside.

We were more naked than we'd ever been, and our nakedness had a consciousness it had never had before. We didn't have sex or even come close to having sex, but what we did was still farther than either of us had ever gone before. Farther into who we were. Farther into who we would be. When it was over, when we were lying next to each other, limbs overlapping, traffic sending its rhythm from floors below, I felt I was allowed to float above my own life, and what I found there was an astonishingly clear peace.

Moshe was right there with me. Until he stood up. Until he put his underwear back on, sat down on the bed, and began to cry.

I moved next to him. I put my arms around him, held him.

"Are you happy or sad?" I asked, because I really couldn't tell.

"Both," he said. "Both."

We got tickets to three more Sunday matinees. We told our parents we were having dinner after, which was why we got back so late.

I took him to see *Into the Woods,* and he thanked me.

He took me to see *Cats,* and I forgave him.

We found out from talking that we'd both come to a certain *awareness* when we'd seen photos of Mark Spitz. But Moshe was careful to make the distinction: It wasn't just because Spitz was sexy in a Speedo. It was his expression. He was a winner, and he was embracing that. We wanted to live like that, so damn sure of ourselves.

For our fourth date, I decided we had to see *The Phantom of the Opera,* since it had, in its own way, brought us together. I waited for him at a kosher deli, which was much better than the kosher pizza place. When he didn't show, I assumed he was running late. I went to the theater, and as curtain time approached, I left his ticket for him at the box office.

Through the first act, I was much more anxious about him than I was about the falling chandelier. At intermission, I found a pay phone and called his house. The angry way his father asked "Who is this?" tipped me off that something was going on. I hung up; it didn't sound like he was there.

I thought maybe he'd be waiting for me in front of the theater after the show was over. I thought maybe he'd meet me in the lobby of the Hotel Pennsylvania. I sat there for two hours, *Goodbye, Columbus* in my lap, unable to read or do anything else besides wait.

I took my scheduled train. When I got to the train station at home, both of my parents were waiting. As soon as they saw me, they said we needed to talk. I wondered if Moshe had called, had left a message. But it was actually his mother who'd called, asking if I knew where he was. She said he'd announced he was going to California. She didn't believe him.

"Do you believe him?" my father asked.

I nodded. And then, to my profound horror, I began to cry.

I told my parents everything. Well, not everything. Not the details. But I told them I'd been dating Moshe. I did not tell them I'd fallen in love, but I'm sure they could hear it in my voice.

This is not the coming-out story I tell on first dates.

There were a couple of phone calls after, from pay phones in California. He apologized for standing me up and said the timing hadn't been his choice. He told me we'd catch another matinee soon, whenever he returned to New York. The word *love* never came up, because it would only make it feel worse—at least for me. Had there been cell phones, texting, email, we probably would have kept in touch. But there wasn't, so we didn't. Our time together became a good dream, possibly the best dream. I never forgot it, but I remembered it less and less, as other dreams joined in.

I've written about him hundreds of times, and I haven't written about him at all until now.

5.

I wish I'd had the experience, the wisdom then to tell him: To me, Jewish is knowing that you can't be asked to have pride in one part of your identity and then be told to have shame about another part. Whoever asks you to do that is wrong. To be proud as a Jew is to be proud of everything you are. I wish I'd seen him crying and had known to say: To be loved by God is to be loved for who you are; to love God is to place no boundaries on who you love. I didn't know this then. I do now. Whether or not I believe in the God of my ancestors, I see God in everyone.

To me, Jewish is holding on to the people you love. To me, Jewish is dancing and kissing and loving no matter who's watching and what they might say. To me, Jewish is helping the world. To me, Jewish is helping each other. To me, Jewish is me and Moshe in that hotel room. It is who we were. It is who we've become.

AFTERSHOCKS

BY RACHEL LYNN SOLOMON

Friday, 5:08 p.m.
Just before sunset

Somehow, Miri had wound up dating the only other Jewish kid in eleventh grade.

She wanted to believe it was an accident. That all the time they spent on Quiz Bowl challenging and teasing each other, blushing when their hands brushed against the buzzer at the same time, his religion hadn't once crossed her mind.

That would be a lie.

Miri liked that Aaron was Jewish, but it also occurred to her that he was *Jewish,* like, really Jewish, in a way she'd never been. He missed school during Rosh Hashanah and Yom Kippur. She not only attended school those days but ate the occasional BLT for lunch. He'd had a bar mitzvah, while she'd never even attended one. He told her once that his family had two sets of dishes, and while she nodded like she knew exactly what this meant, she in fact did not.

And as she stood on his front porch for the first time while trying to remember if she'd locked her car—she was eighty percent sure, but the twenty percent of doubt made an uneasiness settle into her stomach—his Jewishness felt like a massive, physical thing that separated them rather than connecting them.

She was relieved when he opened the door almost right away, his dark hair damp from a shower, his clean-boy smell intoxicating.

"You're here," he said, grinning like the simple fact of her presence had made his entire night, and it wasn't even six o'clock.

"I'm not sure I locked my car," she blurted instead of hello.

His brow furrowed. "It's a pretty safe neighborhood, but—"

"Oh. Okay. Yeah." What was a conversation, even?

Aaron stepped onto the porch, closing the door behind him. He looked cute and Quiz Bowl–championships professional in khakis and a navy button-up. His eyes were the clearest blue. Miri glanced down at the outfit her fourteen-year-old sister, Hannah, had helped her pick out: a striped dress, black tights, and a long black cardigan, plus the thrift-store necklace with a bird charm she wore most days. She'd pinned her wavy chin-length hair back on one side, and her anxious fingers twitched to fiddle with it.

"You look really nice," Aaron said to the welcome mat, his cheeks turning red. The mat declared SHALOM in English and, beneath it, in Hebrew.

Miri felt her face get hot. "It's a pretty attractive mat," she said, which made Aaron laugh.

Their relationship was only five days old, and they hadn't kissed yet. For the past month, they'd been "hanging out" on weekends and messaging each other all the things they were too shy to say in person. On Sunday night after a movie hangout—they never used the word "date"—during which their elbows and thighs had touched the entire time, Miri had finally broken down and decided to be bold. *I think I like you,* she texted once she got home. Three agonizing minutes later, during which Miri had contemplated setting her phone on fire, changing her name, and moving to an isolated cabin in the woods of Vermont, Aaron wrote back. *I think I do too.*

A wild grin took over her face. *Maybe . . . we could date?* Then she quickly added *Each other,* in case it had been unclear. *Maybe . . . we could date? Each other.* This time, Aaron's response was faster: *Okay,* he said. *Okay, let's do this.*

They ignored each other all week at school, save for a few awkward smiles, which Miri's best friend, Lexie, had assured her was normal. Then he'd invited her over for Shabbat dinner on Friday. With his family.

All she wanted tonight was some kind of confirmation that he still liked her, that he wouldn't pull a *Let's just go back to being friends.* She was desperate to close the gap between deciding they were together and actually being together. Maybe they could walk into school on Monday holding hands, even sit with each other at lunch.

If this was what being in a relationship was like, it was a good thing Miri was already in therapy.

Aaron's eyes finally met hers. "Question. What do you call a baby spider?"

"A spiderling, and that's adorable." She felt herself relax

a little, even though she was still unsure about her car, and maybe car prowlers would target a "pretty safe neighborhood" because no one would be expecting it. "What year did World War One start?"

"Nineteen fourteen," he said without missing a beat.

This was a hobby of theirs: challenging each other to spontaneous trivia competitions. Because they'd been on Quiz Bowl since freshman year, they'd accumulated a lot of random knowledge. They'd go back and forth until one of them admitted they were stumped. It was very nerdy, and Miri loved it.

After a moment of rummaging through her mental random-knowledge vault, she lobbed back: "What's the largest freshwater lake in the world?"

"Superior. It's in the name." He crossed his arms over his chest, a mock confrontational stance. "Was that supposed to be hard?"

She swatted his shoulder and felt almost light-headed when her hand connected with the fabric of his shirt. It lasted only an instant, but she could tell his skin was warm underneath. She'd had a crush on him for *so long.* Nearly three whole years of quiet longing, hoping their taunts would turn into something more. It felt absurd and impossible that he was hers now.

"Give me another one," she said. *Are you* sure *you locked the car?* her brain pressed.

They volleyed for a few rounds before he tripped over a question about Henry VIII's first wife, who was Catherine of Aragon, not Anne Boleyn. But Aaron was a good sport, never a sore loser.

Suddenly Miri's mind turned on her, as it was so good at doing whenever happiness seemed within reach. They'd played this game as friends. Did that mean nothing had changed between them now that they were (supposedly) dating? She tried to cling instead to the compliment he'd given her a few minutes ago. *You look really nice.* That compliment was progress. It had to be.

"I'm really glad you came," he said, smiling wide now, which did little to quell her anxiety. "My parents are excited to meet you."

The car definitely isn't locked. If you go inside, someone's going to break in.

"I'm . . . excited to meet Mr. and Mrs. Kaufmann." Was she good with parents? God, she hoped so. She was good with her own parents, stereotypical Seattle liberals who were so invested in their kids that they noticed Miri's OCD symptoms before she even realized what she was doing was out of the ordinary.

He grazed her sweater sleeve with a few fingers, and she wondered if he had the same reaction to these innocent touches. "Should we go in?"

You need to check the car. You need to do it. Just do it. Do it now.

"Sorry I'm so weird; I'm just gonna make sure my car is locked real quick," she said.

Aaron knew she had OCD—most people on the team did, thanks to a Quiz Bowl question she'd answered and then explained sophomore year. But he didn't know the extent of it, that it meant she so often felt like a slave to her own actions, like she did right now.

She hated her OCD. She especially hated it as she knew Aaron was watching, listening as she jogged down his driveway and clicked the lock button on her key fob until her car honked. And then again. And then, just in case her finger had accidentally slipped to the unlock button—you could never be too sure—two more times.

"I'm pretty sure it's locked," he said, eyebrows raised as she headed back to his front porch.

Face burning, she followed him inside.

5:22 p.m.

"Miri! Welcome," Aaron's mom said in the foyer of the Kaufmann home, pulling her in for a hug that crushed the air out of her lungs. Miri realized she'd now gone farther with Aaron's mom than with Aaron, which depressed her a little bit. "I'm Naomi, and this is Aaron's sister, Talia."

A girl with the same blue eyes as Aaron scowled up at Miri. Aaron had warned her that his eleven-year-old sister was a bit precocious. "Talia can introduce herself, thank you very much," she said, sticking out her hand for Miri to shake. "A pleasure."

Miri bit back a laugh as she offered her own hand. "Nice to meet you. Nice to meet both of you."

Over the top of Talia's head, Aaron raised his eyebrows at Miri as though to say, *See? Told you.*

Miri hung her purse on a coatrack but kept her phone in her cardigan pocket. The best word for Aaron's house was "elegant." Every shade of white was represented: the cream of the carpet, the eggshell of the walls, the ivory of the curtains. Family photos were spaced evenly, and the furniture looked almost too immaculate to sit on. Miri's house was a mess of cat hair, mysterious stains, and tchotchkes no one could bear to throw away.

"Miri," Aaron's mom said thoughtfully, tapping a lacquered nail against her chin. "Is that short for Miriam?"

"Yeah, but—" Miri broke off. She'd been burdened with a grandma name, and she'd never really loved it. But she felt weird telling Aaron's mom that. "I've just always gone by Miri," she finished.

"I imagine you know the story of Miriam?"

The story of Miriam . . . from the Bible? The Torah? Miri did not know the story and definitely didn't know how to phrase her answer, so, figuring it was safest, she shook her head. Her parents had only ever said that they'd always liked the name. She knew vaguely that the name had some kind of Jewish origin, but she'd been going by Miri for so long that she'd never really researched it.

"She was the sister of Moses and—and *Aaron*!" his mom said with a laugh. Miri quietly perished from embarrassment. "They led the Children of Israel out of Egypt."

Miri vaguely recalled having watched an animated movie about this forever ago.

" 'For I brought you up out of the land of Egypt and redeemed you from the house of slavery, and I sent before you Moses, Aaron, and Miriam,' " Talia said, and then added: "I'm studying for my bat mitzvah."

"She has a photographic memory," Naomi said, sifting a hand through Talia's thin dark hair. Naomi's hair was a light brown, curling softly onto her shoulders. At her throat was a silver Star of David.

"*Nearly* photographic," Talia corrected.

"You'd be great on our Quiz Bowl team," Miri said.

Aaron's mom checked her watch. "I was just about to light

the candles. Why don't you both wash your hands and meet us in the dining room?"

Miri had only a vague idea of what happened after sundown on Friday nights, most of which she'd formed from research on Wikipedia and JewFAQ.org, which was, apparently, a thing. There weren't a lot of Jews in her Seattle suburb. Until high school, she'd been the only one in her classes. And now there was Aaron, and they were together, and she was trying to figure out what that meant.

In the dining room, Aaron's dad was arranging food on the table. Twin ivory candles stood in the center.

"You're a sport to put up with this one," Aaron's dad said after introducing himself as *Dan! Dan Kaufmann!* and pumping her hand up and down. "I assure you any of his less-than-admirable qualities come from his mom's side."

"I heard that," Naomi said.

"His less-than-admirable qualities," Talia repeated with a snort, and began ticking items off on her fingers. "Where would we even start? He leaves his dirty socks on the table in the TV room, takes *way* too long in the shower, and—"

"Talia!" Aaron's face had gone scarlet.

"What? We all know what you're doing in there."

When Miri realized what she meant, she felt herself blush too.

"Talia, that's enough," Naomi interjected, but in a lighthearted way. Miri liked how this family was able to tease each other. It made their Jewishness slightly less intimidating.

Aaron's mom struck a match, touching the tip to one candle and then the other. Then she held her hands over her eyes and began reciting a blessing in Hebrew. Miri had read about this on JewFAQ: you were supposed to cover your eyes because lighting candles would be considered work on Shabbat, which would officially begin after the blessing.

Once they sat down, Miri marveled at the food. "This is beautiful," she said. "I love challah." That was true, at least. Nothing was better than the fluffy sweet bread, especially the innermost, fluffiest bits.

She reached for the braided loaf, but the collective intake of breath from Aaron's family stopped her as her fingertips made contact.

"Not quite done with the blessings yet," Naomi said gently.

Miri drew her hand back as though a crocodile had just snapped at it. She tried to convince herself it wasn't a big deal, but it dragged her religious insecurities up once again. Her cheeks burned as Naomi and Dan exchanged a glance she couldn't interpret. Maybe she hadn't paid as much attention to JewFAQ as she should have. She'd assumed, if anything, the dinner would be a learning experience. She'd imagined her feet bumping Aaron's beneath the table, which would sustain her until the next time they touched on purpose.

She could tell everyone that they didn't have Shabbat dinners at her house, but she wasn't quite ready to admit the thing she and Aaron had in common was really only his. Before tonight, she'd wondered if sharing a religion indicated they were meant to be together. That if she aced this dinner, it might smooth out the awkwardness in their infant relationship.

Instead, all she could utter was "Sorry" as she stared at her lap.

That was when the table started shaking.

* * *

5:37 p.m.

Miri had been through the earthquake drills, which started back in kindergarten: *Drop. Cover. Hold on.* Once, when she was twelve, she'd come downstairs for breakfast, and her mother had asked if she'd felt the quake in the middle of the night. The news said it had only been a 2.2. Miri had slept right through it.

This was completely different. The house felt *alive,* possessed by some otherworldly force. Photos on the walls bounced in their frames. Their food skidded around on the table. Instinct took over, and Miri blew out the candles in one breath. It was probably wrong to do that on Shabbat, but the alternative could have been much worse.

"Everyone under the table," Naomi said, a ribbon of panic in her voice, but they were already on their way.

The jingles from the emergency preparedness videos looped in Miri's head as they all ducked down. She clung to a table leg. Next to her, Aaron did the same.

It felt at once earsplitting and silent as furniture banged around in this beautiful home. In the kitchen, she heard what must have been plates and glasses crashing, smashing on the floor. Talia whimpered, and Naomi made reassuring sounds. The lights cut out.

Over and over, Miri's heart crashed against her rib cage. *It'll be over soon. It'll be over soon.* She thought about her sister and her cat and her parents, hoped all of them were okay, wondered why she'd thought about her cat before her parents, felt guilty. Her thoughts flew to her car, which was most likely crushed beneath a fallen tree at this very minute. She tried to take deep breaths. Failed.

Aaron was trembling. She wrapped a hand around his. "It's okay," she said, though she was scared too and didn't entirely believe herself. Even in the dark, she could tell his eyes were wide and uncertain.

He swallowed and nodded, gripping her hand back.

It reminded her of one of the reasons she'd started liking Aaron in the first place. So many guys at school were insecure about their masculinity, trapping their true emotions behind layers of testosterone. But Aaron had never felt the urge to prove anything. She'd seen him cry, at school last year when his grandpa passed away, and he wasn't ashamed of it. He'd let his friends hug him with such fearlessness. She'd wanted to hug him too.

"Is it over?" Talia whispered when the ground stopped shaking, seeming for the first time that night like an actual eleven-year-old.

"Let's stay here a few minutes," Dan said. "There might be aftershocks."

Naomi let out a long breath. "Not quite the dinner you were expecting, Miri?"

Her heart was still somewhere in her throat. "Not exactly." Her voice shook. Aaron laid a hand on her knee, which she was too rattled to properly enjoy.

When the house had been still for a while longer, they crawled out from beneath the table. Their dinner now lay on the floor around them, green beans mixed with shards of plates and glasses. The challah had been flung all the way across the room. In the kitchen, the entire contents of the cabinets covered the floor. Half a coffee maker stuck out from beneath a cast-iron skillet. Everything swam in a pool of wine. Apparently, Aaron's parents had had a *lot* of wine. In the adjoining family room, blinds hung crooked from a window, near where books had toppled from their shelves.

It was horrifying how much damage thirty seconds could do.

"No one's hurt, are they?" Dan asked. Everyone shook their heads, but he still examined Talia's face and arms, just to make sure. Fortunately, no windows were broken, and nothing heavy had moved more than a couple of inches.

"Oh no, oh no." Naomi gestured to a small glass sculpture that Miri had seen on the family room mantelpiece before sitting down at the table. It was now in a hundred pieces on the wood floor. "That was my grandmother's."

"Mom, I'm so sorry," Aaron said.

"I should call my—" Miri started, pulling out her phone, then suddenly felt guilty because she couldn't recall whether you were allowed to use electronics on Shabbat.

"Of course!" Naomi said. "Go ahead."

It took her several tries to get through.

"Miri? Are you okay?" Her mom sounded frantic.

"I'm fine, Mom. Just freaked out. Are you guys okay? Hannah? Alfie?" Alfie was their cat, a perpetually grumpy ten-year-old tortie.

"We're okay!" Miri heard Hannah call from the background. "Alfie actually let me hold him the whole time, can you believe it?"

"Alfie! That doesn't sound like him at all."

Miri's dad came on the phone. "Stay where you are for at least a few hours, okay? The roads are going to be a mess. And

I don't want you driving if there are aftershocks. If everything seems safe by nine o'clock, we'll come get you."

That was a relief—Miri didn't want to drive either.

"Love you," her mom said, and Miri echoed it back.

She hung up the phone. "My parents want me to stay here for a while," Miri said. "If—if that's okay. I don't want to impose or anything."

"Absolutely. You can stay here as long as you want." Naomi pulled her in for another hug of the night. "Sweetheart, I'm so sorry."

The floor rolled beneath them, pinballing Miri from Naomi to Aaron. Aaron grabbed her arms to steady her, but the aftershock lasted only a couple of seconds. Somehow that wasn't even the scariest part of this whole thing. She was trapped in someone else's house with a trio of strangers and a boyfriend she still didn't feel entirely herself around.

"We ought to find a radio," Naomi said, "in case we lose our phone signals."

Dan nodded. "There should be one in the office."

"I'll grab it. We should conserve tap water, too, in case the lines get turned off. We have a bunch of reusable water bottles—well—on the floor right there." Naomi pointed. They were scattered among the plates that had shattered. "I'll work on filling them up. Oh—and we should fill up the bathtubs."

Everyone in the Northwest, it seemed, had gone through earthquake-preparedness training.

"Miri and I can do that," Aaron volunteered, maybe a little too quickly. Miri furrowed her brow, and then realized—this would take her and Aaron away from his family, at least for a little bit. And while her emotions were all tangled right now, she felt a burst of excitement sneak in. She tried to make her face look appropriately solemn, or however a face belonging to someone about to fill up a bathtub to conserve water after an earthquake might look.

"Come right back, okay?" Dan asked.

Aaron nodded. "It's upstairs," he said to Miri, and together they waded through the debris.

5:51 p.m.

Once they were in the bathroom with the water running, Miri let out what felt like her first breath since before the earthquake.

Aaron was bent over the tub, his sleeves rolled up to his elbows. Sighing, he moved backward so he could lean against the wall. "I know," he said quietly. "Not how I pictured this night going. I'm so sorry."

"It's your fault, so you should be," Miri said, tugging on her bird necklace.

"If only I'd learned to control my powers. I'm too strong for my own good."

The medicine cabinet had spilled lotions and liquids all over the floor and counter, but fortunately, there was no broken glass. She tried not to look at their reflections in the mirror, but every time she caught a glimpse, she couldn't help wondering if they looked good together. Or what they would look like if they were even closer.

She didn't know how the first move was supposed to happen, but she figured proximity was a good place to start.

"Hi," she said in what she hoped was a flirtatious way, inching closer to him.

He gave her a weak smile and raked a hand through his hair. Then he blew out a long breath, as though coming down from the earthquake adrenaline rush too. "Hi. I like your dress. Did I already tell you that?"

"If I recall correctly, you actually complimented the welcome mat."

"Right. I try to treat all inanimate objects with respect."

"I like yours, too." Daring herself to be brave, she laid a hand on his sleeve. "I mean—I like your shirt. It's very . . ."

"Shirty?"

"Exactly, what with the buttons and the sleeves and the collar."

Aaron glanced down at her hand, at her gray-painted nails. "I really don't take that long in the shower, I swear," he said. "Like. My showers are a very standard length."

Miri bit back a smile and, feeling even braver now, said, "I've . . . had my share of long baths."

When it dawned on Aaron what she meant by this, he turned the deepest shade of red.

Miri pressed on, wanting to pull the conversation back to the topic of Them as a unit, a pair. "So . . . when did you know you liked me?"

Aaron blushed even more fiercely, and for a moment, she was convinced he wouldn't respond. Miri knew he was shy. Was it that, or was he regretting the relationship already? Was their trivia swapping more friendship than flirting? She supposed five days wouldn't be the shortest relationship in history, but she was really hoping to make it at least to ten.

The bathtub continued to fill. They could be doing anything in here, and no one would be able to hear them.

"Last year," he said finally, and she let out what she hoped was not an audible sigh of relief. "The regionals. You were the only one who knew the answer to the final question. The mod told you it was wrong, but you were insistent, politely but firmly asking him to look it up. You knew you were right. And of course"—he gave a little laugh here—"you were."

"Kaffeklubben Island," she said, remembering. "The northernmost point of land on the planet."

"Right. I . . . couldn't stop thinking about you the rest of the weekend. And then I just—kept thinking about you after that too."

"Oh," she said quietly, unable to stop the grin from spreading across her face. They were finally talking about this in real life, not ignoring each other, not relying on their phones to keep them safe, distant. Could it really be this easy?

"When . . . did you know?"

"Hmm." She probably should have had a response prepared. "It wasn't really one singular moment, I guess. I liked being on the team with you, and talking to you, and . . ." With a shrug conveying more discomfort than nonchalance, she trailed off. She wasn't exactly ready to admit she'd liked him for years, but compared to Aaron's, her answer sounded so impersonal. Should she have been able to pinpoint one moment she thought, *Yes, this is a person whose mouth I would like to touch with my mouth,* the way he had? It just hadn't happened that way for her, and she hoped she hadn't disappointed him.

After a silence, he changed the subject. Thank God. "I really am sorry. About all of this."

"On the plus side," Miri said, "your parents have probably forgotten I tried to grab some challah before they were done with the blessings. So thanks, nature, for saving me from embarrassment."

Aaron pushed away from the wall. "It wasn't a big deal," he said as he turned off the bathtub faucet, but there was a tightness in his voice she wasn't used to hearing.

"My family isn't very religious." She rushed to fill the sudden quiet in the room. "I didn't have a bat mitzvah."

"Become a bat mitzvah."

"What?"

"That's the right term. *Become* a bat mitzvah, not *have* a bat mitzvah. It means 'daughter of the commandment,' so it's something you become, not something you have."

Miri really didn't want to see what she looked like in the mirror now, didn't want it to reflect her clear discomfort. She was half convinced her forehead would appear with the words WORLD'S WORST JEW stamped across it.

"Well. I'm not one, then."

"Oh," he said, and she couldn't quite interpret his tone. "That's . . . okay."

Judgmental. That's what it sounded like.

"Knock knock." Aaron's dad pushed open the bathroom door. "How's it going in here?"

Miri hoped he hadn't thought anything had happened between them. She imagined an alternate universe in which she and Aaron had taken this opportunity to steal a passionate kiss, one in which they'd glance at their make-out-mussed hair in the bathroom mirror and laugh. A universe in which he hadn't informed her what she'd already been terrified was true: that she wasn't Jewish enough.

"Bathtub's full," Aaron said.

His dad nodded. "Good. Your mom found the radio."

"Good," Miri echoed, her voice sounding hoarse.

A silence overtook them.

"Since we're going to be stuck here for a while," Dan said, "who wants to play Scattergories?"

6:16 p.m.

The game was a good distraction. They ate what they could before sweeping off the table to play where their dinners had been, though Aaron's parents wanted to wait a few hours before attempting to clean up the rest of the house.

Miri and Aaron sat next to each other, legs crossed but not touching. The bathroom conversation looped in her head. She wasn't trying to keep her Judaism Lite a secret, not necessarily. She'd just hoped she and Aaron could have discussed it during a slightly less emotionally fraught evening. Now he was barely looking at her. All she wanted was more time alone with him, but her words always seemed to take a detour to Awkwardville somewhere between her brain and her mouth. So maybe his family as a buffer was a good thing.

To make things worse—because with her OCD and anxiety, things could always be worse—she itched for her car keys, to hear the jarring but oddly comforting beep when she hit the lock button. She could see through the window that her car was okay, but she couldn't be sure it was still locked. When she got a chance, she'd find her purse, find her keys, and make certain. Her therapist always told her she had to be okay with uncertainty, that there was no way to be one hundred percent sure of anything. "Do you know for certain someone hasn't stolen your car while you've been in this office?" Dr. Dunn would ask. "Do you know for certain Alfie's still alive?" Against all her instincts, Miri would have to tell her no.

She craved certainty, and logically, she knew her quest for it was making her miserable.

"All right, everyone count up their points for this round," Naomi said.

"I've got eight," Aaron said.

"You got me. I only got six," his mom said.

Talia pouted. "Five."

"Nine," Miri admitted, and she could have sworn she saw the corner of Aaron's mouth tip upward in—what? Pride, maybe? It was too dark to tell.

"You're wiping the floor with us!" Dan exclaimed, and Miri offered a weak smile in return.

They tore the sheets off their notepads, and Talia rolled the die for the next round.

"I know this isn't ideal," Naomi said. "But we really are glad to have you here, Miri, and I hope we see you for many more Shabbats."

"Roger that," Dan said. "It sounds like the team is doing well?"

"Going to regionals next month," Aaron said, and Miri nodded.

"Yeah. We have a really solid team this year."

"We'll be there to cheer you on!" Naomi cupped Miri's shoulder. "We always hoped Aaron would date someone Jewish."

Miri's stomach rolled over. Everything she'd felt during their abbreviated dinner and in the bathroom came rushing back. *And I was the only option?* she felt like saying, but then a worse thought gripped her. Was this the only reason Aaron had agreed to go out with her? Was she his default Jewish girlfriend?

"Obviously, it's a challenge in Seattle," Aaron's mom continued as Miri's insides sloshed around. "I grew up in New York. It was completely different there. All my friends were Jewish."

"Did you have a theme for your bat mitzvah party?" Talia asked. "Mine's going to be in June, after I turn twelve, so I was thinking of having a beach theme."

They didn't even blink when another aftershock rocked the house, scrambling Miri's thoughts. She wanted out of this conversation. Out of this house. Her breathing turned shallow, and she struggled to catch it.

"I—um," she started, unable to confess again that she hadn't had a bat mitzvah. No—that she hadn't *become* a bat mitzvah. She sucked in as much air as she could, trying to avoid sounding like she was literally gasping for it. "A—a beach theme sounds great."

"What was your Torah portion?"

"Talia," Naomi said. "Don't badger her."

Miri offered Aaron's mom a weak smile, but her feet urged her to move.

"You never told us what temple you go to, Miri," Dan said. "We haven't seen you at Kol Ami, have we? Do you go to Beth Am?"

Air. She needed air. "I— Excuse me for a minute," she managed, springing out of her chair so quickly she almost tripped on it. Slightly dizzy, she turned back to Aaron's family for a moment. "Bathroom."

She headed for the staircase, wanting only to get as far away as possible before she gave in to her mounting panic attack. In the past, she'd always been at home for them. She'd curl up in a ball on her bed, shut her eyes, and wait for her breathing to return to normal.

She threw open the first door on the left, collapsing onto the bed before fully surrendering to her anxiety.

7:34 p.m.

"Miri?"

Aaron's voice. It had been three minutes or three hours. She stared at the ceiling, one hand on her diaphragm as she breathed in through her nose and out through her mouth, the way her therapist had taught her. The worst of it was over now.

"Sorry," she said, turning her head to face him. "I just needed to be alone for a bit."

"It's my room." He gave her an odd look. "You're, um, on my bed."

"Oh." She'd been too panicked to even take in her surroundings, but now, as she glanced around, squinting in the dark, it felt like Aaron—at least the parts that weren't in disarray. The bookshelf overflowed. The closet was ajar, revealing the plaid shirts he wore most days over T-shirts with sayings on them. There was a poster of Albert Einstein on the wall, and opposite it, a *Star Wars* poster, Einstein and Kylo Ren locked in a staring contest. It didn't look like the rest of the house—or what the rest of the house looked like prequake.

Aaron's bed smelled so very *Aaron* that she couldn't believe she'd missed it.

Suddenly the lying-down part made her feel intensely vulnerable, exposed in a way she was not at all ready for. She shot up to a sitting position too quickly, her head throbbing. She smoothed the hem of her dress.

"I brought this. For your head." He presented a package of frozen peas. "Figured we might as well use some before everything in the freezer melts."

"Thanks." In spite of everything, it tugged at her heart.

She held the frozen peas to her head. The bedsprings squealed as he sat down next to her—not too close, though. She appreciated that he respected her space, but she also wanted him closer. It was a night of contradictions.

"Highest-grossing movie of all time—when adjusted for inflation?" he asked softly. He stretched out his legs so they dangled off the bed, then stared down at his hands as though unsure what to do with them, what to do with his entire body now that there were two people on a bed that had only ever held one.

"Gone with the Wind," she answered, but instead of throwing a question back at him, she said, "You know I have OCD." He nodded. "I have bad anxiety, too, and I get panic attacks sometimes." All she wanted in that moment was for him to understand her, as best as he could.

"Oh. That's okay," he said softly, then backtracked. "I mean—it's not okay, it sucks, but, like, you don't have to be embarrassed about it."

"Your parents must hate me. I'm, like, this total anxiety monster, and a fake Jew on top of that."

"I don't even—what's a fake Jew? Actually, what's a *real* Jew?" He sounded almost amused, genuinely interested in how she'd answer the question.

She crossed her legs, part of her still unable to process that she was sitting on Aaron Kaufmann's bed in the dark with none other than Aaron Kaufmann. "Someone who goes to temple? Someone who has *become* a bat mitzvah?" The emphasis she placed on it was crueler than she meant. "Sorry. I just . . . You shouldn't have invited me tonight. I'm not Jewish enough for you. Or for your parents."

To her shock, he laughed. "Miri. What?"

She covered her face with her nonfrozen hand. "I don't know the prayers. I didn't even know who Miriam was."

"Aaron's sister," he said with a wry smile, and she swatted his arm.

"I eat *bacon*."

"The horror," he deadpanned. "I've seen you eat bacon. You had a BLT when we all went to that overpriced new sandwich place after practice last month."

"Oh." She didn't know why this felt so odd, like he'd observed something about her she hadn't realized she was advertising. Something else was bothering her, though. "Your parents said they wanted you to date someone Jewish." Her face burned despite the bag of peas she held to her head. "I'm the only other one in our grade. So I guess it doesn't matter how little I know about Judaism, just that I'm Jewish?"

He looked stunned. "No! No. I—I liked you before I knew you were Jewish. You don't have one of those Very Obviously Jewish last names. Lowe could go either way." He paused for a moment, and then: "I feel like an asshole. I shouldn't have corrected you about the bat mitzvah thing."

"You shouldn't have," she agreed. The bag of peas was starting to leak water onto her hand.

"I won't lie—I do like that you're Jewish," he said. He opened his mouth again, but then closed it abruptly.

"What?" she pressed.

"It might sound ridiculous. I almost don't want to say it."

"Well, now you have to."

He sighed. "Fine, fine. But—I think I do feel more connected to you because you're Jewish. Because we're both this thing that no one else in junior year is."

Something inside her cracked open, a new understanding. "I think I know what you mean."

"I swear, though, it's not the only thing I like about you," he said quickly.

"My Scattergories skills are pretty impressive."

"You are a Scattergories *master*." He shifted, ever so slightly, closer to her. Was he opening his palm because he wanted to hold her hand? "And . . . you are really, really cute. I've . . . uh . . . thought that for a while."

He was never open like this. Maybe it was the darkness, or the way the natural disaster had upended their evening, or the fact that they were alone in his room.

"You are too," she said, heart leaping into her throat as she laid her free hand in his. His fingers closed around hers, and she closed her eyes for a moment to savor the feeling, thumb against thumb and pinky against pinky. His hand warmed her cold one almost right away. "Cute."

In the dark, he was braver. There was a fearlessness with which he rubbed his thumb against hers, back and forth, back and forth. He dipped it into the grooves between her knuckles, releasing wild amounts of oxytocin into her bloodstream. Holding hands was a freaking gateway drug.

"I'm pretty sure I'm the nightmare boyfriend," he said glumly, as though disappointed in himself. "This is my first relationship, if that wasn't already obvious, given my inability so far to act even marginally human around you. It hasn't been a week, and I feel like I've already ruined it because I'm so . . . *weird.*"

"You haven't ruined it. If I haven't managed to ruin it yet, then you haven't either."

"Maybe . . . maybe it's that I can't wrap my mind around you wanting to be with me? Finding out a crush is mutual . . . it's scary. You're just *together,* and what is that supposed to look like? What are you supposed to say?" He snorted. "I was too nervous to even talk to you at school this week."

"I tried to find you at lunch."

He made a pained face. "I was eating in the library. I'm so sorry. I . . . want to be a good boyfriend. Honestly, I think I'm terrified of messing up. That's why I invited you tonight. I was nervous about being just us somewhere, that I wouldn't know what to do or say because I haven't all week. Like somehow it would be less weird with my parents?"

Both of them laughed at this.

"Little did you know, I'm awkward as hell around other people's parents," she said. Slowly, without releasing her grip on him, she leaned down so she could drop the bag of peas onto the floor.

"Miri." He held up their joined hands to gesture to himself. "So am I. I know we like each other, but . . . what now? That's kind of what it feels like. A big *what now.*"

Her heart slammed against her rib cage. "Can we be awkward together?" she asked in a soft rasp, spreading her fingers out across his knee like a starfish.

"Please," he said, and it sounded like a request for something else.

They were so close now that it was so, so easy to lean in and press her mouth to his. He met her there, his lips warm, gentle.

Their first kiss lasted only a few seconds before they moved apart as though to confirm neither of them was messing this up. Aaron let out this shaky exhale that made her toes curl with delight. *She had done that,* and it gave her the most incredible thrill.

"Hi," he said, and it was maybe the perfect thing to say in that moment. This between them: it was a beginning.

"Shalom," she said back, a joke.

He grinned like he'd just been told their Quiz Bowl team was going to nationals.

They dove for each other again, wilder this time. Aaron tangled his hands in her hair, drawing her closer, and she clasped hers behind his neck. They breathed each other in, exhaled in tandem. Their lips tongues teeth hands fingers arms legs hips were all awkward, but they'd learn. After all, the two of them were nothing if not overachievers.

When the next aftershock shook the floor beneath them, Miri wasn't sure if it was a natural phenomenon or the shuddering of her own heart.

GOOD SHABBOS[1]

BY GOLDY MOLDAVSKY

Kayla and S.T. stood outside of shul, and though the two girls had places to be, neither of them budged. Kayla because S.T. wasn't moving, and S.T. because she was too busy spying on the group of guys huddled together by the men's entrance. Or, more specifically, she was spying on one guy in particular.

"He's not the one with the basketball yarmulke, is he?" Kayla asked.

"Yep," S.T. said.

"You do realize it's a *basketball yarmulke.*"

S.T. ignored the tone in Kayla's voice. She didn't mind the choice of yarmulke—it stood out in the sea of black suits, and it meant that the boy who wore it was quirky. And that could only be a good thing. Maybe. Probably.[2]

"It's the color and texture of an actual basketball," Kayla continued.

---

[1] Shabbos, aka Shabbat, is a time to relax, unplug, and find joy for twenty-five hours between Friday sundown and Saturday sundown.

[2] My money's on no.

"I see what it looks like, thank you."

Kayla, S.T. thought, was way too preoccupied with the topping to notice what was underneath. Which was Moe's truly excellent hair.[3] Not that S.T. was superficial or anything. Moe had a great face, too. He had a lot of *great*s about him. He and S.T. were friendly over two different social media platforms, which was more than one, which meant something. Maybe. Probably. Thanks to his social media, S.T. knew that he davened at this shul, which was the only reason she'd come. And tonight, S.T. had decided, she would talk to Moe in person.

Except shul had been over for ten minutes, and S.T. still hadn't made a move. Kayla was only there for moral support, and even though there was a *basketball yarmulke* involved, she'd come too far to walk away now. She took her best friend's hand and marched over to the group. S.T. was both mortified and relieved. Of the two of them, Kayla had always been the one with beitzim.

"Excuse me," Kayla said, breaking through the knot of guys until she and S.T. stood before Questionable Yarmulke Choice. "You're Moe, right?"

"Yeah."

"You know my friend S.T., right?"

He looked over at S.T., a spreading smile of recognition on his face. "Oh, hey."

"Hey," S.T. replied.

And that was it. If Brooklyn had crickets, they'd be chirping right now. Awkwardness settled in like it'd bought tickets to this show. The rest of the guys were already starting to walk away, and S .T. and Moe didn't seem to have the training to

[3] Debatable.

resuscitate the conversation. Kayla did not have the patience for this. The mission was complete. Saw the boy. Said words to the boy. Time to go.

"Great meeting you," Kayla said, pulling S.T. away. "Good Shabbos."

"Wait, where are you guys eating your meal?" Moe asked.

"The Wexlers'!" S.T. said, quiz-show fast.[4]

"Cool. Hey, there's gonna be a party later tonight. Maybe you guys want to come after your meal?"

"We've got pl—" Kayla began, but S.T. cut her off.

"We'll be there!"

"Awesome—3497 number Two-A East Eighteenth," Moe said. "See you later."

As he walked away, S.T. repeated the series of numbers to herself, etching them into her mind.[5]

"What about the Shabbaton?"[6] Kayla said.

"Doesn't the party sound more fun?"

"So you're just going to go to meet up with a random schmuck?"

Kayla was thinking this, but to her surprise it wasn't her who'd uttered the words. They came from a different random schmuck about their age standing behind them. S.T. looked at

---

[4] Yeah, the type of quiz show where the prize was a lifetime supply of things nobody wanted. Okay, okay, I know I'm being kinda hard on S.T. and Basketball Yarmulke, but just because I'm narrating doesn't mean I can't ship. Or in this case, anti-ship. I'm with Kayla on this one. I don't see it for these two.

[5] Maybe you, upon hearing a convoluted series of numbers, would've written them down or voice-recorded them into your phone. But it being Shabbos, S.T. couldn't do any of those things. Shabbos was a day of rest, and right now that meant a very restful feat of mental gymnastics for a girl who frequently forgot her own phone number.

[6] A celebration held on Shabbos that may consist of a series of programs or activities. Kind of like a corporate retreat, only no one does trust falls. Kayla and S.T.'s school was hosting one.

him sideways. Now she was the one to grab Kayla's hand and pull. "That's none of your business."

"You're right. But I know that guy, and I don't think you'd like his kind of parties."

While Kayla may have totally been on his side—and even thankful for his advice—the chutzpah of him to butt in like this. "Excuse me, but do we know you?"

"No," he said.

"Then stop acting like it."

"Sorry I said anything," he said, but his chortle betrayed him.

The two girls crossed the street, only for the guy to do the same. He was taller than either of them, blond, and kept his head down like he was bracing against the cold, even though it was June.

"And quit following us," S.T. said over her shoulder.

"I'm not following you," he said. But minutes passed, and he remained a few paces behind them.

"Yes you are!" Kayla said. The girls sped up.

"You're going in the same direction I am!"

"Weirdo," S.T. whispered.

"It is decidedly so," Kayla said.

The girls reached the Wexler house and walked up the lawn to the front door. The boy saw them, stopped a moment, and then walked to the front door too.

"Okay, this is getting ridiculous," Kayla said. "We'll call the police."[7]

Mrs. Wexler answered the door. "Hi, girls. And Sruly." She seemed surprised to see him, but not in a get-off-my-front-porch sort of way. "Girls, this is Sruly. He'll be joining us for the meal."

---

[7] A bluff, unless she meant to call the police with the sheer volume of her voice.

S.T. caught control of her bottom lip just as it threatened to fall. She watched as Sruly's mouth turned up into a smirk, directly proportional to Kayla's snarl.

"Good Shabbos," he said to them.

The girls mustered a "Good Shabbos" back, and there was nary a less enthusiastic "Good Shabbos" uttered in all of Flatbush.

* * *

The class Shabbaton would officially get under way the next day, but there would be a small get-together tonight for a kumzits.[8] Until then, everyone in class was split into pairs and put up in the homes of host families.

Mr. and Mrs. Wexler sat at opposite ends of the dinner table, their twin six-year-olds, a boy and a girl, sat on one side, and next to them sat Sruly,[9] the weirdo guy who had followed them home.[10] His presence at the meal was still a mystery, since he was clearly too old to be Mr. and Mrs. Wexler's son. And what kind of teenager was friends with adults?[11] The couple had been too busy serving food—and telling their children to stop playing with it—to explain anything about Sruly, leaving the girls to wonder about him more than they liked.

"So how was shul?" Mr. Wexler asked.

"Really good," Kayla said.

"Inspiring," S.T. said.

---

[8] Sitting around, singing. A proper kumbaya sesh.

[9] Short for Israel.

[10] Except he hadn't really followed them. And this wasn't their home. And "weirdo" seems kind of over-the-top. But I digress.

[11] Maybe one who was mature for his age. I'm just saying.

"What was Rabbi Sherman's speech about?" Mrs. Wexler asked.

In all their time spying on Moe, the girls hadn't even noticed that the rabbi had given a speech, let alone what it was about. Even so, they did not hesitate to answer the question/make something up.

"Doing good?" "Learning stuff?" they said simultaneously.

Mr. Wexler considered the girls' words and nodded thoughtfully. "Sounds like a classic Rabbi Sherman speech."

"That's not how I remember it," Sruly said. The tone in his voice was all innocence, but the look he directed at Kayla and S.T. was pure accusation. "Wasn't it about how on Shabbos we should disconnect from the material world and open ourselves up to the possibility of more spiritual connections?"

He hadn't contributed a single thing to the dinner conversation thus far, and now he decided to articulate the entire meaning of Shabbos? Kayla and S.T. shot him a look across the table, but he didn't even blink, watching them right back as he took a bite of kugel.

"Sounds like Rabbi Sherman covered a lot of subjects tonight," Mrs. Wexler said.

Thankfully, there were no more questions that resulted in lies Sruly could catch the girls at. But he continued to spend the rest of the dinner in his shifty/sullen mood. Kayla made up a nickname for him: Surly Sruly. She'd have to tell S.T. when he was out of earshot.[12]

The meal wound down with Mr. Wexler trying to wax philosophical about spirituality but ending up on tangents

---

[12] Clever, but way too quick to judgment, imho. I would've gone with something more like Simpatico Sruly or Some Kind of Wonderful Sruly. But that's just me.

about how kids don't play with real toys anymore and that car insurance was so much cheaper in New Jersey.[13] As Mrs. Wexler stood up to clear dishes, S.T. popped up too, her own dish in hand. "Well, we've gotta get going if we want to make it to our kumzits."

At this, Kayla bounced out of her chair. Maybe S.T. had changed her mind. Maybe she hadn't spent the entire meal thinking about Basketball Yarmulke. But as soon as the girls stepped outside, all hope of that was gone. "Ready to party?" S.T. asked, her eyebrows dancing suggestively on her forehead.

"So we're definitely not going to the kumzits, then?"

"Tell you what: we'll go to the party first, stay a bit, and then if you really don't like it, I promise we'll go to the kumzits. Deal?"

Kayla didn't want to agree, but in the end it wasn't like she had a choice. She'd asked to be paired off with S.T. this weekend because they were best friends. And best friends stuck together. Plus, even if they were ditching the kumzits, they were still ditching it together, so really, she couldn't complain. "Fine. Which way do we go?"

S.T. paused to think and looked down one side of the block and then the other, as though somehow that would signal the correct direction. "Okay, I'm pretty sure there was a *three* in the address."

"You forgot it?"

"It's not my fault. That was more of a zip code than an address, I mean, right?"

"Sigh," Kayla said. She actually said the word out loud,

---

[13] Nisht Shabbos geredt. (And if you think I'm adding a footnote to this footnote, think again.)

having trouble with the line between sarcasm and sincerity. "If only you could ask him on Facebook."[14]

"I know of an oneg happening close by," Sruly said. As was apparently his MO, he'd sneaked up behind them. "Might be the one your guy was talking about."

"He's not my guy," S.T. said low, the blush creeping up her cheeks much louder.

"Is eavesdropping a hobby for you or . . . ?" Kayla snapped.

"I was just trying to help," Sruly said. He was already bounding down the porch steps. "But if you don't want any—"

"Wait," S.T. said. "Where is this party?"

"Come on, I'll walk you."

* * *

"You know, we don't need an escort," Kayla said as the three of them walked. "We can take care of ourselves."

"It's Brooklyn and dark out," Sruly said. "You could get mugged."

"Don't talk ill of Brooklyn like that," Kayla said.

"Yeah," S.T. said. "And it's not like they'd have anything to rob.[15] Plus, what would you do if we did get robbed? Fight off our assailant?"

Sruly shrugged. "Yeah."

S.T. and Kayla both snorted. They'd heard boys talk about the fights that broke out in yeshiva alleyways, but neither of

---

[14] Again, no.

[15] Very true. With no need for money on Shabbos and no phones on them, Kayla and S.T. really were terrible mugging targets. The thing of most value between them were Kayla's shoes, and considering they were a faded mouse brown, there was little chance anyone would want them.

them had ever seen any frum boys fight, didn't even know of any that *would.*[16]

"Well, we don't need a man to save us," S.T. said. "Because . . . feminism."

"Okay," Sruly said. He stopped walking, and the girls nearly bumped into him. "We're here." They stood in front of a building on Ocean Avenue, one of the taller ones. "Apartment Eight-B. Have fun."

"Wait, where are you going?" Kayla said.

"Chavrusa's waiting for me at shul. It was nice meeting you. Kind of."

Sruly walked off, and Kayla and S.T. were left standing in front of the building.

* * *

The girls were on the sixth floor of the stairwell, and although they were only two floors away now, it might as well have been thirty. "Who makes a party"—Kayla paused for breath—"on the eighth floor?" Another breath. "On Shabbos?"[17]

"Monsters," S.T. wheezed.

"The worst kinds of humans," Kayla agreed.

The two wordlessly decided to stop and take a break, but once their breath was caught, they kept climbing the stairs. "That was weird with Sruly, right?" Kayla asked.

"What do you mean?"

---

[16] Though if there ever were a frum boy who'd throw down, Sruly seemed to fit the bill. Confident yet steady. Head-down attitude. And buff. What I'm saying is, Sruly was buff.

[17] Can't use pens, phones, or Facebook on Shabbos, but did you also know you can't use elevators?

"Avoiding a party to go *study*? I didn't take him as the studying type."

Neither did S.T. Nothing about his casual Shabbos clothes,[18] messy hair,[19] or confidence in talking to girls struck her as attributes of a learned mensch. And yet.

"Aside from the fact that he butts into other people's business and that he's clearly a stalker, he wasn't technically *not* cute."

S.T. knew better than to try to untangle the compliment buried under Kayla's insults and double negatives, so she wasn't even going to try. "You like him?"

"No way. Boys are garbage.[20] But at least he doesn't go around wearing a basketball yarmulke."[21]

"Will you get over the yarmulke already?" S.T. said, finally landing on the eighth floor. The door to 8B was left slightly open. S.T. lifted her knuckles to knock, but Kayla got to it first, swinging it wide open. It was definitely a party, all right. Too many people, too many loud voices. "But also keep your eye out for that yarmulke," S.T. said.

* * *

In lieu of music,[22] sounds of chatter filled the tight apartment space. Laughter and schmoozing and political arguments,

[18] A checkered blue button-down. Which, among the light-colored button-downs, kind of made him a rebel. Maybe. Probably.

[19] Messy or expertly tossed? Let's go with the latter.

[20] Way harsh!

[21] Excellent point.

[22] No electronics, remember? Keep up!

which were enough to repel the girls whenever they caught whiffs of those. But there was something in the air. Something that made this unlike any party the girls had been to before. It became instantly clear just what kind of party this was.

"Kayla, is this what I think it is?"

Kayla nodded, recognizing the signs all around her. There was the age of the partygoers (college and above) and the manner by which people were approaching one another (shy, flirty). The aggressive conversation starters and bold style choices. The crumbly snack foods and overflowing wineglasses. Kayla had an older sister who spent plenty of nights meticulously applying her makeup for parties like this, all while whining about how much she hated going to them. "This is a singles party."[23]

S.T. and Kayla didn't need to consult each other before turning for the nearest exit, but a girl stepped up to them, drink in hand and eyebrow cocked. "You guys look really young."

"We're not," Kayla said, and apropos of nothing added, "We've been friends for twenty-seven years."

S.T. elbowed Kayla in the side. "No we haven't. She's kidding." But the girl who asked the question seemed to already regret it and walked away. "*Twenty-seven years?*" S.T. hissed. "People are going to think we're ancient."

"So?"

"I don't want people thinking I'm old at a singles party. And when did you get that drink?"

Kayla stared down at her cup, then back at S.T. for a prolonged moment. "Before."

---

[23] This is, like, a Thing. It is an established mark of Jewish life, as cemented as latkes on Chanukah. The fact that the girls stumbled into a singles party by accident wasn't all that surprising. More surprising was that they'd never stumbled into one before.

"*What?*" S.T. said. She was really good at the whisper-hiss. "You can't drink."

"But there is so much booze here," Kayla marveled. "And you said we were going to have an adventure tonight." Somehow, while saying all of this, Kayla had managed to walk over to the drinks table and refill her cup. She took another sip. "You've got Basketball Yarmulke—let me have my fun."

"Okay, we're going," S.T. said. She took her friend's hand. "Moe clearly isn't here."

"But wait. Over there. A sports yarmulke!"

S.T. followed Kayla's gaze, and there, indeed, was a yarmulke designed like a ball. Only not a basketball this time. White with red stitching. A baseball.

"I know who that is," S.T. said.

S.T. didn't need Kayla to find her courage this time. There was a new determination in her. The situation was a little bit more desperate, and if she was ever going to find Moe, she was going to have to make some moves. She marched right up to Baseball Yarmulke and interrupted his conversation with his friends. "You're Moe's brother."

He looked at her and Kayla a little strangely. "Yeah?" he said slowly.

"We're looking for him."

"*She's* looking for him," Kayla corrected, though nobody heard her, as her mouth was obscured by her cup.

"He's probably at Aaron Dwelig's house," Moe's brother said. "He goes there every Friday night."

"We need the address," S.T. said.

One of the guys listening laughed and made a comment about Moe having more game than his older brother, and

Kayla did not have enough drinks in her to put up with sports analogies.

"Uh," Moe's brother said. "I don't think it's a good idea for you to—"

"Don't try to tell us what we can and can't do," Kayla said. For the second time that night, she'd surprised herself by being combative with a guy who was clearly on her side of things. But, feminism. So. "We're capable of making our own choices."

"Fine," he said. "It's 3497 number Two-A East Eighteenth."

* * *

Outside, S.T. was still repeating the address to herself, increasingly wondering if she got the numbers in the correct order. She wished she could reach for a pen. Though what Kayla said made her stop muttering altogether.

"I don't want to go."

"What do you mean?"

"It's like ten blocks away. And the kumzits is actually five blocks away." She hiccupped. "It's *faaar.*"

"You really want to go to the kumzits?" S.T. took a step closer to her friend, the urgency with which she moved matching her tone. "It's going to be a bunch of girls we already see in school. Sitting on the floor. *Singing.*"

"Well, maybe I want to do that," Kayla said. "You know, I was excited about this Shabbaton. I thought it'd be like a fun sleepover where our parents wouldn't be around to bug us, but all you want to do is go chase some boy all night."

This gave S.T. pause. She knew Kayla was right. All they'd talked about tonight was Moe, and all they'd done was try to find him. A boy who wore a basketball yarmulke. And it was all S.T.'s fault. "Okay. Let's go to the kumzits."

"Really?" Kayla said.

"Yeah. I already forgot the address, anyway."

Kayla let out a tiny, excited squeal.

* * *

The kumzits was held at the home of S.T. and Kayla's earth science teacher, Mrs. Bingheimer. It was kind of embarrassing going to a teacher's house on a Friday night. Made even more embarrassing by the fact that when she saw S.T. and Kayla at the door, she quipped, "Girls! Come, sits."[24] Based on the decor in the living room, it seemed that when Mrs. Bingheimer wasn't busy grading tests, she was majorly obsessing over cats.

Cat photos in frames, cats embroidered on couch cushions, even a few actual cats meandering between girls' feet, some settling comfortably on laps. An evening of cats and singing. S.T. sat and began planning her escape, though a quick glance at the cat clock on the wall told her they'd only been there three minutes.

Kayla plopped down next to S.T. like a life raft. She'd been in the dining room and kitchen, helping herself to a selection of snacks Mrs. Bingheimer had laid out for the evening. In one hand, Kayla clutched a handful of Viennese crunch and lady-fingers. In the other, a cup. You only had to be standing an inch away from Kayla to know immediately what was in the cup.

[24] Fun fact: "come sit" is exactly where the Yiddish word "kumzits" originates, so while still a painfully unfunny joke, let's cut Mrs. Bingheimer some slack.

"Where the hell did you find booze?" S.T. whispered. "Again."

"It is literally all over the house," Kayla said. "In the back of her spice cabinet. And Mrs. Bingheimer told us to make ourselves at home."

"Is this what you do at home?"

"You know it's strictly Manischewitz at my house. But if I can handle that, I think I can handle this."

"I can't believe you're drinking in a teacher's house. You're a lush."

"And I think you're very luxurious too, thank you."

"Girls," Mrs. Bingheimer said. She spoke over the harmonizing vocal stylings of the rest of the girls in the class, directly at S.T. and Kayla. "Less talking, more singing, please."

And so Kayla sang. She sang loudly. Good singers sing with their diaphragm. Bad ones with their head. Kayla sang with the contents of her cup, the booze making her words and musical notes swirl together until she was standing in the center of the room, her voice loud enough to drown out everyone else's. In time, all the girls stopped singing, leaving only Kayla to perform, which meant there was no melody in the room at all, just loud, shrieking words that may have been Hebrew or a language none of them knew.

"Kayla!" Mrs. Bingheimer said. "You're disrupting the kumzits."

Kayla stopped, genuinely confused. "I am?"

"If you can't participate n—"

"Hey!" S.T. said. She came to stand beside Kayla. "Kayla wanted to come here so bad tonight. She wanted a spiritual experience. She wanted inclusivity. And she wanted to sing. If you're just going to kick her out, then we don't want to be here anyway."

"I wasn't going to kick her out," Mrs. Bingheimer said. "I was going to suggest she wait until she knows the song before she joins in. I don't think anyone here is familiar with what she's singing."[25]

"Oh," S.T. said. The word started off indignant but ended up sounding defeated. Now the whole room was staring at her and Kayla. It was time to get out of there. "Yeah, we're still gonna go."

* * *

"I'm sorry," Kayla said. She and S.T. walked with their arms linked. "I ruined everything."

"I didn't even want to go to the kumzits, remember?"

"Yeah, but I made you stop looking for Moo."

"Moe."

"Whatever."

S.T. let it go. At least Kayla wasn't calling him Basketball Yarmulke anymore. "No, you were right. This Shabbaton was supposed to be about us, and I made it all about a boy. And anyway, even if I did want to go find Moe, we can't. I forgot the address again."

"I didn't."

S.T. stopped walking, and since she and Kayla were attached, Kayla stopped short too. "Photographic memory for

[25] It was "Despacito," by Luis Fonsi, and everyone in the room besides Mrs. Bingheimer was definitely familiar with it.

useless information," she explained. "All these other parties were a bust. We might as well stop by Moe's."

This time S.T. was the one to let out a tiny, excited squeal.

* * *

When Aaron Dwelig opened the door to his house, it was as though he had never seen girls before in his life. Kayla and S.T. were only midway through with the explanation for their presence there, but Aaron cut them off, inviting them in and immediately ushering them through the house. It was quiet, with the lights all on but nobody there.

"So where's this party?" S.T. asked.

Aaron stopped at a door beside the kitchen and opened it. "In the basement," he said.

"This isn't sketchy at all," Kayla muttered so only S.T. would hear, though she was pretty sure Aaron was listening to every word. "We should get out of here. We should go now."

S.T. poked Kayla discreetly in the side, which was when she noticed the bottle in Kayla's hand. "Where the hell did you get that?"

"It was right there in the fridge," Kayla said.

S.T. rolled her eyes and turned to Aaron. "Lead the way."

The finished basement was a teenage boy's dream, or at least a place a teenage boy would come to hibernate without the meddling interference of parents or cleaning ladies or Febreze.

"Please, let's go," Kayla whispered.

The place indeed had a faint whiff of canned boy mixed with feet. Flickering lamplight illuminated the wall decor, which was little more than haphazardly hung street signs.

YIELD, STOP, and DO NOT ENTER. Kayla took these signs literally. "Now. We should go now."

There were way too many couches lining the walls, all with sports-themed wool blankets strewn over them that you couldn't pay any girl to touch. Blue-and-orange Nerf bullets littered the floor like the world's most juvenile war had just broken out. In the distance, a toilet flushed, and then a boy walked out of the bathroom, holding his abdomen. "Well, I just lost about two pounds," he announced proudly.

"Immediately. *We need to get the hell out of here.*" Kayla wasn't even whispering anymore.

In the center of the room were five guys, all sitting around a table, cards in hand. "Hey!" Moe said when he saw S.T. "You made it."

S.T. lit up. "Hi."

"Are you guys playing poker?" Kayla asked.

"No, Magic: The Gathering."

"What?" S.T. and Kayla said.

"Magic: The Gathering," Moe repeated.

"Sorry, I don't think I heard you right," S.T. said.

"Yeah, it sounded like you said you were playing Magic: The Gathering," Kayla said.

"We are," Moe said.[26]

An extraordinary silence fell over the room.[27] The boys, their cards frozen in their hands, watched the girls carefully. S.T. and Kayla exchanged loaded glances in which so much

---

[26] Although Magic: The Gathering is one of the most popular games in the world, it is a well-known fact that its players lose their attractiveness almost as soon as the cards come out. There's really no way around that.

[27] Akin to a gathering of magic, some might say.

was said and so much was decided. It was the kind of glance that only girls who had been friends for a mythical twenty-seven years could have.

"We need to go," S.T. said.

* * *

"I am so sorry."

"No, I'm sorry," Kayla said.

They were outside again, holding each other close like they'd just escaped hell.[28] Running, stumbling as far from 23982397276456323 #2A East Eighteenth Street as they could get.

They got as far as the mailbox on the corner, because Kayla bumped into it.[29] "S.T.?" she said. "I think I'm drunk."

"No kidding." S.T. wasn't going to be able to guide her back to the Wexlers' all by herself. She looked around, and that was when her eyes fell on the shul across the street.

* * *

Sruly carried Kayla.[30]

"Thank you for doing this," S.T. said. "But this doesn't change anything. We didn't need an escort or a man to protect

---

[28] And let's face it, a party of Magic: The Gathering nerds is a certain kind of hell.

[29] "Bump" may be too light a word. She crashed into it. She struggled against it. And the mailbox won.

[30] If you wanna know the truth, there were so many issues with this. Among them, a boy and girl touching and him carrying, which is technically work, which—like cell phones and elevators—is not allowed on Shabbos. But, considering the circumstances, I'd give the guy a break. Plus, Kayla didn't mind being carried around. And did I not tell you this boy was buff?

us or anything like that. I would carry Kayla myself, but she's . . . like . . . way heavier drunk."

"I wasn't going to say anything," Sruly said, though the mirthful twinkle in his eye made that questionable.

"I am not drunk," Kayla said.

"You're slurring your words," Sruly said.

Kayla laughed. "I'm slurry, Surly Sruly?" The fact that she was able to keep all that straight proved that she was at least sobering up. She swung between the two extremes. Right now her pendulum seemed to swing toward "out of it." She may have even been dozing off.

"She got this drunk at the oneg?" Sruly asked.

"And a few other places," S.T. said. "We ended up at the right party after all. But they were playing Magic: The Gathering."

Sruly visibly shuddered. "I tried to warn you."

"Don't worry—we left immediately. How did you know it wouldn't be our scene?"

"Those guys invited me to play cards once before," Sruly said. "I thought it would be poker, and then the cards had, like, ogres on them. I left and never looked back."

"Maybe I like ogres."

Sruly cocked a skeptical eyebrow, and a laugh bubbled up in S.T. that she couldn't tamp down. Both of them laughed, actually, and it was sort of nice. In the back of S.T.'s mind, if she really thought about it, it was even kind of flirty. Which made her suddenly self-conscious, and a moment languished awkwardly between them, where the only sound was that of the cars whizzing by.

"So, you eat by the Wexlers a lot?" S.T. asked.

"Pretty much every Shabbos."

"That's a lot."

"My parents aren't religious," Sruly said. "They don't really do the whole Shabbos thing. But I love it, so . . . the Wexlers have been really good to me."

Another moment. Though not as heavy. This time Sruly picked up the slack. "So was your Shabbaton everything you thought it was going to be?"

"Not exactly. Still not bad, though. We met some interesting people."

"Yeah, I once heard something about Shabbos and surprising connections."

S.T. smiled, but her unmatched ability for letting conversations die slow, painful deaths came back with a vengeance. She didn't know why it was suddenly awkward, and thinking about it made her cheeks burn. A sneaky look at Sruly revealed that his cheeks were looking kind of ruddy too. Though that could've easily been explained by the exertion of carrying Kayla around.[31] Thankfully, there wasn't any pressure for more convo, because they were back at the house. They spied Mrs. Wexler in the window.

"We can't let her see Kayla like this," S.T. said.

Sruly put Kayla down. She stayed on her feet but leaned on S.T. for support. "I'll distract her," Sruly said.

"Really?" S.T. said.

"Sure. Just promise that next time, she takes it easy on the drinks. Or at least invite me to join."

S.T. nodded, her blush coming back as her mind lingered

---

[31] That wasn't it.

on that "next time." She would have to figure out a way to finagle an invite back to the Wexlers' in the near future.

Sruly took off toward the front door and knocked. S.T. and Kayla stood off to the side of the house and waited. Mrs. Wexler let Sruly in, and through the window S.T. could see that he led her to the kitchen. She helped Kayla up the porch steps and then straight to the guest bedroom in the basement.

* * *

Kayla was all tucked in, and though there were two twin beds, S.T. climbed in beside her friend. She thought Kayla was asleep, but then she spoke.

"Thanks for bringing me back here."

"Sruly's the one who carried you."

"Surly Sruly's strong. He probably could beat up muggers."

S.T. agreed, and her mind wandered to a scenario where he did just that. She was thankful that it was dark and that Kayla couldn't see her face.

"He's not a garbage person."

"No, he's not," S.T. said. "I'm sorry everything turned out awful."

"It wasn't that bad," Kayla said. "We got to spend Shabbos together. That's a win in my book."

S.T. thought of the whole night—of running around town with her best friend, of discovering the other side to a surly boy, even of the disappointing "party" in the basement. It all lived inside a sort of bubble she didn't want to pop. "The biggest win," she agreed.

They curled up like best friends do, and went to sleep.

JEWBACCA

BY LANCE RUBIN

"Dude, no one is gonna know how Jewish or not Jewish you are. It's just people hanging out."

Rye had heard this from Josh before, but for whatever reason, this time it actually worked, which is why he was now at an open mic hosted by the Temple Beth Shalom youth group, nodding his head to an unimpressive acoustic guitar rendition of Ed Sheeran's "Galway Girl" as he clutched a cup of Sprite. He didn't feel like he belonged, exactly, but he didn't feel like he *didn't* belong either. So. That was something.

Josh was next to him, talking with two girls. One of them was Jamie Stein, who'd gone to school with them since first grade, but the other—tall, sparkly-eyed, gesturing a lot—Rye did not recognize. He instantly liked her, which created a weird tension in the center of his chest, the desire to endlessly stare countered by the desire to look literally everywhere except at her.

"Oh," Jamie said, possibly noticing Rye's brain melting down. "This is Rye. He goes to our school too. Rye, Dara. Dara, Rye."

"Hey," Rye said.

"Hi," Dara said.

And there it was, the full extent of their interaction during the open mic. Rye generally thought of himself as a quick-witted person, but in the sanctified space of Temple Beth Shalom's all-purpose room, he felt more like an amoeba.

Luckily, the universe or Jewish God or some beneficent force smiled upon him, somehow aligning his stars so that after the event wrapped up—with a rhyming spoken-word poem about nuclear disarmament—and everyone headed to Friendly's, Rye ended up squished into a booth next to Dara.

"Hey," he said.

"Hi again," Dara said, twisting her body to take off her purple coat.

He then stared forward, elbows held tight to his body, fingers tapping the table, no clue what to say next. His body tingled from the close proximity. He could smell strawberry lip gloss.

"You didn't perform anything," Dara said.

"Oh," Rye said. "Nah. I don't really do that."

"Me neither." The relief and gratitude that coursed through Rye upon finding a shared experience was palpable. "Jamie and I and one of our other friends did a song from *Pitch Perfect* at the last one, and I was shaking the whole time. I don't think I'm designed to perform in front of other people."

"Are you designed to perform *not* in front of other people?" Rye asked, surprising himself with how calm and confident he sounded.

"Oh, definitely," Dara said. "At home in my room I'm *amazing*. I win Grammys."

Rye laughed, and Dara smiled. A server came by and took

the table's orders. Rye pointed blindly at something ice cream related on the menu, scared that if he stopped talking to Dara for too long, the moment would end, and it would be too hard to get one started again. "At least you can sing," he said, turning back to her. "All I have is a Chewbacca impression."

"Seriously?" Dara said, her face lighting up. Rye wasn't sure she'd even know who Chewbacca was, which he realized was probably sexist. "Why didn't you do it?"

"Um," Rye said, "I don't know. Because it's weird. And really short."

"I love weird, really short things."

Rye laughed again, reveling in that flirtatious "love," uttered to him by a girl he was liking more every second.

"Can you do it?" Dara asked.

"Wait, what? The impression?"

"Duh, yes. You can't mention a Chewbacca impression and not do it."

"Oh!" Josh shouted across the table. "Yes! It's so good."

"What is?" Jamie Stein asked.

Rye felt his face getting warm.

"Rye's Chewbacca impression."

"Who's Jewbacca?"

"Do it, dude," Josh said, and Rye felt all eyes at the table on him—and some from the tables behind and in front of them too—though he was, of course, most aware of the shiny green eyes immediately to his left.

"Okay, okay," Rye said, ignoring the panic welling in his chest, never having done his impression for an audience larger than his family or Josh.

"This is so exciting," Dara said, giving Rye the necessary

boost of encouragement to turn off his mind and unleash his inner Wookiee.

He knew he'd nailed it.

"Whoa-my-god," Dara said, one hand over her mouth as she laughed in disbelief, everyone else joining her.

"Easy, Chewie," the server said as he walked by.

Rye was elated, adrenaline pumping, endorphins dancing.

"My parents would love that," Dara said. "They're *Star Wars* freaks."

"Not mine," he said. "They're just regular freaks."

Dara laughed, her shoulder pressing into his with extra pressure, and that's when he knew something was starting.

* * *

Still cracking up about that impression, Dara texted later that night, sending a jolt of electricity through Rye's body.

That wasn't actually an impression, he texted from bed. *I'm part Wookiee.*

I KNEW IT

Rye sent a cry-laughing emoji as he laughed in real life.

Win any Grammys lately? he texted the next day.

Oh yeah, Dara replied. *All the time. Best Female Vocalist in My Room for over a decade now.*

I'm so proud of you. Rye held his breath, unsure if that response, which he'd spent ten minutes deciding whether to send, was too much.

Dara emoji-blushed.

The texting grew exponentially every day until, almost a week in, Rye texted: *I'm worried we're gonna run out of inside jokes to make about the night we met.*

Me too, Dara wrote back within seconds. *Guess we should meet up. Get some more material.*

Good call, Rye said, unable to stop smiling.

Is your temple having another open mic anytime soon?

Rye's breath caught in his chest as he read the words, wild panic squirming around his insides.

Dara thought Temple Beth Shalom was his temple. Of course she did.

Rye *was* technically Jewish—his last name was Silverstein and everything—but it was more complicated than that. Or maybe it was simple: His family never went to synagogue, didn't fast on Yom Kippur, had no problem devouring yeasty foods during Passover. Oh, and also, Rye's dad had become a Buddhist right after college and had a shrine room in their house, where he meditated, sometimes multiple times a day.

See? Simple.

The whole situation had been a perpetual source of anxiety, especially when Rye was younger. Everyone assumed he was Jewish, and Rye, knowing it was at least kind of true, never corrected them. "What'd you get for Hanukkah last night?" Josh would ask in elementary school, and Rye would scramble to fabricate a gift, the truth being that most of his presents weren't coming till Christmas. Because, oh right, Rye's mom hung stockings every year, and he, his parents, and his younger brother, Cliff—none of them even part Christian—celebrated Christmas. Because, as his mom had once said, "It's fun!" To this day, it was a relief when Christmas fell during Hanukkah.

Presents weren't the only thing Rye had lied about, though. In second grade, his imposter angst had compelled him to google a temple a few towns over and tell Josh his family went there. It was a falsehood that he had maintained for years, until they both turned thirteen and Rye realized manufacturing a fake bar mitzvah was a lie too cumbersome, perhaps impossible, to run with.

Josh thought it was hilarious that Rye had gone to so much trouble for no reason, but he hadn't actually cared.

And here Rye was again, mistaken for someone who belonged.

He knew he needed to respond, that Dara had been staring at three dots for at least two minutes now. He couldn't start their relationship with a lie.

It's actually not my temple, he wrote.

But before he hit send, Dara wrote, *I'm totally kidding. We obviously shouldn't wait for another open mic to meet up.*

Rye replaced what he'd written with *Haha good* and sent that instead.

* * *

Rye was hoping it wouldn't come up again for a while, but halfway into their first date, eating a couple of greasy slices at Antonio's, Dara said, "My parents love that I'm out with a nice Jewish boy."

Rye knew this was the moment to clarify. A text could be misread, but not speaking now would be a more active form of deceit. Still, he didn't want to risk the look of disappointment on Dara's face when she learned the truth.

And so: active deception it was.

"That's me, all right!" Rye said, wiping his mouth with a napkin to catch any stray tomato sauce.

Turns out, Rye's knack for impressions extended beyond

hirsute aliens from the planet Kashyyyk. Over the next couple of weeks, he became the nice temple-attending Jewish boy Dara and her parents assumed he was. And it wasn't that hard! Just had to throw in the occasional reference to going to services with his family. Sure, part of him felt a little guilty, but the rest of him felt great. At Rye's homecoming dance, he and Dara barely left the dance floor, decided they were officially boyfriend and girlfriend, and made out afterward in Dara's car for forty-seven minutes straight. It all felt vaguely unreal, this private joy Rye carried around every day.

But, not even twenty-four hours later, things became more difficult.

Rye and Dara were on the phone—yes, they liked each other that much—talking about the freakishly warm November weather, and climate change, and what the world would be like by the time they were adults. "It's so disturbing," Dara said. "My dad puts it into his sermons a lot, so there's that."

"Oh cool," Rye said, sure he'd misheard. "Wait, puts it into his what?"

"His sermons. Hopefully reprogram some of the more conservative brains in our synagogue."

"Oh yeah, that's great," Rye said, trying to disguise the alarm in his voice. *Sermons.* " 'Cause your dad's a . . . rabbi?" He barely got out the last word.

"Ha, yeah," Dara said. "At Temple Sinai. You didn't know that?"

Rye was doubly caught off guard, as that was the very temple he'd lied to Josh about belonging to for almost six years. For the first time, Rye thought there might be a God. One who enjoyed messing with people. Like him. "Um, oh wow," he said, trying not to throw up into the phone. "I think I . . . Yeah, I maybe did, but— Oh, right, yeah, now that sounds— Yeah. I think I did."

"He's really good. You have to come hear him sometime."

"For sure, yeah," Rye said. He didn't know how he'd been picturing Dara's dad, but it certainly wasn't as a rabbi. He did not realize rabbis could be *Star Wars* freaks.

Either way, the jig was up. Keeping up his charade for a couple of ordinary everyday Jewish parents he could handle, but for a *rabbi*? That was like trying to fool a Jewish superhero. There was no way.

The problem was Rye had never liked a girl even half as much as he liked Dara.

He would have to push forward.

And really, how much would he have to interact with her parents, anyway?

This strategy worked well enough for a few weeks. When Dara invited Rye over for dinner, he unfortunately already had plans with his own family. When she invited him again the next week, he had to help his brother, Cliff, with his algebra homework. (This made no sense on multiple levels. Rye was terrible at algebra.)

After the second refusal, Dara seemed slightly skeptical but was kind enough not to push him on it. But then, days later, she invited Rye to her house again. For a Hanukkah party.

"We've been doing it since I was a baby," she explained. "It's always really fun. And my dad's latkes are amazing."

Rye immediately understood how much Dara wanted him to come. He also understood that refusing this would be the third strike. He'd be out.

But this rabbi-hosted celebration would very likely expose him as the imposter Jew he was, and once that happened, he might be out, anyway.

"Uh . . ."

"You don't have to come if you don't want to. Or if you're busy again or whatever."

"No, no, it's not that . . . ," Rye said, stalling for time, working through the various permutations of how the party could play out, trying to identify the best-case scenario, which was probably wowing Dara's rabbi dad with his Chewbacca impression early on and not having to speak the rest of the night.

"Lemme guess," Dara said. "You have to help your sister with her geography homework."

"I don't have a sister," Rye said.

"Exactly."

Rye laughed nervously. "Good one. But actually, it's that . . ." He wanted to tell her. He knew he should probably tell her. "I'm very bad at dreidel spinning," he deadpanned instead.

Dara laughed. "Well, that is a problem, but we can work through it together."

So there it was. He'd be taking his nice-Jewish-boy act on the road.

* * *

When the fourth night of Hanukkah arrived, Rye felt as prepped as he possibly could be. He'd done thorough research, both on the Internet and using Josh as a primary source. The Temple Beth Shalom rabbi? Sheila Lipkin, beloved by all. The cantor? Ross Kramer, very nice man with terrible pitch. Rye walked into his girlfriend's house, a list in his head of the imaginary presents he'd so far received, ready to do his new impression for his biggest audience yet.

"You must be Rye," a shorter, older version of Dara said, appearing in the foyer of the house and shaking his hand. "I'm Robin. We've heard so much about you."

"Oh, hi," Rye said, wondering if he seemed Jewish enough, if he was already failing some unspoken test. "Same. It's really nice to meet you." He had to raise his voice to be heard over the din of chatter.

"You're so sweet!" Dara's mom gestured to the yellow tulips in Rye's left hand, the ones his mom had forced him to bring.

"Hanukkah tulips," he said, handing them to her.

Dara's mom laughed. "That's cute. Thank you." Maybe it was that easy: Rye only had to add the word "Hanukkah" to whatever he said, and he could charm his way through the entire party.

"Dara's around here somewhere. Follow me." Rye involuntarily held his breath as they walked into a well-furnished family room filled with people of all ages, including four kids taking turns chasing each other with a Swiffer. "She's probably in the kitchen." Dara's mom barreled forward, but Rye was cut off mid-stride by a clean-shaven man wearing a white button-down shirt, thick glasses, and a blue yarmulke made of yarn.

"Hello," the man said, extending his hand. "I'm Shelly."

"Hi. I'm Rye." Shelly's handshake felt like a threat, extra firm and vigorous.

"Short for Uriah?" That was new. Usually people asked if it was short for Ryan.

"No. Just Rye."

"Huh. You're Jewish?"

Rye nodded.

"Interesting. You don't hear of many Jews named Rye." Shelly smiled disingenuously. "Your parents must love a good corned-beef sandwich, huh?"

Rye tried not to wince. The irony of his parents inadvertently naming him after a Jewish deli staple (while trying to name him after one of their favorite novels) was not something he enjoyed.

"Like rye bread," Shelly added.

"Yeah." Rye made a sound he hoped resembled a laugh right before his legs got whacked by the tail end of the Swiffer, more startling than painful.

"Elijah," Shelly said sharply to the ten-year-oldish boy who'd swiffed him. "You have to be careful with that." Shelly shook his head, then gestured a hand in Rye's direction. "What brings you here?"

"Um, I'm Dara's . . . friend."

He wasn't sure why he'd said friend instead of boyfriend. Probably because he didn't trust Shelly.

"Oh, wonderful," Shelly said, no longer smiling. "My son Matthew is also a friend of Dara's." Shelly called out across the room, where a group of guys were in conversation.

"What?" Matthew said, looking over with a peeved expression. He was Rye's age, maybe a year or two older.

"Come over here."

Matthew had light hair and broad shoulders and wore, like his father, a crisp white button-down and a yarn yarmulke, except his was orange and blue.

"Matthew, this is Rye," Shelly said. "He's friends with Dara."

In a heartbeat, Matthew's eyes shifted from disinterested to magnetic, and a chill bounced down Rye's spine. "Nice to meet you," Matthew said, not unkindly. "How do you know Dara?"

Rye searched the room behind Shelly and Matthew, wishing he was not in this conversation. "We met at an open mic night. At Temple Beth Shalom."

"Is that your temple?" Matthew asked, and for the second time in five minutes, Rye felt like he was being subtly threatened.

He tried to seem confident, to believe the lie before he said it. "Yup. It's a, you know, it's a great place. Cantor Kramer is . . . very nice."

Rye was unimpressed with his own performance, but Matthew and Shelly seemed to buy it.

"Sorry, gentlemen," Dara's mom said, mercifully poking her head among them. "But Rye's been requested in the kitchen."

"Oh," Shelly said, eyebrows raised. "Well then."

Rye finally exhaled as he left Matthew and Shelly and entered the kitchen, which was even more of a scene than the family room, people flitting around an island in the center of the room, arranging platters, shouting things. A lanky man in an apron stood in front of the stove, flipping potato latkes. Dara was next to him, also aproned, holding the plate that served as the latke landing pad.

"Yay!" she said as she spotted Rye, breaking out in a huge smile that made his heart inflate. "You're here!"

"I am!" he said.

"The famous Rye," the aproned man said, turning from the potato pancakes to look right at him, inciting a wave of nausea. "The Rye man. Rye guy. Pleasure to finally meet you. I'm Jake. But you can call me Rabbi Goldfarb."

"Dad!"

"Okay, fine, I guess you can call me Jake." He smiled at Rye, who was charmed and taken aback by this joker of a rabbi. His name was *Jake*? Rye would have thought men named Jake wouldn't qualify to be rabbis. Only Mordecais and Bens and Levs.

"Here," Dara's mom said, taking the plate out of Dara's hands, "let me take over and you can show Rye around."

Dara passed her apron to her mother and took Rye's hand, leading him into another room. As her fingers intertwined with his, Rye felt something unwind within him. "How's it going? I hope nobody pressured you to spin a dreidel."

Rye laughed. "No, not yet. I did get cornered by Shelly and Matthew, though."

"Ugh." Dara rolled her eyes. "Sorry. They're family friends. I mean, also Matthew and I were dating for a little while, but it's not a big deal."

It made sense now. The vaguely threatening handshake, the flip from apathy to intense interest. Dara already *had* dated a nice Jewish boy. And Rye's high-wire act this evening would now be that much more challenging to pull off.

"Hey, Becs," Dara said as they crossed paths with a teenage girl even taller than Dara. She wore huge clear-rimmed glasses. "This is Rye."

"Oh," Becs said, barely looking at him. "Hi."

"This is my sister, Rebecca," Dara said. She'd often mentioned how awesome her older sister was, so Rye was thrown to learn that Rebecca's awesomeness didn't seem to extend to making her sister's new boyfriend feel welcome.

"Do you know where more candles are?" Rebecca asked Dara.

"Like, Hanukkah candles?"

"Duh."

"I don't know. Maybe in the bathroom linen closet?"

Rebecca sighed and walked past them.

"She gets really stressed when we host parties," Dara said.

She pulled Rye back to the family room, toward a folding table covered with a blue-and-white paper tablecloth, a pattern of lit menorahs, dreidels, and Stars of David peppering its edges. Rye was struck by how similar the table's spread—cheese, vegetable crudités, and crackers next to some kind of spread, probably whitefish salad—was to the kind his mother would put out while hosting.

"My mom's friend Rhonda made the whitefish salad," Dara said, cutting herself a piece of cheese. "I don't do smoked fish, but everyone says it's incredible."

"My mom's obsessed with whitefish salad," Rye said, noticing Matthew out of the corner of his eye, kneeling on the floor with a bunch of kids, guiding them through a game of dreidel. *He's like the Jewish Pied Piper,* Rye thought to himself. He hadn't clocked Matthew's boyish good looks earlier, but he definitely did now.

"Oh well, you got nun," Matthew told one of the kids. "So none for you!"

Rye's stomach dropped.

In all of his extensive preparation, he'd been so focused on Temple Beth Shalom that he'd forgotten to do any research on Hanukkah. It was a huge oversight. Sure, he knew how to spin a dreidel, but he always forgot the names of the Hebrew letters. And what they meant. *Nun means none,* he mentally noted now, trying to soak up whatever he could on the fly.

"Are you okay?" Dara asked. "You seem kinda . . . nervous. You don't actually have to play dreidel."

"No, I know," Rye said, dipping a celery stick. "I, uh, I just . . . you know, meeting your parents for the first time and everything."

"Aww, that's so endearing. I think they really like you." Even though they'd literally met him within the past half hour, Rye was comforted to hear that.

"Agh!" one of the kids shouted as Matthew wrestled him to the floor.

"I'm sorry I didn't tell you about Matthew sooner," Dara said, probably noticing the forlorn look on Rye's face. "It's so not a big deal, which is why it didn't even occur to me."

"He seems like a good Jew," Rye said, almost involuntarily.

"What?" Dara asked.

"Just, you know," Rye said, "that he wears a yarmulke and knows a lot about dreidel and stuff."

Dara stared at Rye as if he'd just explained he was part guinea pig and was wondering if she had a wheel he could run on for a while.

As if out of nowhere, Dara's mom appeared with four other women, descending upon the table and clearing away all of the apps in under a minute.

"You need help, Mom?" Dara asked.

"We got it, we got it," she said, balancing three separate serving dishes in her arms.

"Here," Matthew said, swooping in and grabbing two of the serving dishes before Robin reached the kitchen. Dammit. It was like page 1 of the *How to Be a Nice Jewish Boy* handbook.

When Dara's mom and her entourage came out of the kitchen again—this time carrying steaming platters of brisket, noodle pudding, potato latkes, and carrot soufflé—Rye was ready. "Here," he said, intercepting Robin a moment before Matthew could. "I'll take that."

"Oh, that's sweet," she said as she passed him a platter piled high with latkes, so many latkes.

"No problem!" Rye said. The platter smelled amazing, though it was heavier than he'd expected. *Don't drop them,* he thought, taking slow steps toward the table. *Don't drop them.*

"Ya got that?" Dara asked.

"Definitely," Rye said as much to himself as to her. The table was only two feet away now, and he was about to start breathing easy when his foot stepped onto something round and plastic.

The goddamn Swiffer.

It had somehow ended up on the floor right next to the table.

Rye lost his balance as his foot rolled with the Swiffer's handle, but he was determined not to fall, drawing on every muscle in his body to counter the forces of gravity. He wobbled forward, close enough to the table that he was able to put the platter down.

He felt triumphant. For a moment.

But then he realized with horror that he'd placed it onto a previously unnoticed seam, one side of the table's surface slightly higher than the other, and as three women pointlessly shouted "Watch out!" Rye observed the platter slide and then topple off the table's edge. He stuck out his hands at the last moment, blindly fumbling. He caught half a latke.

I dropped them, Rye thought, his vision a blur of potato pancakes and light blue platter shards strewn on the floor. *I dropped the rabbi's latkes.* "Sorry, so sorry," he said.

He looked up for a moment and immediately wished he could unsee Dara's shocked expression. This was not going the way he had planned. He crouched down, about to start picking up latkes with his bare hands when Dara's mom swooped in.

"No no," she said. "Let me." She cradled each fallen latke in a paper towel as she placed it onto a new platter.

"I'm really sorry," he said again. "I'd love to— Can I go buy some more potatoes? Or, I could— I'm sorry about the platter. I'll definitely replace—"

"Oh come on, don't be silly," Dara's mom said. "Mistakes happen."

He couldn't help but think of himself as the mistake that had happened to her daughter. The entire party had stopped what they were doing to watch. Rye was crouching next to Dara's mom as she inspected latkes, placing some on the new platter and others into a garbage bag. He didn't want to look for Dara, afraid she would wordlessly point a finger at the door: *Go.*

Instead, he heard her voice in his ear. "You can stand up. It's okay. And you can stop holding that." He still had the half of latke.

"Oh." He gingerly placed it into the garbage bag. "I'm sorry I just, like, ruined everything."

"You haven't ruined anything, Drama Queen. Come with me."

Dara grabbed the hand that wasn't coated in latke oil and passed Rye a napkin to clean the one that was. She wasn't done with him yet. Thank God.

She led them through a throng of people, awkwardly brushing by Matthew, and, much to Rye's immense relief, up a staircase to her bedroom. It had green carpet and smelled like her. "Take a seat," she said, gesturing to her bed, which had four posts and a canopy above it. "I begged forever to have one like this when I was six, and now I hate it. But I don't want my parents to know they were right, so I pretend I still like it."

"I admire that commitment," Rye laughed, trying to wipe the slate clean, erase the horrifying moment of five minutes ago.

"I admire *you,*" Dara said, plopping down next to him on the bed. They looked at each other for a moment, the air buzzing. Rye was shocked to realize that not only would he be allowed to stay at the party, but they were about to make out. Dara leaned in.

As Rye placed his hand on her neck, his fingers just below her ear, he felt more like himself than he had all night. Maybe they could stay up here and mess around till the party was over.

Dara started laughing, even as their mouths continued to touch.

"What?" Rye asked, smiling, too.

"Your face when you dropped the latkes," Dara said, now pulling her head back a few inches. "It was so sweet. Like a scared little puppy."

"Oh God," Rye said. "I should probably go home. Learn how to hold latkes on YouTube."

Dara laughed harder. "I always think of you as being so chill; I never realized how neurotic you are."

"I mean . . . ," Rye said. Now was the time to come clean.

"I like it." Dara smiled. "Jews are supposed to be neurotic. It's built into our DNA." She kissed him again, but Rye was so struck by her words he wasn't able to fully enjoy it.

Dara was right. No matter how he'd been raised, the Judaism was *inside* him. In his freaking DNA! So he didn't have to pretend. It was like some odd logic problem: his neurosis about not being Jewish was, in some ways, the very thing that confirmed he *was* Jewish. He felt simultaneously relieved and proud and was about to start focusing on the kissing when Dara pulled away. "We should probably get back downstairs," she said.

Rye returned to the party with a new confidence. He ate dinner next to Dara at a folding table, and for the first time all night, he felt like he belonged.

The feeling didn't last long. Some of the older women kept glancing his way and whispering. And, even though at least half of the latkes had been salvaged, Dara's mom was looking at him differently, less warmth in her eyes.

"That's a lot of menorahs," Rye said as about a dozen of them replaced the dinner platters on the main table. It was partly to prove that he knew at least one thing about Hanukkah.

"You brought one, right?"

Rye's eyes widened.

"I'm kidding," Dara said, shaking her head in wonder at this new neurotic Rye.

Within minutes, everyone at the party was crowded around the table. "They were in the garage, btw," Rebecca said to Dara, holding up three boxes of candles and passing them around.

The rabbi appeared next to Rye. "Heard you had a little spill," he said, a subtle smile playing at the corners of his mouth.

"Oh man," Rye said. "I'm so sorry about that."

"You're no longer welcome in this house."

Rye knew he was joking—all the social cues were there—but it stung nevertheless. Rabbi Goldfarb put one hand on Rye's shoulder, as if to further convey that all was good, and began to speak.

"Hello, everyone. It is so nice to have you all here with us tonight. We've been hosting this party since . . ." He looked to Dara's mom. "Robin, this is our, what . . . ?"

"Sixteenth year," she said.

"Sixteen years!" Rabbi Goldfarb said. "It's our sweet sixteen!" People cheered and laughed. "But seriously, we are so grateful that we've been able to gather together during the Festival of Lights for so many years."

"Us too," Shelly said, one hand cupped over his mouth like a megaphone.

"Thank you, Shelly," the rabbi said. Rye was thrilled by the hint of sarcasm in his voice. "Now, every year, we invite someone to tell the story of Hanukkah, usually one of our younger attendees. Any volunteers?"

The kid who Rye knew to be Elijah shot his hand up in the air.

"Elijah, wonderful," Dara's dad said. "Please tell us the story of Hanukkah."

"Okay," Elijah said. "Well, there was this small amount of oil, right? So the Maccabees decided to rub some on their butts—"

"Elijah," Shelly snapped.

"Not exactly the telling we were hoping for," Rabbi Goldfarb said, laughing. "So, thank you, Elijah, but I think we'll find someone else." Elijah ran off snickering with another kid.

"Any of our other young guests want to have a go?"

There were a few other kids, but none volunteered.

"Hmm," Rabbi Goldfarb said, scanning the group before his hand again landed on Rye's shoulder, freezing his insides. "What about you?" Rabbi Goldfarb asked, his eyes burning into Rye's soul.

"Daddy," Dara said from Rye's side.

"Everyone, this is Rye," the rabbi said to the crowd. "He's the schmendrick my daughter Dara brought home, and even though he dropped all my latkes on the floor, we're so happy to have him here tonight. What do you say, Rye?"

"Oh," he said, though it came out more like a squeak. He tried to maintain balance as the room gently spun around him. Here it was, the moment all of his preparation had been leading up to, and he had studied the wrong material.

"Go, Rye!" a woman he didn't know said.

"Sure," Rye said. "I'd love to."

"Excellent!" the rabbi said, patting his back twice before removing his hand. "Take it away."

Rye's mouth was so dry it took a few tries before he could swallow. "Hello, everyone." He decided to start with a joke that had occurred to him moments before. "Makes sense that Elijah couldn't be here to tell the story. But we'll save a place for him."

Staring faces, zero laughs.

"Wrong holiday, honey," one of Dara's mom's friends said.

"Oh, yeah, I know," Rye said, though he hadn't remembered which holiday it was, just that one of them had this guy

Elijah who Jews saved a place for. "So, um, the story of Hanukkah." Why hadn't he hopped on Wikipedia earlier? He only knew key bullet points, gathered from school and life and Hanukkahs with Josh. "It's a powerful story. And moving, too."

Just be a nice Jewish boy, Rye thought, though it wasn't helpful advice. "The oil is the main thing. That it's about. Because these Jews were trying to light a lamp, and it seemed like they would only have enough oil for a night, but it lasted for eight nights. Which is really, you know, that's a lot more than one night."

"Antiochus," Dara said quietly into his ear. "Mention Antiochus."

"Oh," Rye said. "Also Auntie Okus. Is another big part of the story. Because she, uh, was the one who . . ."

"It's *he,*" Rabbi Goldfarb corrected.

"Huh?"

"Antiochus is a he. He's the one they were fighting against."

"Why couldn't it be a she?" Rebecca asked. "We don't know for sure." She gave Rye the tiniest of nods. He now recognized her awesomeness.

"Well . . ." The rabbi shrugged at his older daughter. "In this case I think we do know, but. Go on."

"So, right," Rye said. "Auntie Okus is probably a he. Because back a long time ago men could be aunties." Some people chuckled and others stared in bewilderment, and Rye understood that aunties had no place in this story. "But anyway, the Jews fought him, and then had enough oil to last more than a week, and it was a miracle. And, to commemorate that miracle, we give each other presents for eight nights. And spin dreidels." Rye had officially run out of things to say, so he stopped there, sitting in an awkward silence until Dara's dad popped back in.

"Well, okay, Rye," he said. "I'm not sure which temple you go to, but clearly they taught you the abridged version." The room erupted with laughter. "Maybe someone could pick up from there to flesh out the story a bit?"

Rye's inadequacy sat heavy in his chest, like he'd swallowed a couple of dreidels.

"I gotcha," Matthew said, putting down his cup and sauntering up next to Rabbi Goldfarb, forcing Rye to make space for him. Of course. Stupid Matthew. Rye noticed his yarmulke featured the NY Mets logo, and for some reason this infuriated him.

"So, to build on what Ryan was trying to say," Matthew began. Rye was almost positive Matthew knew that wasn't his name. "King Antiochus and the Syrians had been persecuting the Jews for a long time, but, led by Judah and the Maccabees, the Jewish people defended themselves. They fought back."

Matthew continued with a spellbinding telling of the story of Hanukkah. Even as Rye resented him, he couldn't deny that he was learning a whole lot.

As Matthew finished, Rye was about to turn to Dara, who he hadn't looked at since his own pitiful telling petered out, but suddenly it was time to light the candles and say the blessings. Dara stood next to her mother, father, and sister at the menorah, lit candle in hand, Rye a moon hovering behind them.

The moment when he believed that being neurotic was all it took to be a Jew was a distant memory, a cruel joke. It wasn't enough. No matter how much research he did, it would never be enough. Rye stared at all the families huddled together around the candlelight, seething with anger at his own parents. *I'm Jewish,* Rye thought. *I should know the goddamn story of Hanukkah. Why did they never tell me the story?*

Everyone in the room began to sing in Hebrew, and Rye pretended to sing along, hating himself for not being brave enough to keep his mouth shut. He knew the beginning of this one from hanging out with Josh: *Baruch atah Adonai, Eloheinu melech haolam . . .*

It was unlikely anyone was listening for Rye's voice, but now he felt like he had even more to prove, raising his volume on the random syllables he remembered. He sounded like someone singing prayers on the other end of a bad cell phone connection. Matthew's rich baritone, meanwhile, soared over the other voices. Frigging Matthew. Why couldn't he just go by Matt, like the other ninety-eight percent of people with his name?

The blessings finished, presents were passed out to the younger kids, and the speedy process of bringing out dessert began. Rye wanted to melt into a pool of slime and ooze out the door, but first he needed to get proper closure on his and Dara's relationship. He cautiously walked over to her as she was putting down a plate of dreidel cookies.

"Hey," he said, grimacing. "I did a terrible job with that story."

"Oh, it was fine," Dara said, not very convincingly. "I mean, you missed a lot, but the overall ideas were there."

Rye looked at Dara. Her dimples, the speck of makeup under her right eye, the asymmetrical birthmark on her jawline. He had to tell her the truth.

"I'm not really that Jewish," he said.

"Ha, what?" Dara smiled and blinked twice.

"I mean, technically I am Jewish, both my parents are by blood, but my family doesn't go to temple. I wasn't bar mitzvahed."

"But you said you belong to Temple Beth Shalom. You go to services, like, all the time."

"Yeah. No. I don't." Rye figured he might as well rip the Band-Aid off entirely. "And also my dad's Buddhist."

"Oh, wow," Dara said. "That's interesting."

"I'm really sorry." Rye looked down at his bright blue dress shoes. They were a little over-the-top.

"It's weird that you lied," Dara said, "but you don't have to say all this as if it's, like, a tragedy." She took Rye's hand in hers, and he looked up. "I'm not with you because of your deep connection to Judaism. You could be zero Jewish for all I care."

"Dar, could you help me for a sec?" Dara's mom asked. "I can't find the cake cutter."

Dara gently smiled at Rye. "Are you gonna be okay if I leave you here for a second, my sweet not-really-that-Jewish boyfriend?"

Out of habit, Rye opened his mouth to defend himself, then smiled instead. "Probably." Dara walked with her mom into the kitchen.

So she didn't care. It wasn't as big a relief as Rye thought it would be.

Which begged the question: What was bothering him? He had been shamed by Dara's father in front of the entire party, so there was that.

Rye wandered down the hall to the bathroom, but when he saw it was occupied, he kept walking and found himself in the garage. It was chilly without his jacket, but Rye didn't care. He deserved the cold.

He paced around the two parked cars, replaying his Hanukkah story over and over, astounded that he was somehow able to top the latke debacle.

"Hey," a voice said, pulling him out of his own brain. Rye turned and looked over the top of a red Hyundai to see, of all people, Matthew.

Pretty much the last person he wanted to see.

"Hi," Rye said, trying to omit anything resembling friendliness.

Matthew stood in the doorway to the garage, looking like he wanted to speak.

"Do you need something from out here or . . . ?" Rye wanted him to go.

"I'm not really Jewish either," he said.

"What?" Rye said. He was ninety percent sure he was being messed with.

"Sorry. I heard what you were saying in there to Dara. I wasn't, like, eavesdropping or anything, but I was just, like, nearby."

"Uh. Okay."

"My mom's not Jewish," Matthew said, staring up at the garage ceiling. "So technically that means I'm not Jewish either. That's the way it works, through the mother's family line. If you're conservative, like my dad."

Rye could now tell he was not being messed with, but he was still very confused.

"So I know what you're feeling," Matthew continued. "Is what I'm trying to . . . I mean, like, feeling like a fake. I get that."

"But . . ." Rye was bewildered not just by the words, but by the sudden vulnerability presented by someone who up till now seemed completely impenetrable. "You're, like, totally Jewish. You know all the Jewish things. You told that story so well."

"Thanks, man." Rye thought Matthew might have been

blushing. "But . . . doesn't matter, because I'll never actually be Jewish."

It seemed so ridiculous. "That whole thing about the mother's line," Rye said. "What does that even mean? What does any of it mean?"

"You said both your parents are Jewish?" Matthew asked.

"Well. Yeah. In theory."

"So you're Jewish."

Rye wasn't sure how things had flipped so dramatically in the past two minutes, but hearing Matthew say that did carry a lot of weight. He realized suddenly that, unlike his Chewbacca impersonation—done for a laugh, to impress Dara—his impersonation of a nice Jewish boy had been done expressly for one person: himself.

Matthew shrugged, wiped his face. "She really likes you."

"Who?" Rye said, in that involuntary way where of course you know the answer but feel like you have to ask anyway.

"Dara. She never liked me like that."

"Oh." Rye of course loved hearing those words, but he felt bad, too. "On the bright side, I'm still a total mess."

Matthew laughed. "Your story did leave something to be desired."

"Yeah, no kidding."

"But I can tell you're a really good dude. You're just, like, very relaxed or something."

Rye was again skeptical before realizing that, since Matthew had appeared in the garage, he *had* been pretty relaxed. Maybe he'd absorbed more of his dad's Buddhism than he'd realized. And maybe he was also Jewish. Maybe he was a lot of things.

"Thanks," he said.

"Absolutely."

It only took a few seconds of them standing there nodding at each other for Rye to remember that, other than their mutual feeling of Jewish imposterism, he had no idea what they had in common.

He wanted to get back inside to Dara, but he didn't want to be rude, so he searched for something to say, landing on a reference to Matthew's passion for the Mets. Matthew, however, beat him to the punch.

"So, uh, you get anything cool for Hanukkah?"

EL AL 328

BY DANA SCHWARTZ

The plane lurched down with such urgency it was like it had disappeared through a wormhole and reappeared a few yards lower. Several of the passengers on El Al 328 to JFK gave small involuntary yelps. Fi's guts climbed into her throat. She gripped the armrests on either side of her until the tendons in her wrists bulged. *Please, God,* she thought, a little self-consciously, wondering if she should have included an introduction, a brief *Hello there, remember me? Please, God,* Fi thought as the plane dipped and righted itself, hurtling across the Atlantic. *Please don't let me die before I have sex.*

Neither Emma nor Dean seemed to pay any attention to the turbulence. With the plane's lights still off, Fi wasn't certain at first whether they were even awake. Maybe they had fallen asleep with their limbs entangled under a single blanket in the space between the middle and aisle seats of the row in which Fi was crouched into the window. But no—the bracelets on Emma's thin wrist jangled as she curled her arm, like a rhinestoned snake, farther around Dean's neck. To the best of

Fi's observational skills, the two hadn't come up for air since the cabin lights dimmed.

They had been in the air long enough for the hours to bleed into each other, and Fi felt like a failure. She had wasted Birthright, and she was coming home not only *not* devirginized, but also completely unkissed. How had she managed to go ten days with purposefully minimal adult supervision without finding someone who was interested in her?

That was what Birthright was for, wasn't it? Fi thought bitterly. Meeting eligible Jewish spouses? There was a rumor that if you met your significant other on Birthright, you would get a honeymoon to Israel for free. She was *trying* to have sex on a trip *designed* to get kids to have sex, and she had still managed to fail.

Even sweet Dean, with his bad skin and eyes a little too far apart, had been only politely friendly when she had attempted flirtation—offering a bite of her shawarma, sitting next to him on the bus and pressing her knee into his—during the trip's early days. And now he was here. Next to her. Giving Emma a dental exam with his tongue.

It's not that Fi was surprised Dean would go for Emma—she was probably the prettiest girl on their trip, with a sort of undone gorgeousness that always made her look like an off-duty model backpacking through Nepal. What was surprising to Fi was that Emma would be interested in Dean. For the first half of their ten-day trip, Emma had been playfully fending off the flirtations of Eitan, the obvious ringleader of the Israeli soldiers who had been assigned to accompany their college group. The morning that the group was supposed to hike Masada, Eitan and Emma were conspicuously missing, and Fi had heard that the two had been having sex at the hotel and received a formal reprimand from Corinne, the trip leader.

Dean was a full head shorter than Eitan. He and Fi had usually gone to eat lunch in the same group, and he used a fork and knife to eat falafel sandwiches. *If he asks me out when we get back to Iowa,* Fi remembered thinking back during orientation, *I will probably say yes.* The memory of her own presumptuousness now that he was chosen by Emma made Fi's stomach sink with humiliation.

Emma's bracelets jangled again, and her fingernails (painted black) clawed at the back of Dean's head. Where did Emma even get those bracelets? How old had she been when she pierced half a dozen rings through the cartilage of her ears and through her septum? There were a thousand questions she wished she could ask Emma, interrogating her in a white, locked room away from the rest of the world for as long as she wanted without anyone else ever finding out: Did she shower in the morning or at night? How was her skin so smooth and poreless? Did she purchase her jeans like that—soft and worn, dotted with fraying holes—or did she wear them in? Were her band T-shirts actually vintage, or did she buy them, like Fi, at Forever 21? How did Emma look cool wearing a backward baseball cap, when Fi looked like a prepubescent male clown, with her hair poofing out on either side of her ears, demented uncontrollable triangles?

It was as if Emma and Fi were entirely different species, with disparate grooming habits and education levels. Fi's own mother had taught her how to shave her legs (carefully, from the ankles up to the knees) and had purchased her jewelry, like the small gold Jewish star she had worn continuously since her sixteenth birthday, even in the shower. She knew how and when to wash her bras and apply makeup, but it seemed as though there was an entirely separate education that Emma had received. Who had taught her these things?

But there was only one truly important question: Would Emma even acknowledge Fi after the plane landed, when they were back on campus? That was how Birthright was supposed to go, right? You meet people who you go to college with, share a life-changing experience, and then stay friends throughout the rest of your college life, sharing inside jokes about falafel and how that kid Max went to the Holocaust museum while he was hungover.

Fi and Emma had become close over the past week, rooming together all but once, but Fi was aware that tours of community farms and long bus rides were a universal equalizer. Back at Grinnell, their paths had never crossed. Emma had her own friends; she went to parties; she had easy fun in a way Fi never did. Plus, Emma wasn't a virgin.

It's not like Fi wished she were the one making out with Dean, but having someone to make out with on the nine-hour flight would have been nice. Having someone who wanted to make out with her, ideally the same person who could have made her not a virgin before she returned to campus, because the turbulence hadn't stopped.

The plane tossed up and down, left and right, a deranged roller coaster in the dark. Fi wondered briefly if she was going to die. She prayed quickly again as the plane gave its most violent shudder yet. What would her funeral be like? She probably wouldn't even get her own memorial at Grinnell—if this flight went down, the campus would be mourning the entire spring break Birthright trip, all twenty-four of them, without anyone caring in particular about Fi more than anyone else. She and her college roommate, Vivie, had been on touchy terms since Vivie had decided that she wanted to be premed and would need to stay for a fifth year on campus to complete her degree. "You're distracting me," Vivie would hiss every time Fi forgot to use headphones while watching Netflix, or let the microwave beep to alert her that her popcorn was done instead of stopping it with a second or two left on the clock. Vivie would probably secretly be relieved that she got full use of the room for the rest of the semester.

Fi was contemplating turning off the movie so she wouldn't die watching *America's Sweethearts* (VIRGIN DIES WATCHING CRITICALLY UNDERWHELMING ROMANTIC COMEDY) when the plane veered so violently to the side the books in Fi's backpack tumbled out under her seat, and someone behind her screamed. The lights in the cabin flashed on with a ding.

"Jesus," Emma said, extracting herself from Dean's arms and righting herself in the middle seat. The plane's audio system crackled to life, and a low, male voice boomed invisibly throughout the plane.

"This is your captain speaking. As you're probably aware, we're going through some, eh, turbulence here, and, eh, we're going to need to divert our course to avoid the worst of the storm. We'll be, uh, making an emergency landing in Dublin in order to make sure you all safely make it back to JFK, uh, New York."

"It's not even raining, is it?" Dean asked, leaning over toward Fi to peer out the plane window. Fi obligingly lifted the shade a bit for him. Pitch-black. If it were raining, or snowing, or hailing fist-size diamonds, there would be no way of knowing.

The cabin lights stayed on, and although the FASTEN SEAT BELT sign bleated out its ever-present reminder, their trip leader, Corinne, still managed to make it up the aisles, crouching as if lowering herself six inches would make her invisible to the flight attendants' wrath.

"Hey, guys, you doin' okay up here?" she said, gripping the back of the seats to protect herself against a particularly vicious bump of the plane.

"So what's the deal, then?" Emma purred, not bothering to remove her legs from where they rested across Dean's. "We have to do a layover or something?"

"Your guess is as good as mine," Corinne said. She was still wearing her laminated name tag on a lanyard around her neck, even though they were on the flight home. Fi guessed she was somewhere around forty, still working an indeterminate job at the campus Hillel. Fi had been surprised when Corinne mentioned her husband casually, while they had been at the Wall. "Just wanted to make sure the gang is okay!"

"If we have to stay overnight, do they put us in a hotel?" Emma asked. Corinne's eyes passed over where Emma was entangled with Dean, but she didn't seem to care at all.

"I'd assume so," Corinne said with an earnestness that made Fi sad. Corinne gave a little laugh. "God's hands!"

"Excuse me, ma'am," said a flight attendant with an Israeli accent. "Please return to your seat." Corinne gave Emma, Dean, and Fi a conspiratorial grin and floated to the back of the plane.

"You hear that, Fi?" Emma said. "Hotel. You can finally

bone Max, like you've been planning this entire goddamn time." Fi and Dean gave matching involuntary scoffs of disbelief. Emma turned to Dean. "What? She has. I've seen the way she was moon eyes over him. They shared a water bottle on the hike! That's, like, first base."

"He was thirsty," Fi mumbled, a blush creeping down her neck.

Max. Why had she not thought of Max? He was tall, maybe one of the tallest boys on the trip, at least six foot three, with curly black hair that looked like a Brillo pad and was already balding in the back. But Fi and Max hadn't exchanged so much as a dozen words between the two of them. It seemed like he had been more interested in quoting Will Ferrell movies with his friends, and trying to sneak booze back into their room, than talking to Fi at all.

"You two are adorable," Emma said. "You're going to pop out his Jewish babies before we're even back home."

Maybe Fi had been wrong. Maybe *she* had been the nervous one, the shy girl who hadn't initiated conversation. By the time the plane landed in the pitch-black, Fi had rewritten a version of the previous week in her head in which she had been standoffish and distant to the boy who had been pining for her, and now—thank God—she had been given a single night to rectify her mistake.

The Dublin airport could have been any airport in the world. Same white linoleum floor, same fast-food-mixed-with-cleaning-fluid smell, same bleary-eyed children dragged along by exhausted parents, same tight-lipped, chignoned flight attendants in too-tight polyester. Corinne gathered the group at the gate when they had all stumbled off the plane. Max gave Fi a drowsy, two-fingered salute when she made eye contact. She smiled back.

"Okay, gang, looks like we're spending the night in Dublin!" Corinne said, slapping her hands together, after she returned from talking with someone at the counter.

"Like, can we hang out? Do we get to explore or whatever at least?" said Tova.

"Unfortunately, no," Corinne said with more patience than Fi would have thought a human being was capable of. Maybe a prerequisite of leading a Birthright trip was the surgical removal of your eye-roll reflex. "We're just going to be popping down to the airport hotel and be back here in a few hours for a five a.m. flight." There were a few groans and a few sleepy blinks.

"Is it even worth going to sleep?" asked Maddie-with-an-*ie*. "Like, that's like four hours."

"Whether you sleep or not is up to you," Corinne said, again with complete astonishing earnestness. "But I know I'll be catching some much-needed shut-eye!"

After a silent shuttle-bus ride and an awkward shuffling in the predawn darkness, Corinne assigned rooms, using their seat numbers as a template. Fi and Emma were in the same room together; that was the only reason Fi was there when Dean, Evan, Max, Tova, and Maddie-with-an-*ie* showed up to hang out. There had been no communication as far as Fi could see as to when or where they would meet—popular kids communicated by telepathy, on a wavelength that was inaudible to normal people.

Fi had already changed into her pajamas—just the T-shirt she had been wearing on the plane, no bra—and brushed her teeth, and she had just gotten into bed when the door burst open.

"Let's get this party starrr-ted," Tova said, bouncing onto Fi's bed and crossing her legs.

"Too bad we don't have any booze," said Max.

Evan removed his sneakers and sat next to Tova. "Who needs booze when we're riding on severe lack of sleep. I heard somewhere that not getting enough sleep is basically the same as being drunk." Max sat on the bed too, close to Fi, and smiled. Fi smiled back and then pulled the thin blanket higher up over her body.

"Should we play Truth or Dare?" Tova asked. Fi tried to meet Max's eyes to give him a coquettish look from beneath her eyelashes, but he was distracted untangling a knot in his sneaker laces and didn't look up.

"What are you, ten?" Evan said. "Spin the bottle."

"How about . . ." Emma rifled through her backpack.

"Looking for your dildo, Em?" Evan sneered. Emma hit him and laughed. She pulled out a hairbrush.

"Found it. Spin the hairbrush."

"This is dumb, guys," said Maddie-with-an-*ie,* and Fi's heart expanded with involuntary relief. "We're not in fucking middle school." Dean murmured his assent. Fi tried to gauge Max's expression, but he was still fiddling with his shoelace.

Tova swung her legs back onto the floor. "Come on, it's our last night. Not even our last night. It's a bonus night. It's like Leap Day. Nothing we do on a layover counts. Just play—who even cares."

"I'll go first," Evan said, grabbing the hairbrush and giving it an awkwardly forceful spin on the carpeted floor. It careened to the side, making two and a half rotations before it stopped, its handle pointing squarely at Emma. She rolled her eyes and lifted her body up to accept a peck on the lips from Evan.

"Okay, okay, my turn," Maddie-with-an-*ie* said, clearly all her misgivings dissolved. She squared herself against the group, which was still more of a clump than a circle, and gave the hairbrush a jerky spin. It barely moved and landed on Evan. "You rigged this!" she squealed, giving him a kiss on the lips that lasted more than a few seconds.

Tova spun next, landing on Dean. Then Emma (Max), then Evan again (Dean and then a re-spin, Tova). No one asked Fi if she wanted a turn. Maddie landed on Tova, and the girls kissed for a few seconds while Dean and Evan hooted. Tova landed on the space between Fi and Max, and spun again and landed on Evan, and kissed him for a good fifteen seconds, until Emma said, "All right, kiddies, time to break it up."

Fi felt like a voyeur for not playing, but this was her room, wasn't it? It wasn't her fault if they were doing this in front of her. It was like being granted a backstage pass into a social life she never would have seen otherwise. Emma landed on Max. Watching them peck on the lips made Fi's chest hurt.

"Maxie's turn!" Tova sang. Fi sat up straighter. The universe had willed this all to happen—the turbulence, the emergency landing, the night in the hotel room—just for this moment.

Max rolled his eyes. "You realize this is a game for seventh graders, right?"

Fi's heart buzzed like a hummingbird. Of course he was playing it cool. He didn't want his first kiss with Fi to be during some dumb game.

"Everyone is ageless during spin the bottle," Emma said sagely, gnawing at a protein bar she'd pulled from her backpack.

Max sighed and pulled the hairbrush toward him, and then spun hard. It spun.

Every force in the universe tugged at the hairbrush.

The polar magnets flared.

Gravity upended itself.

All of Newton's laws dissolved and rebuilt themselves so that this hairbrush, on this one night, would do what Fi couldn't during the trip.

The hairbrush slowed, drifting slightly sideways on the hotel's thin carpet.

And stopped.

And landed directly between Fi's eyes.

Fi swallowed. Hard. She wiggled herself out from beneath the blanket, wondering if Max could see her nipples under her shirt and secretly hoping he could. She could hear her heartbeat in her ears.

She had willed this moment to happen, and it did.

"This is dumb," Max said, shifting uncomfortably. "We're not fucking twelve-year-olds. Nothing personal, Fi."

"No," Fi said, her face pulsing with blood and shame. "Obviously not."

The rest of the group stirred. Shoes began to be returned to feet. Tova unpretzeled her limbs and stretched. "Time to try to grab literally a second of sleep," she said.

"Hey," Max said, gesturing to Fi. "Will you grab me my shoes?" She complied. "Thanks, yo." Fi wasn't sure whether he meant it like "Thanks, yo," or whether he was making his own nickname for her: Yo, for Fiona. Fi-YO-na. No one had ever called her Yo before, but she was too embarrassed to ask if that's what he was doing.

Before the group had even filed out, Fi began crying, despite herself. She rolled away from the door and curled up as tightly as possible, like a pill bug. She did it silently, with the tears pooling in the lumpy fabric of the pillow, and didn't move until the rest of the group had left the room and she heard the door slam behind them. Fi knew that moment with Max would replay in her mind for the rest of the trip home.

This, she thought, *is how it's always going to be.*

"You okay?" Emma asked, slinking toward the beds after she had brushed her teeth. But the tone made her question sound more like *When are you going to stop with the annoying crying?* Fi couldn't speak, and she couldn't face Emma without showing her bloated, wet, red face.

"Mm-hmm," she said, without moving.

Emma didn't ask again. She turned the lights off. Fi tried to go to sleep—they would need to be up in an hour anyway to leave for the airport—but there was a crack of light that found its way through the curtains. And so while Emma slept, Fi stayed awake, frozen, until an alarm went off, when the two girls put on their jeans and left the room.

* * *

Emma was already seated by the time Fi boarded the bus to get to the airport the next morning. As Fi turned sidewise to make her way through the aisle of the bus without making eye contact, Emma sighed loudly. "Ugh, Fi? Have you seen my headphones?"

Fi could say, *Yes, maybe*. She could use the question as an excuse to sit in the spare seat next to Emma. She could rifle through her bag as the rest of the group sleepily filed onto the bus, and then maybe Max would sit right across the aisle from her, and then—

"No. I haven't," Fi answered. Instead of sitting next to Emma, she took a seat in an empty row. She plopped her bag down in the aisle seat, marking her territory.

"Maybe they got mixed up with your stuff!" Emma called out. "Are you sure you don't have them?"

"I'm sure," Fi responded. As the bus pulled away from the curb, Fi took out a book, but she didn't bother to open it. Instead, she pressed her head against the window. She watched the sun rise as she began the journey home.

SOME DAYS YOU'RE THE SIDEKICK; SOME DAYS YOU'RE THE SUPERHERO

BY KATHERINE LOCKE

Title: parties and dancing, takeoffs and landings
Author: Makeabeat02
Rating: PG
Tags: au, I just have feelings okay, not really fluff, I tried, I was going to use Justin Bieber lyrics as a title but I am afraid of being sued, same with Nirvana lyrics, everything gets meta after this, apologies, makeup fic, no romance, if you came here for a hea lol get out, well actually, I don't know how it ends, I am alarmed by how many of these tags are actually already tags, who is in charge of me, please stop me, I am the worst, no beta reader, no hate mail please, desperation smells like the entire box of Goldfish I ate while writing this, I hope you're okay, I'm here, I screwed up, and I'm genuinely sorry, apology fic, OC, the OC is me
Notes: I can't decide how this story starts.
I could start it in three different places.

I think you'd hate me in all of them.

So I guess if it doesn't matter, if they all end up in the same place, I'll start it here.

I'm not tagging you, but you know who you are.

* * *

CHAPTER 1: MASOCHISM IS AN ART

Mom's waiting for me and Davey outside the school. She's got the windows down and Mariah Carey blasting, and I'd tell you that it was embarrassing, except I love her, and I secretly love Mariah Carey (please don't tell anyone).

Davey's also outside, hanging out with their friends by the picnic table under the pine tree. They're sitting on the part you're supposed to eat on, and their feet are on the bench, while a half dozen girls sit around them, fawning over their every word. I don't know if Davey's interested in girls, or anyone, but it's clear that my younger sibling is much more popular than me. It's not that I'm not popular. It's just that Davey moves as fluidly between groups at school as they do between genders, and I am more of a—fine. I'm a nerd. I stare at Davey's perfectly tied bow tie and down at my IRON MAN'S THE WORST DON'T @ ME shirt.

I'm not saying it's the reason that I'm generally shunned by the popular kids at school, but Briana Henderson did ask me what "don't @ me" meant, and it occurred to me that I might spend more time on Tumblr and Twitter than most kids my age. And that's slightly alarming.

Mom honks, and I trip down the last few steps. "Davey! Come on!"

"Coming!" calls Davey, and the way I know they're still in middle school is none of their friends laugh at this. I haven't said the word "coming" in a solid three years now. I slide into the passenger seat while they hop in behind me and shut the door.

"Hi, sweethearts," Mom says with a smile. "How was school?"

"Awesome. I'm going to audition for the school play," says Davey. I can see them in the mirror posing for a selfie. "It's *The Music Man*."

Mom and I instantly begin singing "Gary, Indiana" while Mariah croons at us through the radio. I should definitely mention that neither Mom nor I can sing. Davey groans and pretends to hate it, but I can tell they secretly love it.

"What part?" asks Mom.

"Marian the librarian," says Davey, surprising me. They clearly don't miss the looks Mom and I shoot each other. "There's no reason why that role has to be played by a cis girl in 2019."

"Go get 'em, sweetie," Mom says. "As long as it doesn't interfere with your b'nai mitzvah practice, I'm all for this."

"It probably won't," says Davey vaguely, which means it definitely will. That'll be a fun battle.

I decide to come to their defense. "You let me skip a few lessons for cross-country."

"True," Mom says thoughtfully.

Davey kicks the back of my seat. I think it's a thank-you. It better be a thank-you.

"Did you look at the links I sent you?" Mom asks me.

I looked at the email and just seeing *Can't wait to tour these colleges with you!* made me want to puke. College-searching stress is really getting to me, and it feels like everything I do must be marketable to a college. Like my parents *hate* how much time I spend on Tumblr and this one fandom site called Milk & Honey, but I kid you not, this past spring, Dad was like, *Hey, do you think you can call that creative writing?*

I mean, it *is* creative writing. (Why do people think only girls write fanfic? Why is it only okay for girls to write fanfic? Uh, I've got things to say about the canon too.) But if I put it in a college app, don't I have to share it with the admissions counselors? No thanks. I don't even let my nerd friends read my fic.

"Hellllooo? Gabe?" Mom waves her hand in front of my face without ever taking her eyes off the road.

"What? Also, I'm pretty sure you're supposed to keep two hands on the wheel," I tell her to deflect.

"You can critique my driving when you manage to park a car without hitting a wall," says Mom simply.

"Ouch," I mutter. But we've successfully dodged the college question.

"Burn," crows Davey from the back seat.

I'm tempted to flip them off. The *one* time I happened to put the car in drive instead of reverse, there was a brick wall in front of me. That's why Mom picks us up on Friday afternoons to go to synagogue for Shabbat services instead of Davey and me driving together straight from after-school clubs (me: lit mag; Davey: theater and music).

We don't live in a super-Jewish area, so we drive about forty-five minutes to the nearest synagogue for services and religious school. We always get Friendly's before services, and today's no exception. It's kind of fun, in some ways, to drive to a new part of town. I see people in the Friendly's and then at services I only see once a week. I don't go to school with any of my temple classmates, and that division makes me feel a bit like Clark Kent.

Plus, I think if Samantha Robinson and I went to school together, we'd have murdered each other by now.

Wait, that's not exactly right.

She would have murdered me by now, and she would have been justified.

But neither of us has figured out how to leave Judaism (can you?) or convince our parents to switch to a new congregation away from this one, which I think we both genuinely love, so we're still subjected to each other's presence every week.

Sure enough, Mom parks behind Sam's mom's car.

"Look who it is!" Mom says cheerfully. Like she hasn't noticed that Sam and I don't hang out anymore. She hands me the button-down shirt she brought for me, because I never remember to bring synagogue-ready clothes to school. (In my defense, it's *really early* when I get up.)

I cannot get out of the car fast enough. If I keep my head down, maybe we'll be like ships in the night or whatever that saying is. We'll just pretend we don't see each other. We pretend so well, Sam and me.

Mom slows down to chat with Sam's mom, so Davey and I walk into Beth Israel right behind Sam and this other girl I've known my whole life, Bethany Elwin. The guard at the door nods to all of us, recognizing us, and we all smile back, quiet for a few steps before conversation starts up again. Beth's dyed her hair a shocking shade of purple, and she's telling Sam the entire process while Sam keeps saying, "But it's so . . . *bright*."

"I know, right? The box didn't lie!" sings Beth, tossing her hair.

"A box dye? You're doing so much damage to your hair," Davey pipes up. "You should really make sure you're washing with a color-safe conditioner that can help heal the follicles."

Beth turns. "How do you know that?"

"I read," Davey says cheerfully. "I follow a couple of people on Instagram. I can give you their names if you want. They have great hair tips."

"If I wanted tips from a—" Beth begins to say.

"Think about where that's ending," I cut in smoothly.

Beth's mouth hangs open for a second, and then she shuts it and presses her lips together.

I sling an arm around Davey's shoulder. They don't look the least bit rattled. Their resilience is incredible. "I don't know how you follow so many Insta accounts and keep up with them."

"It's easy," Davey says, rolling their eyes. They look me up and down. "And you could use some help. I'll send you some links."

"This is my best T-shirt," I protest as I head toward the bathroom to change.

"It's atrocious, and it smells like a gym," Davey calls back. They don't need to change, because they dress well *all* day instead of just for two hours on Friday nights and Saturday mornings.

Beth rolls her eyes and walks down the hall, and for a beat, Sam hangs back, a faint smile on her face. Then she seems to realize that she's lurking outside the men's room, and a flush runs up her cheeks. She ducks her head and hurries down the hall to catch up to Beth.

It's always like that. Every time I've seen her for the last year (which feels like forever), I know I should say something like *Hi, how are you?* or *I'm sorry,* but the words stick to the roof of my mouth.

I don't even know where to start. It replays in my head over and over and over again, constantly. It's behind me everywhere I go. And that's stupid—because I'm not the wronged party here. I'm the wronging party. I'm not even sure that's a thing. But it feels like this black cloud that follows me everywhere. It's been a year. It feels like too long ago to apologize now without seeming like a creep or a weirdo. I should just get over it, except I can't. And obviously Sam can't either.

In the coat closet where I stash my T-shirt (and Davey's right, it does smell a bit like a gym; I hope no one notices), I rub at my face and check my phone, a useless attempt in this dead zone to refresh Milk & Honey. (You know what it is, yeah? I mean, you're here. How'd you find this without knowing? But just in case this is the first fic you've clicked on—you've made a mistake. Read something else. This is a whole site dedicated to reimagining every canon character as Jewish. It's pretty fantastic, and I'm obsessed with it. Click my favorites if you want to see what I'm reading.) I joined basically as soon as it opened last year and I heard about it on Tumblr, and it's basically saved my sanity.

I posted a new chapter to my fic last night. I had a handful of new comments this morning, but I haven't checked all day—no phones at school, and Davey uses so much of our family data plan that I usually don't bother trying until I'm home and on Wi-Fi. But right now I really need a distraction, and the only escape I have, here and everywhere, is through fic and fandom.

Then Davey comes around the corner, a little breathless. Services are about to start, and Mom wants to know why it's taking me so long to change a shirt. I reluctantly follow them into the sanctuary, letting out a breath of relief when I see that Mom's not sitting next to Sam's family.

I like being here, I remind myself, because I do. I swear I do. But every time I bow, I can feel guilt rolling around in my stomach like a cannonball.

Endnotes: You probably don't care about this part. But for once, I'll give you the truth instead of the fiction. I'll stop asking you to read between the lines, because you deserve more than that. You deserve the whole truth and nothing but it. You deserve the apology.

And I swear it's coming. But let me get through all of this first, okay?

You can take this down when it's done. I don't mind. I know I'm probably violating the terms of service and a dozen rules.

* * *

CHAPTER 2: MILK & HONEY AND HOME

Author's Note: n/a, see endnotes

The first thing I do when I get home from school on Monday is dump my backpack by my desk and log on to Milk & Honey. I've got a half dozen new comments on my fanfic where I reimagined the X-Men as Maccabees.

This is pretty awesome, dude. When's the new chapter going up?

Omg I love it. MOOORRREEE

UM YOUR WRONG ABOUT ICEMAN—HE IS WAY TOO SENSITIVE FOR THIS. DELETE YOUR FIC.

Please update soon? Also is it going to earn that M rating?

bookmarks

"And this isn't what they expected. They expected it to be easier. They expected it to be harder. But they didn't expect that the cold in the mountains, looking out over their city under occupation, would turn to steel in their veins. They did not expect to find a new camaraderie in the face of defeat. But they did." <= MY FEELS. HOW DARE YOU.

The "please update" comments make me laugh, because I *just* posted a chapter last night. How often do I need to update to make them happy? (Do not answer this.) According to the moderator and founder of M&H, and probably my best friend, but don't tell them that, YaelLouder, you can't make everyone happy, no matter what you write. Still, it's hard to wrap my head around that in the moment when I'm scrolling through the comments. At least I don't get harassed much on M&H. My handle is gender-neutral, but I've been clear on the forums and in my fic that I'm a cis guy, and I'm pretty sure that's why.

Sometimes, if I can't sleep, I stay up on M&H's forums and help Yael with the harassment that comes through. Yael—who always has third singular in their profile despite their gendered username—gave me moderator privileges so I can go through and issue public or private warnings, put people in time-out, or ban them. I've never had to ban someone, but I like helping Yael out.

I'm still responding to comments when a chat message pops up on the site from Yael.

YaelLouder: *hey Mabface ☺ looks like people are enjoying your new fic!*

They call me Mab because it's the shorthand for my handle: **M**ake **A** **B**eat.

Makeabeat02: *hi yourself! How's it going today? People are . . . apparently I need to update every hour?? Send help. I can't do homework anymore. Just fic.*

YaelLouder: *lol people are so demanding sometimes.*

Makeabeat02: *haha I know, but it's nice. I mean, that's why I write it, right? For people to read it? Imagine how unbearable I'd be if no one read my fics.*

YaelLouder: *I would probably have to go into invisible mode just to avoid you. You're emo enough as it is.*

Makeabeat02: *omg*

Makeabeat02: *I am not emo*

Makeabeat02: *take it back*

YaelLouder: *have you even read your own fic?*

Makeabeat02: *feeling v attacked right now tbqh*

Mom calls up the stairs, "Are you starting homework? If you haven't done your homework, you can't get on the computer!"

"I need the computer for homework!" I call back.

YaelLouder: *the truth hurts*

Makeabeat02: *blocking you*

YaelLouder: *:p you would never*

Makeabeat02: *haha yeah.*

Makeabeat02: *that would be weird.*

Makeabeat02: *also I don't think I'd have any friends if it wasn't for you*

YaelLouder: *Somehow I doubt this*

Makeabeat02: *no joke though. Anyways, how was your day?*

YaelLouder: *don't think I'm not circling back to that friend thing. My day was . . . meh.*

Makeabeat02: *meh doesn't sound good*

"Gabe!" calls my father, slamming the door behind him as he comes home. "Come down and help your mother with dinner!"

"One second!" I yell back.

I type to Yael, *Hold that thought, okay? I'm sorry. Have to go do dinner with the fam. I'll be back soon.*

I can see them replying, but I leave before I get sucked into more conversations and Dad has to call me a second time.

After dinner, I go upstairs and log on to M&H right away.

Makeabeat02: *hey, I'm back*

YaelLouder: *:)*

Makeabeat02: *your day get any better?*

YaelLouder: *Ugh. No? Not really. I had to block two people this morning for being asshats and violating their warnings, and I can't stop thinking about this weird thing that happened this weekend and—I think one of my friends is homophobic. I mean, I knew that she was kind of uncomfortable with gay people but I think she's straight up homophobic. I don't know what to do about it.*

Makeabeat02: *ugh that sucks. Can you talk to her about it?*

YaelLouder: *I don't know. Does it make me a bad person if I avoid it?*

Makeabeat02: *I mean, I don't think you are a bad person and I don't think this makes you a bad person? But it's not going to help her—or any gay people she runs into*

YaelLouder: *What would you do?*

Makeabeat02: *Hmm. First, I mean, it's personal for me? A family member's queer. That's all I'm going to say because it's not my story to bring online etc etc. It happens. But I guess the best thing I can do is be there for them and make sure people know they can't turn to me with their bigoted bullshit, you know?*

YaelLouder: *Yeah, I think that's the part that I'm realizing hurts the most. The part where she thought she could be that person in front of me. She never should have felt like I had her back. Anyways, I have to figure out how to handle that. Thanks for listening.*

Makeabeat02: *no problem <3*

Sometimes I wonder why it's so easy for me to say all the right things online, when I'm typing, and say and do all the wrong things in real life.

YaelLouder: *what's up with you?*

They aren't subtle when they're changing the topic, that's for sure.

Makeabeat02: *I'm working on the next chapter of X-Maccabees and brainstorming the next fic. I think I'm going to write one-shot of Clint Barton taking Natasha Romanoff to Israel for the first time. Not on a mission. Obviously she's been there on a mission.*

YaelLouder: *obviously*

Makeabeat02: *I can't decide if it's serious or fluffy though*

YaelLouder: *All of your Clintasha fic is kind of fluffy.*

Makeabeat02: *what?!*

Makeabeat02: *THEY BASICALLY ALMOST ALWAYS NEARLY DIE*

YaelLouder: *it took me a few seconds to understand that sentence and yeah, near death experiences do not automatically make something not fluff. You always tag it hurt/comfort and it is not h/c. It's fluff.*

Makeabeat02: *wow. It's like I don't even know you. It's like you don't even know me.*

YaelLouder: *I do know you. You're one of my best friends. This year would have been impossible without you.*

Makeabeat02: *it's raining on my face*

Makeabeat02: *alternatively my roof has a leak*

YaelLouder: *take the compliment, Mab.*

Makeabeat02: *here's a new fact about me. I am allergic to kindness.*

YaelLouder: *false. You love those gushing comments on your fic*

Makeabeat02: *that's about fic. This is about me. I have hives all over me. It's really gross and itchy.*

YaelLouder: *you are ridiculous* ☺

After the conversation moves to the forums and trouble-makers there, I eventually have to sign off to sleep. But my day feels made now. There's something about M&H that makes me feel at home, but there's something about Yael that makes me feel *seen* and heard and understood like I don't get in my real life. We talk a lot about treating others like we want to be treated, but really, I think we ought to see others like we want to be seen.

Endnotes: See? I can write fluff. Tempted to tag this h/c just to be that way.

I'm getting there, by the way. I promise. I'm the worst, but I don't break my promises. Even that one from a year ago.

CHAPTER 3: SOME DAYS YOU'RE THE SIDEKICK; SOME DAYS YOU'RE THE SUPERHERO

Author's Note: God, this is getting to the part that's hard to write, and I can feel myself looking for anything other than the truth. It's this throbbing ache in my chest. I've written and deleted this chapter so many times. I'm trying. I'm trying so hard.
When I wake up Tuesday, there's a message from Yael waiting in my inbox on M&H.

YaelLouder: *I joke that I don't know what I'd do without you, but I really mean it: I don't know what I'd do without you, Mab. I know we don't talk too much about real life, except for last night I guess, but I don't actually have that many friends—and definitely none (anymore) that understand fandom. I wish* *there was an instruction manual—I don't know how to interact with people without being like "Is Stucky canon?" What I'm saying is, when I talk with you, I feel like you get it. I love this site, but I love it* more *because it means I get people like you in my life. It makes me feel less like Pluto and a little more like Mars.*

"Gabe!" yells my mom. "If you want a ride, we're leaving now. Otherwise, it's the bus."

I type out a quick reply.

Makeabeat02: *I'm running late this morning and I need to catch my ride to school. This deserves a longer reply, but for now this will have to do: I get it. Hang in there, Yael.*

Then I shut my laptop and go off to school. It's the same drudgery all day. Mostly, I can't pay attention. I can't stop thinking about M&H and Yael and their message.

At the end of the day, Mom texts me that she's not picking Davey and me up until Davey's play audition is over, so I walk to the coffee shop, Grounds for Change, next to school. I base almost all of my coffee shop AUs on this coffee shop, but I've changed all the details. I guess mostly I love the feel of this place. They have tables by the front windows, and booths along the side opposite the bar, and couches and chairs throughout the middle. In the back, they have tons of single tables, and upstairs, they have more couches and a small stage for open mic nights. There's an outlet at every table—probably the eighth wonder of the world, to be quite honest—and the music is the perfect volume. If I could hang out here all the time, I would.

I order a latte and flop onto one of the couches with my phone.

I've been thinking about it all day, and now I'm ready to reply to Yael.

Makeabeat02: *I know what you'd do without me, Yael. You'd be just fine. You'd read fic, and pretend you weren't secretly writing it, and you'd write code and you'd develop widgets and modules and all those fancy things that you plug into the website and make it cooler than ever, and you'd turn down all the interview requests you get from the* Forward *and that cool Jewish fangirl podcast because you're modest and private, and then you'd find your people. I'm not talking about Jewish people—you've clearly found those—but the ones who know the truth, the most important truth of all: that Stucky is canon.*

Makeabeat02: *also, I'm not going anywhere. I'm the Nat to your Cap.*

A text from Mom pops up. *Davey threw up on the stage. I'll be there in fifteen.*

Are they okay?? I text back, sitting up on the couch. My latte isn't even cold yet, but I guess it's time to go. I drain it quickly, toss the cup, and head for the door. My nose is basically in my phone—I guess I might need those glasses Mom's been suggesting—as I can see the little dots from Mom indicate she's typing.

But that's definitely why I walk *right* into the person in the doorway as they open the door. I yelp and almost drop my phone, jumping back a step. "Oh crap, I'm sorry!"

It's Sam. She's gripping her phone in one hand, staring at me wide-eyed. Her long brown hair is pulled into a messy bun, and she's wearing makeup and *earrings.* I've never seen her so dressed up.

"Hi," I say stupidly.

"Hi," she says, a little breathless. She tightens her grip on her backpack strap and her phone. "What are you doing here?"

"Um, I go to school right there." I point at the brick building across the street.

"Oh, right." Pink colors her cheeks, and I have to look away, because I don't want Sam to feel embarrassed, and I have a horrible, *horrible* ability to accidentally humiliate her.

"I'm—sorry." I stumble over the words. "I was looking at my phone. That was my bad."

"I was too," she says.

"This is cute and all," says someone behind Sam. "But could you get out of the way? I'm trying to get coffee?"

We both turn bright red and scoot to the side as some older woman slides past us, winking at us. Or maybe just Sam, since she turns even brighter red. She clears her throat and looks around the coffee shop, worrying her bottom lip with her teeth. "Are you . . . ," she begins.

"I'm leaving," I say quickly. She doesn't want to be here if I'm here. I get it.

Her shoulders slump a bit. In relief, I'm willing to bet. "Okay."

"See you Friday night?" I ask, because it seems weird to just run away.

"What? Oh yeah," she says faintly. "Shabbat. Yeah. See you there."

I push out the door and back into the sunshine, feeling like I've run a thousand miles and I need to catch my breath. I don't turn around and look over my shoulder after I cross the street, and I don't think about anything other than putting some distance between me and the coffee shop. Mom's waiting in front of the school when I get there. Davey's already in the back seat, their hat pulled low over their face.

"Where were you?" Mom asks, but she's not scolding. She's frowning at me like I said something confusing.

"Um, nowhere," I mutter. "I mean, Grounds for Change."

"Did you get my text message?" She locks the door and pulls forward.

I buckle my seat belt and slouch. "No, sorry."

It comes up now on my phone. *They got stage fright, I think. They think they have the stomach flu but it came on quick and seems to be better. They're very embarrassed so please don't mention it.*

"Davey," I say.

Mom shoots me a warning look.

"What?" Davey asks sullenly from the back seat.

"Want to go to the new Marvel movie with me this weekend?"

I hear them shift in their seat. "Really?"

"Yeah," I say, smiling a bit. "I don't think it's going to be very good, but it's Marvel. It'll be fun. What more do you want?"

"I'm in," they say, and I can feel them flop back again, their knees in the back of my seat.

It's only inside our house that I realize Sam was thirty minutes from hers. She was in *my* hometown, in *my* café. Why would she come here, when we've spent the last year trying to avoid each other the best as we could?

Endnotes: I feel like *I'm* going to throw up. Davey's fine, by the way. Disabling comments won't stop the lot of you from sending me all-caps messages about that dangling thread. I wouldn't leave you like that, would I?

CHAPTER 4: I WISH I WERE BETTER

Author's Note: Okay a hundred (just kidding, just a dozen) comments about how I *would* leave you dangling on that cliff-hanger about whether Davey was okay or not. Just because I did it in fiction doesn't mean I'd do it here.

As soon as I get home, I check M&H. I have a crapload of homework to do, but 10/10 would choose M&H over history homework again.

Yael has replied.

YaelLouder: *In what world am I Cap and you Nat?*

Makeabeat02: *That's what you took from all of that? Are you serious?*

YaelLouder: *I took a lot from it. This is just the part I'm questioning.*

Makeabeat02: *Well, for one, I'm obviously prettier than you.*

YaelLouder: **spits out dinner onto keyboard**

Makeabeat02: *And funnier, apparently. I am your wing-man. You're the captain of this ship/war/team of misfits.*

YaelLouder: *brb, changing the name of this site to On Your Left*

Makeabeat02: *a subtle nod to our political leanings and a fandom reference. I like the way you think, Rogers.*

We banter our way through until I have to log off, and they admit they should log off too.

But even after their chat icon turns gray, I stare at the screen. I have plenty to do, but the first thing I reach for is story. I want to put this down in words somehow, this weird itch at the space Yael and I create. I love it when we're in that space, but as soon as we log off, it fades so fast that I question if it's real. Or if I'm the only one they talk to like that. Maybe Yael gives every down fic writer that spiel about how they're special and they mean a lot to them, that they don't know what they'd do without them. I've been there. I've texted people the same lines. I get it. But—I thought it was different here in M&H. And I thought what Yael and I had was different. That it was deeper and more personal.

And our *chats* feel that way. But something's tight in my chest.

I want it in real life too. Maybe it's because I understand Yael saying that they want friendships that get fandom. Or maybe it's because I've seen Sam an extra time this week. Maybe it's the guilt nagging at me. Maybe it's because I miss what we had. Or I'm mad at myself. I guess that's it, though—when I look at Sam, it's not just guilt that I feel. It's this longing for what I ruined.

So maybe I'd mess this, with Yael, up too, if it was in real life. Maybe I don't get to have this in real life, even if I want it.

I feel like an idiot, feeling all these feelings—and I'm not even sure what they really are—for someone in a screen. I don't know them. I don't know what they're like or if they feel the same things or if they're catfishing me or if they're sharing everything I'm saying with someone else. For all I know, they're writing a fic just like this one but about me. Gullible Gabe.

I wipe my sweating hands off on my jeans and close my eyes. Characters swim toward each other, snippets of dialogue unwind in my head, and when I open up my eyes and a fresh document, the words come tentatively but steadily from my fingertips. I don't even know what I'm writing until it's written, one word spilling after another by instinct or feeling. It's rough and raw and full of confusion. I've probably switched verb tenses at least once, but I don't care.

I hit post, and then close the browser. It'll take me about point zero three seconds to open it up and check to see who's read it, but at least I can pretend to work on homework.

As stupid as it is, the assignment takes all of my attention, and by the time I'm done, I realize I haven't checked M&H in a few hours. I log on again, and a message from Yael is waiting for me along with a few comments and dozens of likes.

This fic is a MOOD

Same, bro.

*Been there. <3 *hugs* I'm sorry you're feeling like this.*

I see you, if that helps.

I hesitate before I open Yael's message.

YaelLouder: *Hey. You okay?*

What do I even say to that?

I opt for a half-truth.

Makeabeat02: *sorry. Rough weird day. You know when you think a place is yours and then worry it isn't?*

I start to type, *Or that you'll ruin a friendship so you might as well not even start it?* But then I delete it before I hit send. It's too much. It's too obvious.

YaelLouder: *Yes.*

Makeabeat02: *that kind of a day.*

YaelLouder: *you mean M&H or somewhere else?*

I mean both. I mean Grounds for Change and M&H. I mean worrying that what's happening online isn't real, even though I know it isn't real—but it is. Isn't it? This is real too, in its own weird way.

Makeabeat02: *meh, I'll get over it. Sorry for the emo-ness. Catch you later?*

Makeabeat02: *good luck with the code*

YaelLouder: *Sure thing. Ttyl. And thanks.*

We're quiet through the week, but things get busy. I'm not too surprised. I can't expect Yael to be around all the time, even if I kind of want them to be.

But by Friday morning, I'm so tired from staying up late and from sleeping so poorly, it's only in the car and after our Starbucks run that I realize I didn't use shampoo on my hair that morning. I used *shower gel.* I want to thump my head against the dashboard repeatedly. Neither Mom nor Davey shows me much sympathy either.

The best part about Fridays, other than Friendly's and Shabbat services, is that even early in the year, teachers give up on teaching pretty quickly. I mean, they try. They do. Kudos to them for their best effort. But we're so done by Friday at 1:20 and sixth-period English. Mrs. Nessbaum capitulates and takes us to the library, where we're told to do research on our nonfiction reader responses for our Vietnam unit.

In my defense, I do open Wikipedia. But I also open up a tab and log in to M&H. I rarely get the chance to do this without someone hovering over my shoulder, and I didn't get to check my story stats this morning. People are still loving my X-Maccabees series and demanding updates, and a lot of people have feels about the weird Avengers fic I threw up last night along with my feelings. I almost want to delete it, but I don't.

YaelLouder: *You're on in the middle of the day. Is this the* *apocalypse? Did something happen? Are you dying? Is someone else dying?*

Makeabeat02: *careful, Yael. You jump into my messages so fast when I log on I might think you're waiting for me.*

YaelLouder: . . .

Makeabeat02: *no, I am "working on an essay"*

YaelLouder: *Oh yes. I can see. Working very hard.*

Makeabeat02: *I am a diligent student who would never ever abuse the privileges I've been given at school to check fanfic stats.*

YaelLouder: *clearly lol*

Makeabeat02: *I am having a Friday but this is making it better.*

YaelLouder: *What kind of a Friday?*

Makeabeat02: *Washed my hair with shower gel type of a Friday.*

YaelLouder: *Does that work?*

Makeabeat02: **jazz hands* NOPE*

YaelLouder: *oh no*

Makeabeat02: *I know.*

YaelLouder: *this is tragic*

Makeabeat02: **suspicious* I suspect you're laughing at me*

YaelLouder: *I would never *covers mouth so laughter is muted**

Makeabeat02: *how dare you*

Makeabeat02: *i am going through a deep and troubling time in my life right now and though it's only a few hours until i can wash said gel out of my hair, i expected you to be there for me in my time of need*

YaelLouder: **pats Mab's head* poor bb*

Makeabeat02: *hahaha*

"Mr. Roth," says Mrs. Nessbaum. I click over to the Wikipedia tab so fast I think my eyeballs get whiplash. "You're making progress? There's lots of typing happening over here."

"Yes, ma'am," I say, and then wince. I never say "ma'am." I add quickly, "I'm learning a lot."

"When you lie, Mr. Roth," says Mrs. Nessbaum calmly, "make sure you're not pretending to research Vietnam and grinning at your screen like a lovesick fool. Close out of that screen and get some work done."

I do not say *That was a sick burn, Mrs. Nessbaum,* but I do think it.

I wait until she moves past me to click back to M&H.

YaelLouder: *okay but how did you mix up shower gel and shampoo? They are usually v different textures now that I think about it.*

Makeabeat02: *I was tired!*

Makeabeat02: *I have to go. Teacher caught me. Byyyyyeeeee.*

I log out before they can reply. But I walk a little lighter through the halls because that's the first time we've talked in two days. Maybe I didn't screw everything up.

At synagogue that night, I try to make my hair as respectable as possible, but it still looks like I tried to style it by using an entire bottle of that gel deodorant Davey uses. I give up, shrug on the jacket Mom brought me, and get out of the car. Davey's in their favorite suit-and-jeans combination, carefully applying purple eyeshadow in the rearview mirror.

They blink at me. "Look good?"

I shrug. "Looks like it always does."

They narrow their eyes. "What does that mean? Mom, does it look good?"

Mom appraises them and then nods. "Good. I think that purple looks better when you do a cat eye with the eyeliner, but we don't have time for you to redo it now."

Davey looks doubtfully at her. "You're sure it's okay, though?"

"Totally," Mom reassures them. "Come on."

We walk into synagogue, nodding at the guard at the front, who nods back, just like he does every Friday night. Board members are there, greeting people along the hall. I walk past all of them with a faint fake smile, echoing back "Shabbat shalom" to everyone who says it to me or makes eye contact.

"Marilyn!" calls Mom, and I shrink back into myself as Sam and her mom turn in the hallway. Sam's wearing a purple dress I've seen before and star tights, and her hair's loose. She fidgets, not exactly looking at me, but not ignoring me. Mom and Sam's mom are good friends, and they start chitchatting, turning away from us kids. Davey sees one of their classmates, and before I can grab them and make them stay, they skip off. That leaves Sam and me standing awkwardly next to our parents, who are talking about some synagogue sisterhood meeting or another.

I'm not even sure how to make small talk with Sam. Do I start with *I'm sorry about that thing a year ago*? Or do we keep pretending it never happened, and I skip to *How was Grounds for Change*? But the real question pounds like a steady pulse. *Will you ever forgive me?*

"What happened to your hair?" Sam asks abruptly.

I touch it, grimacing. "Uh, I . . . used shower gel instead of shampoo by accident."

Something lights up in her face, and she looks happy for a

second, amused. "Ha. That's so weird. That's the second time I've heard of that happening."

I snort, rolling my eyes. The words come out more bitter than I intend, though. "The bottles are pretty similar, you know. And it's early in the morning. Honest mistake."

"I wasn't making fun," she says quietly.

I flinch. Swallow. "Oh. I'm sorry. I mean. I was trying to joke."

"Oh," she says, her voice small.

We stand there awkwardly for a while, desperately looking around for someone else our age that we can pull in or one of us can go talk to, but it looks like we're the only two teenagers right now in the synagogue. It's weird to come here only once or twice a week now, after coming three or four times a week when I was younger and studying for my bar mitzvah and confirmation. Sometimes this space feels like mine, like it's talking just to me, and sometimes this space feels totally different, like it belongs to *all* these people, and I'm just standing on the periphery. It's like the coffee shop that I've gone to for years, and then finding out Sam knows it exists. And it's not mine anymore. It's hers, too, and I'm not sure how I feel about that.

"You know when you think a place is yours, but it turns out it's not?" The words slip out before I can stop them.

Sam turns to me, frowning. "Yes . . ."

I don't have a follow-up, but her frown is disconcerting, so I have to turn away. I end up looking at some of the old people with such intensity that they give me tentative smiles and murmur, "Shabbat Shalom."

"It's you," Sam says.

That makes me turn. "What?"

She's staring at me, wide-eyed . . . like she's afraid, or shocked, or horrified. Something big. Something inside me quivers. She takes a step away from me, and then a step toward me, and a step back again, like she can't decide what to do.

There's a wrinkle on her forehead as she stares, her head tilted to the side. And her mouth quivers, like she's about to smile, but she doesn't. "It's you. You're Mab. That's why Grounds for Change feels like something out of one of your fics. And the shower gel. You are Mab."

And that knot inside of me detonates. If I'm Mab—*if I'm Mab, then she's Yael.*

She's *Yael.* I don't think my heart's breaking, but *something* is breaking—nothing is mine anymore, because she's *everywhere.* The first flash of anger surprises me, and then it sinks like a stone in my chest. I press a hand to my sternum, trying to breathe.

We stare at each other, and the rest of the synagogue melts away.

Her mouth opens—Yael's, Sam's—and she starts to say something, but I say hoarsely, "Please."

She closes her mouth, looking stricken. I need to say something, but I'm scrambling for words, and none are coming. Words are my superpower, and I can't find a single one. I only have "please." And that seems like such a *small* word right now. Such a powerless word right now.

Then my mom's hand lands on my elbow. "Hey. Gabe. Come on. Time to get seats."

And I want to scream that I can't *take a seat* because *Sam is Yael and I am Mab and—this isn't real. This doesn't happen to real people.* But Mom and Davey's momentum carries me away from Sam, and I leave her there, standing in the atrium of the sanctuary, swaying slightly, like the leaf at the end of a branch.

Endnotes: If you ask me what the rabbi's sermon was, I couldn't tell you. If I stood up and sat down and said the prayers and did anything, it was sheer muscle memory.

CHAPTER 5: WHAT HAPPENED LAST YEAR

Author's Note: n/a

It's a short story, really. For once.

At someone's little brother's bar mitzvah, some other older teens, Sam, and I were all having this fantastic time. Running around like goofs, like we were still little kids. There's something about b'nai mitzvahs that brings it out, I guess. Playing games, dancing like clowns, flopping into chairs breathless and sweaty and laughing. We took videos on our phones and put them on social media and tagged people who weren't there, which was both hilarious at the time and terrible in hindsight.

Then Seth, a kid from our confirmation class last year, decided to start a livestream of the party. We all got up and started dancing for the livestream, not that anyone was watching, but it was a trip. It was this rush of adrenaline. Someone *could* be watching.

But Sam tripped on the edge of the dance floor, where the

DJ had taped down a ton of wires. It was dark, and the lights were going, and I probably would have tripped too. It's just that I wasn't wearing a dress at the time. So Sam tripped and fell, and when she did, she flashed the camera. She landed kind of awkwardly on her shoulder and splayed there for a second before sitting up. This girl Amber helped her sit up, and Sam looked at me, tears on her face. I think that it was more from the shock of falling or the pain of landing on her shoulder than flashing the camera. I'm not even sure she knew what had happened just then.

But I didn't know what to do. I just stared back at her for a second. Seth was screeching and laughing along with a few of the other guys, because they'd caught Sam's fall and the flashing on the livestream. That no one was watching—but someone *could* be watching.

And—God. I hope this is the worst thing I ever do in my entire life, because it is the worst thing I have ever done to date.

I started laughing too.

In hindsight, they were laughing, and I was laughing because I didn't want to be the guy who wasn't laughing. But the second I chose to laugh—and it *was* a choice—my friendship with Sam was over.

Our parents saw the whole thing, and Dad took Seth's phone, ended the livestream, deleted the archive of it. I hadn't even known he was that tech savvy. But I just remember Mom helping Sam off the floor and taking her to the bathroom to wash off her face and her scraped palm. And then I remember feeling heartsick and violently ill as Mom sat with Sam, alone on the stairs, until her parents came to pick her up.

She hadn't said goodbye to me.

But I hadn't said I'm sorry, or goodbye, or please forgive me to her.

I hadn't said anything about that time since then.

I don't even know how Sam felt about it, because I've never asked her. One whole year. One ruined friendship later. One humiliation. One cowardly act.

This isn't an apology. I intend to do that in person, on Sunday, or Wednesday, or whenever I see her next. I owe her that much. But here's this:

When we were six years old, someone pushed you out of a tree at the playground, and you broke your arm. And I held your other hand while one of the big kids went to get your mom, who took you to the hospital. I wrote my name on your bright green cast, and it took up the whole length of your arm, because my handwriting was too big in first grade and your arm was so small. But you didn't mind. And when we were ten years old, our families went to Disney World together, and you cried when the Beast tried to dance with you, but you weren't afraid of the Tower of Terror, and I knew it was because you didn't like dancing, but you were never afraid of heights. (That's how you'd gotten into that tree in the first place.) And when we got separated from our parents, I was the one who cried, and you were the one who knew what to do, because you weren't afraid of being lost. I don't remember my childhood without you. I told you we'd be best friends forever, and you made me promise.

I broke that promise.

Did you ever think we'd find each other again? I didn't. The girl I met on this website is the same girl who wasn't afraid to climb the trees with the big kids on the playground, and who hated to dance but wasn't afraid of falling. You make every space your own. You always did.

I'm sorry for any breach of confidence I made in writing this, but I wanted you to know. I'm sorry. I wish I could have been better to you and for you.

Endnotes: I think this is probably the end, folks. I'm going to keep comments disabled. Thank you. I'm stepping away for now out of respect for this space and who it belongs to. You can still find me over on tumblr and twitter. The usual names.

CHAPTER 6: EPILOGUE

Author's Note: Been a hot minute, hasn't it? Okay, three weeks. I was told that you'd all appreciate an update. So here it is.

She doesn't come to Shabbat the following week. Or the week after that. But then the third week, she's at Shabbat services. She's wearing a new black dress, and her hair's done up, and she looks like she's going to a funeral. For our online friendship, I guess.

My parents don't know what happened, just that I've been moody as heck, but Mom doesn't say anything when I branch off from them to where Sam's standing by the windows that overlook the Holocaust Memorial Garden.

"Hey," I say quietly.

I can see her swallow hard, and she wrings her hands in front of her. "Hi."

I take a deep breath. I've had a speech prepared for weeks now in my head, but what comes out isn't a long explanation. She already has that. I'm sure she's read what I posted three weeks ago. "Sam, I'm sorry."

She bites her lower lip. "For what, exactly?"

I glance sideways at her, trying to read her expression. "There's a lot. I know. I mean, I'm sorry for what happened last year. I shouldn't have laughed." And then I add, "And I'm sorry that it took me a whole year to say it."

She nods a little bit, tears in her eyes. She's not looking at me, and I really want to hug her, but I'm not stupid. She doesn't want a hug from me right now. "Okay."

I want more. I want *something* more. I want *I hate you and I don't forgive you* or *Thank you* or *I'm sorry too* or *I accept your apology* or *something*. I don't know what to do with "okay." But I told myself, coached myself, made myself promise to an invisible Sam in my room that if she didn't say anything or she slapped me or she walked away, or whatever she said or did, I'd take it.

"Can I ask you something?" I didn't plan this part.

Her look's a little sharp. "What?"

"You use 'they'/'them' on Milk & Honey," I say, keeping my voice down. The question's implicit.

She lets out a slow breath. "Yeah. I'm okay with 'she'/'her' in real life." Then she pauses and adds, "Thank you."

I nod a little and say quietly, "You're still Cap to me."

I shove my hands into my pockets and walk back toward the sanctuary doors. I'm sweating and shaking, but it's over.

I did it. And now both of us can stop walking on eggshells around each other and pretending that what happened didn't happen.

I take a seat next to my family, and Mom gives me a curious look. I shake my head. It's too complicated to explain to other people. Davey gives me a sympathetic smile, and I elbow them back, smiling.

Then someone sits down on my other side. I twist, and freeze. Sam's staring straight ahead, her cheeks flushed, tonight's program gripped tightly in her sweating palms.

I don't know what to say. Then Sam says, "Did you see what we're singing tonight?"

I turn over my own program. "Matisyahu?" I'd forgotten we'd gone to a Matisyahu concert when we were kids. I laugh a little bit, slouching in my seat. "I don't know this one."

"It's catchy," says Sam, relaxing too. "It'll be stuck in your head. I bet you write a fic based on it by the end of the weekend."

I don't ask her if she forgives me, because maybe she doesn't. Maybe she never will. And that's okay.

"Okay," I whisper as the rabbi walks onto the bimah. "But can you imagine Logan at a Matisyahu concert?"

"Yes," Sam whispers back. "Think bigger."

"Iceman," I suggest.

Her eyebrows go up. She knows I'm at the mercy of the Iceman stans again. "Interesting. Make it an accident, though."

"Done," I say.

"A five plus one," she whispers as the rabbi greets the congregation.

"I hate writing those," I mutter.

"I love them. And you owe me." She gives me a sidelong glance.

I do owe her.

"I would say you're the worst," I tell her, "but I'm pretty sure I have that superlative on lockdown."

A smile twitches in the corner of her mouth. "For at least another decade."

The banter between us hurts my heart a bit. We could have had this the whole time. Not just online but in person. We could have been Yael and Mab for the last year instead of the last five minutes. Or maybe that's not the point. Maybe we could have been *us* again, Gabe and Sam, for the last year instead of the last five minutes. I can feel shrapnel from whatever exploded in my chest weeks ago flicking against my nerve endings.

"At least," I agree.

And this time she really does smile.

Endnotes: And that's why you'll see a 5+1 fic from me later this weekend. And I've been given strict instructions. It's five concerts Iceman hates and one Iceman loves. I secretly love writing it, but don't tell Yael. Shhhhh.

HE WHO REVIVES THE DEAD

BY ELIE LICHTSCHEIN

For the third time in the two and a half hours since the plane departed, Raysh decided to go to the bathroom. It wasn't easy. As soon as the seat belt sign went off, the woman in front of her had leaned her chair back as far as it would go, and the enormous-bellied man with the gray beard and black hat in the aisle seat was snoring, which meant she had to wake him up, which was tricky, since she'd read enough about Hasidim to know that he'd flip out if she touched him.

"Excuse me," she said, tapping the armrest, leaving a few inches of space between her and his beefy arm. "I have to use the bathroom."

The man opened his eyes and spoke to her for the first time. "Again?" His accent was thick, Israeli. "What's your secret? They have special coffee back there? Bring me a cup when you come back. I've been clogged since Shabbos."

Raysh didn't actually have to use the bathroom. But as she walked to the back of the plane, passing seats filled with dozens of kids her age, none of whom she knew but all of whom carried the same energy of the first semester of college, she felt the clamminess she'd felt every day, at least a dozen times, since she was pulled out of the river.

She shut the accordion door and turned to face herself in the mirror. Her eyes looked small, but that was mostly compared to the bags under them. Sleep didn't come easy these days, and when it did, it was full of dreams of rushing, pushing water, a swampy subsurface smell she associated with rot, and the particular wet darkness that had compressed her body. That was the worst part. It was enormous, the weight of the feeling that something dark, huge, and impossible to understand was out there, waiting for her.

"You're not dead," she whispered to her reflection. "One foot in front of the other. You're not dead." It seemed to work. She lifted up the toilet seat, stopping only when she felt her chest heave. There was a tiny pool of clear water at the bottom, but to her it was as deep, muddy, and suctiony as the bottom of the Hackensack River. She kept her eyes on the water as her hand found the flusher. She plunged it down, and, as the water was sucked away, her eyes spilled over. She lowered the seat cover and sat down hard, sobbing.

Three minutes later, red-eyed but dry-cheeked, she emerged from the bathroom. She made her way back to her seat, planning on popping a few Tylenol PMs and letting the diphenhydramine carry her away, but the aisles were crowded with life.

A group of fratty-looking guys in muscle shirts reading ALEF BETA KAPPA blocked her path, talking loudly and punching each other in the biceps. "Excuse me," Raysh said. "I need to get through." They ignored her. She tapped the closest one on the back. He turned, looked her up and down, and turned back to his buddies. Raysh felt something inside her sink.

"You have to go full-on Israeli at them," a voice said beside her. She turned. A dark-skinned guy was grinning at her. He had a gap between his front teeth and a cartoonish Theodor Herzl as Abraham Lincoln on his T-shirt. "Let me show you." He got up from his seat and turned to the group. He took a deep breath, but Raysh wasn't ready for the volume that blasted from his mouth. "YALLA, CHEVREH! Let's go, let's go, let's go! Move it or we'll *re*move it! Yalla! Yalla! Yalla!" The fratty guys glanced over, annoyed, but communicated via nods and slunk off.

"I'm like Moshe," the guy said. "Only I'm parting a sea of douchebags."

"Impressive," Raysh said. "Thanks. You on Birthright too?"

"As a madrikh. Counselor," he added at Raysh's look of noncomprehension. "I'm studying at Ferkauf. PhD. But I'm from Netanya originally, and being a madrikh gets me a free flight home." He stuck out a hand. "They call me Yaron." His hand was tan and knotted and reminded Raysh of the jagged tree limb that had grazed her face under the water; she wore the scar, a long pink crescent, on the bottom of her jaw. For a moment, she felt clammy, but she swallowed and pushed the feeling aside.

"Raysh," she said, and took his hand.

"I'm a nondenominational-identifying-per-se but pansympathizing, Israel-loving Jew. I don't have a kippah on my head, but I've got little baby tikvah in my arms and the sandalim of the old yishuv on my feet." He lifted a foot, and Raysh saw his tan sandals. Each one had little Stars of David sewn into the crisscrossing straps.

"Nice speech," she said.

He grinned. "Life is easier when you come prepared."

She nodded and made her way down the aisle, stepping into the vacant row behind hers so she could climb into her seat without waking the big-bellied Hasid. She reached into her bag and took out two Tylenol PMs. Thirty minutes later, she was passed out against the window, her breath fogging it up. She didn't wake until the wheels touched down.

* * *

The first thirty-six hours on Israeli soil were such a whirlwind that Raysh barely had a minute to think about water and near drownings. They disembarked from the plane and spilled like rivers of loud American twentysomethings through Ben Gurion Airport to the outer terminals, where they met up in an ocean of hundreds more loud American twentysomethings, all spending the third week in December taking advantage of the free ten-day trip to Israel that their Jewish identity (and serious philanthropic funding) gifted them. Raysh followed signs to her bus number in a far corner of the terminal, where she was surprised to see Yaron standing on a bench, waving his bus mates over.

From there, she and two dozen kids her age loaded onto a large green bus manned by a surly, chain-smoking driver. He drove them to Caesarea, a coastal site of Roman ruins two thousand years old, and as Yaron and the other counselor, a woman with red hair named Shiri, led an icebreaker introduction

("Who are you, where are you from, and what do you want to get out of this trip?"), Raysh watched the sparkling blue of the coastline grow nearer, feeling the clamminess increase with each jerk of the wheels, and felt glad to be there, forced to participate, because thinking up a good answer and the best way of phrasing it gave her something to focus on that wasn't her memories ("Rachel Tannenbaum—Raysh—from New Brunswick. Hoping for a new stamp in my passport. And to do some swimming"). On the beach, Raysh kept her distance from her bus mates, staying as far away from the water as possible and turning her back to it, staring at the ruins like they were the most interesting thing she had ever seen. They ate dinner at a kibbutz a few hours north, where they were spending the night, and after more icebreakers and get-to-know-your-neighbor games that left Raysh feeling like an outsider watching everyone befriend everyone else, they broke off into gendered fours and retired into small rooms with two bunk beds apiece.

The next day was overloaded with activities, starting with an early-morning hike up Masada, the mountaintop fortress, where Yaron told them that in 30 BCE, the Jewish rebels who lived there committed mass suicide rather than give in to the conquering Romans. "In a way, Masada is the world's biggest mountaintop cemetery," he said. "It's this whole area." He pointed at a blue seam in the hazy brown distance. "Look, you can see the Dead Sea. That's the story of all of Israel in a way. Death here. Death there. Death on all sides. But in the middle"—he gestured at Raysh and her bus mates and the dozens of tourists scrambling on all sides of them—"*life*. So much life."

They ate lunch at the peak (turkey and lettuce on rolls, chocolate wafers, and Capri Sun–esque pouches of a medicine-y grape drink) and then boarded the bus for the Banias Nature Reserve, which had enough springs in it to make Raysh's skin crawl. By the time the bus stopped in front of their hotel in Tiberias, Raysh felt like she might collapse; she'd spent the whole day hiking in the sun, and even though she drank bottle after bottle of water (cursing the peanut-sized bladder her father gave her), she felt like her skin and brain were fried. All she wanted was a bed.

But her bus mates had other plans. A pair of light-haired twins from Milwaukee invited her to join them for a chill in the hotel garden. "We're thinking late-night spirits and hookah," the girl, Orlee, said. Her brother, Oren, nodded, asked, "You in?" and before Raysh could answer, handed her a hookah pipe and a small bag of strawberry tobacco. "I'll get the rest of the stuff."

"So what do you think of Israel so far?" Yaron asked twenty minutes later, joining the eight of them sitting around a fire pit in the hotel's surprisingly lush back garden.

Everyone said something positive; Raysh guessed that it was hard to focus on the negative when someone was footing a multi-thousand-dollar travel, food, and hospitality bill for you.

"Crazy. There are soldiers literally everywhere," Oren said, taking a sip from a bottle of vodka. He chased it down with a mango fruit drink.

Yaron smiled. "We're a small country with a lot of enemies. Protection matters. Like how having a McDonald's on every street matters to you Americans."

This got a round of laughter. Someone passed Yaron the vodka bottle, but he shook his finger and sent it to the next person in line.

"Yeah, but why do they carry their guns so openly?"

Raysh knew what Oren was talking about. On the hike up Masada, in the streets of Tiberias, at a rest stop close to the Banias, she had seen the men and women in green fatigues, with huge black semiautomatic weapons strapped to their backs.

Yaron looked surprised. "For protection. Life is always worth defending."

"Whoa, check out the stars," someone said. Raysh turned and saw everyone crane their necks back. She looked up and was amazed by how much the heavens looked like a curtain, a great black cloth with thousands of holes in it thrown over a terribly bright beam. But the more she stared, the shakier she felt, and instead of the sky, she saw the green-and-black murk of the Hackensack River, remembered the crushing weight that had overwhelmed her lungs, and sensed the dead light of the thing that was waiting for her.

"Hey, what's that?"

Raysh turned. Oren was staring at her jaw. She pressed her fingers to the jagged scar.

"That looks brutal. How'd you get that?"

"Don't be a jerk!" Orlee hissed. To Raysh she said, "Ignore my brother. He gets drunk and loses his filter."

"No, it's okay," Raysh said. "I was in an accident. I . . . I almost drowned."

She pictured the night it happened and felt a jolt of déjà vu. Friends hanging out in a park, drinking and laughing and staring at the sky. Only that night, they decided to go swimming. "We had just finished finals," she said, "and were feeling, I don't know, reckless or something. So we jumped into the river." She didn't mention that it was her idea, or how when Matt, with his cartoonishly wide biceps and relentless sex mind, suggested they all get naked, she immediately agreed and even slipped off her pants first, which was enough for the other guys and girls to start hooting and disrobing. "It was fun," she said, her mind on Matt's abs and the nest of hair underneath, calling attention to his groin. "We were just splashing and spitting water at each other, but then someone suggested that we see who could hold their breath the longest, and . . . I mean, I won, but not really by choice."

"What happened?" Orlee asked. Everyone else was quiet, their eyes on Raysh.

Raysh exhaled. "I heard this thing once that the trick to holding your breath underwater is to go down as far as you can and stay there, keeping your mind as blank as possible. Like, remember that it's just your brain telling you you need air and that you're dying. If you ignore it, you're fine. So I did that. I dove as deep as I could and found a sunken tree. I . . . kind of straddled it so I wouldn't float up, but I put my foot on this part that was rotted through, and it got stuck. And . . . I lost my mind. I was thrashing and pulling, trying to get out. I smacked into the tree and cut myself on a branch." She traced her finger along her jaw.

This was where it got tricky. Raysh didn't know how much to share. She looked at Orlee, who was smiling kindly, but with something sad in her eyes, and gestured for the bottle. "I swallowed half the lake and . . . died, basically. It took three people to get me out, and I had all these . . . death rattles in the ambulance. I learned that later, because I was unconscious at the time."

Raysh finished speaking to a silent garden. Everyone's eyes

were on her. She lifted the bottle and took a sip. She didn't even taste it.

Yaron cleared his throat. "Baruch atah Adonai, Eloheinu melech haolam, michayeh hamaytim. Blessed is he who revives the dead." He paused. "We're so glad you're here."

Raysh stared at him. "Thank you." It was all she could say.

* * *

In fact, Raysh knew where to draw the line when it came to sharing. To tell her bus mates that the main reason she signed up for Birthright was to conquer the fear she felt every day since that night was a definite overshare. So was explaining that she wasn't ready to return to the Hackensack River just yet, but there were tons of bodies of water in the Holy Land for her to use to baby-step her way back to New Jersey. She really felt like she had died under the water, and a third-year med student at the hospital where she recovered backed it up. "You were dead, clinically speaking," he said. "Dying for a few seconds or minutes, even, and then coming back to life is common. But don't worry. You're not a zombie. Literally, of course."

But the first few bodies of water her bus encountered were all huge and terrifying, so Raysh focused on distraction. She came up with a game called "count the soldiers" with Orlee, Oren, and a tall guy named Simon. It was simple. They counted every soldier they saw. You could only count each soldier once, so whoever spotted him or her first got the points. It was great, since you had to be focused and paying attention pretty much the whole time. Which didn't leave much brain room for memories.

The four of them soldier-counted their way through the candle factory and DIY art galleries filled with paintings of Hebrew letters in the mystical city of Tzfat, past the ritual baths and vacant fire pits on their hike through Meron, and along the gleaming golden streets of Jerusalem, where Raysh lucked out when she and her bus mates entered a falafel shop, and she spotted three soldiers on line ahead of them wearing steel-toed boots and sucking on red cigarettes.

Just before they reached the Kotel, the holiest place in the Jewish world, Yaron stopped them. "We're about to get our first glimpse of the wall. You'll have plenty of time here, but first, I want to share something. For two thousand years, Jewish bodies have turned here in prayer. Your ancestors all wished for the privilege of what you're about to see. For many, it kept them going. The thought of Jerusalem, the city of their religion and so many of the stories and prayers they heard their whole lives, being rebuilt—not at the expense of the previous tenants, I'm not getting political here—was, how you say?" He looked down at the Stars of David on his sandals. "A huge motivator in many of their personal interests and passions moving forward. All right, we ready?"

They turned the corner and saw the Kotel. Raysh felt let down. It was beautiful and swarming with people, but it looked exactly like the pictures she had seen her entire life in Hebrew school and on social media.

They walked to the plaza outside it. Shiri handed out two small notebooks. Yaron passed around a few pens. "There's a custom to write a note and stick it in the cracks of the wall," he said. "Take your time. Write your note. And then go to the wall, say a prayer, and find a place to put it in. Men on the left, women on the right."

Most people took a pen, scribbled something, and waded into the sea of people, fighting to get close to the stones, but Raysh lingered. She thought about it, and when she finally found the words, she was surprised by how short her note was. As she reread it, she realized that instead of a prayer to God, she had written one to herself.

Let me go under, but this time let me come up.

She pressed her way through the women crowded around the wall and waited until an opening presented itself. When she was up against it—she saw thousands of slips of paper stuck into every conceivable crack and wondered how this towering wall could possibly fit all the notes people wrote and shoved in it, every single day—she stopped and repeated the prayer Yaron had said the night before.

"Blessed is he who revives the dead."

She spotted a ledge full of rolled-up pieces of paper with space for one more and pressed her note into the stone.

* * *

The next day was the Sabbath, and they spent it in the Old City. They went to a synagogue and visited the Israel Museum, where Oren spotted a group of thirty-three soldiers and rubbed it in the rest of her bus mates' faces. After that, they returned to their hotel, ate fatty kosher food, and spent the rest of the afternoon lounging in the lobby, basically observing the Sabbath. Raysh liked the slowed-down change of pace, but without the distraction of movement and things to look at, she felt near-drowning thoughts creeping in. She was glad when Sunday morning came around, and they boarded the bus and headed down to Ein Gedi.

But the drive was tense. A heated argument broke out after a tall boy with a yarmulke objected to Oren's use of the word "occupation" to describe Israel's disputed territories.

"Don't call it that," the boy said. "It's an unnecessary description."

"How is it unnecessary?" Oren asked. "It's literally an occupation. There are people living their lives oppressed by Israeli occupiers."

"They're not oppressed by occupiers. They're watched over by soldiers protecting Israeli citizens. When there are no soldiers there, they launch rockets and bombs into Israel. If they stopped doing that, the military would stop guarding them." The boy's face was red. He pulled out an asthma inhaler.

"If the military stopped guarding them, then they wouldn't do any of that!"

"That's ridiculous!" The boy took two long puffs on his inhaler. "You're asking Israel to lay down its weapons! We've all seen what happens when Jews don't defend themselves!"

"Why does it always come back to the Holocaust? You can be critical of Israel without saying you want to murder six million Jews!"

And so on.

Other people joined in, but Raysh didn't care to. She just watched. Yaron was in the seat in front of her, watching too, not saying a word. At one point he turned to Raysh and shook his head. "Like everything, there are strong arguments on both sides," he said. "But what bothers me, what's always bothered me, is how we Jews are expected to make peace with the Palestinians when we can't make peace with ourselves. How can there be external peace when there's no internal peace?"

When they reached Ein Gedi, Shiri told them to bring their bathing suits so they could change before the hike, which had a few natural springs on it, including one used as a swimming hole. As they shuffled off the bus, Raysh turned to Orlee. "Can I ask a favor?"

"Sure. Whatever you want."

"Um. Okay, so you remember my story about almost drowning, right?"

Orlee nodded.

"Well, I haven't been in a body of water since it happened, but I feel like I really need to. You know, to prove that I can."

"Makes sense."

"I'm going to try to go in the spring, but can you just make sure I don't freak out?" Code for *Please make sure I don't clinically die. Again.*

Orlee smiled. "Of course. I got your back. I'm actually a certified lifeguard, so you're super in luck."

Raysh smiled back. "Thanks."

The hike was easier than the other ones, just a trek up a sloping incline surrounded by short cliffs full of stubby trees and prickly flowers. It was peaceful, as long as Raysh didn't think about what waited at the end of it. Already her breath was jagged, and her body felt clammy, which was partially because of the sun, but mostly not.

She lagged in the back, with Orlee and the bus's security guard, who was always the last person on every hike. She started talking to him as a distraction.

"It's beautiful here," she said, gesturing all around them.

He nodded and pressed a cigarette to his lips. "It's the miracle of the Jews."

"What do you mean?"

He stopped walking. "We are in the desert. And yet there are trees and plants and perochim . . . how you say? Flowers. It's the miracle of the Jews. When Herzl came it was all . . . mah hamilah? Swamp. The miracle of the Jews is they come to the desert and make it this. Where there is death, they made life." He dragged on the cigarette.

Raysh walked in silence, thinking. She caught up with Orlee, and as they came closer to the spring—the splash and roar of a waterfall was the giveaway—she realized that she believed him. She believed it in her bones. Where there was once death, she could make life.

But the sight of the spring was overwhelming. Two other buses were there, a few families, and a handful of solo hikers. About fifty people were already in the water.

Yaron led them to a spot away from the others. He gestured to a small clearing under a few trees and took off his shirt and sandals. He grinned at them and then, like Moses at the Red Sea, he led them into the water. A lot of people followed him in, and there were cries of "It's so nice!" and "Oh my God, yes!" and "Marco!" but Raysh stayed put.

"How are you feeling?" Orlee asked.

"It's too crowded," she said. "If I freak out, I'd rather it be less public."

"There's another spring over there," a voice behind them said. Raysh turned and saw Simon.

"I'm not stalking you or anything. I just overheard."

"How do you know that?" Orlee asked.

"He told me." Simon pointed at the security guard, who was leaning against a boulder, holding a cigarette in one hand and reaching into a bag of sunflower seeds with the other. "I asked if he was going in, and he said no, but if he were, he'd go to the spring behind that boulder. Want to check it out?"

"Sure," Raysh said. She took a deep breath and, for a moment, felt like she was back on the banks of the Hackensack River. "But you guys don't have to."

"We don't have to," Orlee said. "We want to."

"Want to what?" Oren said, joining them.

"Go swim in a private spring. For Raysh."

Oren looked at her. "Ahh, got it. Yeah, totally. What are we waiting for?"

Raysh smiled, but it wasn't easy. "Thanks, guys," she said.

They walked past the security guard. He nodded at them and pointed. "Over there," he said. "Beautiful, I tell you. Mamash yafeh."

They climbed up the path and then veered off it, toward a huge boulder that sat at the top of a short incline. It was a tight squeeze through the trees around it. Raysh had to suck in her stomach to fit, and even then she was just barely able to, but it was worth it. On the other side was a deep burbling stream of crystal-clear water the size of a large Jacuzzi. Totally empty.

"Do you . . . do you want us to do something?" Orlee asked.

Raysh didn't answer. Just looking at the water clammed her up. She was shaking and felt like she might vomit. But she thought again of what the guard had said. *Where there was death, they made life.* And even though she was in panic mode, she told herself she was ready.

But she wanted to do it right, and that meant re-creating the original experience as much as possible. "Um, this might sound weird, but can you guys turn around? I want to go in without a bathing suit."

"Skinny-dipping! Woooo!" Oren shouted, but he turned

his back. Simon did too. Orlee didn't. "I'm on guard duty," she said.

Raysh nodded and unzipped her shorts. She slipped out of her T-shirt, unhooked her bra, took a deep breath, and slid down her underwear.

It was now or never. In her mind, the water swung between looking dark and quicksand-like to the clearness it actually was. Better to get it over with. "One . . . two . . . three!" She jumped.

The water hit her like a grenade. She prepared to sink and was amazed to find herself floating. She shrieked and moved her arms and legs.

There was the rustle of cloth, a flash of naked body, and Simon was in the water. More rustling, more nudity, and Orlee was in too.

"I'm not going in," Oren said on the shore. "I'd rather not accidentally bump into my sister's naked body, thanks."

Orlee rolled her eyes, treading water. "We were naked roommates for nine months. Get over yourself." But he just stood on the shore and turned away.

The three of them treaded water. Orlee and Simon splashed and laughed. At one point, after making sure they were ready and watching, Raysh summoned all her bravery and dove as deep as she could, praying there were no branches on the floor but ready if there were, and pressed her feet to the bottom, which was alternately muddy and stony. She stayed there, trying to keep her mind as blank as possible. Dark thoughts swirled, memories of the muck and rot of the Hackensack River and the awful clamminess of being trapped, feeling the end coming for her, reaching out to touch her like an underwater tree trunk.

She concentrated, doing her best to push the thoughts away. It worked. She felt months of heaviness roll off her like sweat. She waited there as long as she could and then breached the surface. "I did it, you guys! I fucking did it!"

Orlee and Simon cheered. Raysh cheered too, and did a little dance in the water. And she dove again. And then again and again. She stayed there, treading water, grinning, listening to her friends sing and the water splash.

By the time they climbed out of the spring and back into their clothes (Raysh avoided staring at Simon's pubes but got a nice look at his skinny butt), Raysh felt different. At peace. Like a war between two ferocious enemies had ended. She walked back to the bus with Orlee, Oren, and Simon. They were shouting and joking, and there was a lightness to the four of them that hadn't been there earlier.

"How do you feel?" Orlee asked.

Raysh thought about it. Her heart was thumping, and her skin felt sparkly, like it was covered in a glaze. She didn't know how to tell them how it felt to have two different parts of yourself in combat, each pushing and pulling and trying to sabotage the other. How calming it was to attempt the impossible, to rise from below, to zombie yourself back to the living. How going into the water and facing the thing that was out there, after her, waiting for her, took away some of its power. She might be surrounded by desolation, but going after it did something to her, something powerful.

She smiled at Orlee. "I feel revived."

BE BRAVE AND ALL

BY LAURA SILVERMAN

"Holy Jews, Batman," Rachel says.

I nod. "Seriously."

We're riding the glass elevator down from the twenty-third floor of our hotel, probably the only one brave (or foolish) enough to host a thousand teenagers for the national JZY convention. The lobby is packed. Kids sit on the floor in circles, hang out by the check-in counters, and play Hacky Sack where there definitely isn't enough room to play Hacky Sack. There are kippahs and curls and chapter T-shirts with sayings like CHALLAH BACK and ONE FISH, TWO FISH, WHITEFISH. Rachel and I are wearing the shirts from our local chapter: ATLANTA JEWS ARE HOTTER.

My pulse races as the elevator stops at the fifteenth floor and more people pile on. Rachel and I scoot back to make room. But there are strangers' shoulders and feet and warm breath all up in my personal space. My body tenses, and Rachel reaches out and squeezes my hand. "You good, Naomi?" she asks.

I squeeze her hand back and shoot her a nervous smile. I

don't do conventions. I don't do massive crowds and fourteen-hour days packed with scheduled activities like icebreakers and group dinners. Even my local chapter events can be social-interaction overload, so this is next-level out of my comfort zone.

But Rachel is my best friend, and she begged me to go, and she promised I would have a good time. And to be fair, she has held up her end of the bargain so far. On the ten-hour overnight bus ride from Atlanta to DC, she scored us that row of three seats in the back, so we got to spread out in our own little domain, away from the sounds, and smells, of our fellow passengers.

Still, it was a long trip, followed by just a quick two-hour nap in our shared hotel room. And now it's only noon, which means there's a full day of social interaction between me and introvert heaven (i.e., a closed door and HGTV).

The elevator stops on the lobby level, and everyone squeezes out one at a time, squishing and pushing to make room between those waiting to go back upstairs. This seriously has to be a fire hazard. Hmm, maybe it is a fire hazard. Maybe I should call the fire department and tell them this is a fire hazard, and we'll all be sent home early. . . .

"I wonder where Zeke is," Rachel says, craning her neck to look around. Shouting voices bounce off the walls, and groups move as herds, blocking every pathway. She slips out her phone and twists her lips. "Ugh. There's no service in here."

Because there are too many people. Because this is a fire hazard.

Okay, Naomi. Deep breath. Chill out. Be in the moment. Go with the flow—the flow of packed people shuffling forward one centimeter at a time. I lean into Rachel. "We'll find him eventually. Maybe he's in our tour group."

"Maybe," Rachel says, doubt in her voice.

Zeke lives in South Carolina. Rachel met him three regional conventions ago, and she hooked up with him at the two most recent, because JZY is basically a front for Jewish matchmaking wrapped up in "educational social events."

Eventually, the crowd breaks up enough for us to move forward. Rachel and I make our way toward the sign for group C, our tour group for the day. I look down at my feet as we walk, mentally trying to move people out of my way, like an introverted Moses trying to part the Red Sea.

We come to a stop in front of our group. Rachel leans left and right, searching for Zeke. I know what he looks like from his Instagram, which Rachel swears she doesn't stalk, and his page just *happens* to be up every time I glance at her phone, so I help her look for him.

There are so many people here. And they're alive and loud and taking up space. My pulse races, and I try to calm myself down by thinking of the nice crinkly comforter and Twix bar waiting for me in the hotel room. It helps, a little.

As I'm scanning the crowd, I notice a guy leaning against the far wall. He's strumming a ukulele, the strap much too small around his broad chest. His eyes meet mine, and in that long moment, my pulse calms. But then the crowd shifts, and my glimpse of him is gone.

"Off we go!" Rachel says, following as our group spills out onto the streets of DC. "Ready for the best weekend ever?"

I spot him again, the polka-dot strap cutting across his T-shirt. His hair is ruffled in the back, like he just woke up from a nap. I get the urge to smooth it down for him. "Yeah," I say, smiling. "I think I am."

* * *

Rachel is eating peanuts, cracking the shells and tossing them into the grass as we walk. It's bright out but cold, and I'm grateful I packed a warm jacket. The National Mall bustles with tourists and residents alike. Groups like ours walk in matching shirts, families shepherd around their little kids, and men and women stride quickly down the paths, texting and talking on their phones.

"Maybe Zeke is with him," Rachel says. "Can you tell?" I pointed out ukulele guy to her, and she noticed he's wearing a Charleston chapter T-shirt, Zeke's chapter. But now he's up at the front of the group, and we'd have to push in front of people to find them, if Zeke is even there. Rachel checks her phone again. "Whatever," she says. "I'll find him when we stop. So you're into ukulele guy?" she asks.

"'Into' even feels like too strong of a word. I mean, who brings a ukulele to the National Mall? Is he trying to look cool?"

"He probably only knows three songs," she says.

"Probably," I say. Then, after a pause: "He's hot, though."

"Super freaking hot," Rachel agrees.

We both laugh, and Rachel loops her arm through mine. I feel better now that we're outside. There's space to breathe and be. We walk for another ten minutes before our group slows to a stop. There's some statue up ahead, but it's hard to see from here. "Gather round!" our guide shouts, clapping her hands together.

Rachel shifts on her feet, trying to see the front of the group. "Should we go up there now?" she asks. "I don't know.

I mean, should we?" She twists a lock of curly hair around her finger. "What do you think?"

It's weird to see her anxious.

It's weird to see her acting like me.

I glance ahead. Everyone is packed in tightly. I'd have to say "excuse me" a hundred times to get to the front of the crowd. "Um, maybe we should wait."

"Yeah." She nods. "Yeah, whatever. C'mon, let's sit. My feet are done for."

I look at her ballet flats. "I told you to wear your sneakers."

She rolls her eyes, grinning. "Whatever, *Mom*."

We find a grassy area a bit farther from the group and sit down, leaning against a tree. Now it's really impossible to hear the guide, and the ground is a bit cold, but it's kind of nice to depart for a moment and just be alone with Rachel. My body relaxes as I shred a piece of grass.

"What do you think they're saying up there?" Rachel asks.

I shrug.

"C'mon, Naomi." She nudges. "Take a guess."

I glance up. The guide waves her arms around and marches up and down. And now there's a second guy with her, and they're obviously reenacting some sort of scene. I laugh and say, "It's like *Whose Line Is It Anyway? US History Edition.*"

"I do say, Mary Todd," Rachel says, dropping her voice to a deep octave to mimic Abe Lincoln. "I love the theater. Shall we go see a play?"

I grin, then clap my hands together and make my voice high-pitched. "Ooh, how delightful, Abe. I'll get us box seats, only the finest. It'll be the *last,* I mean *best,* night of your life!"

We both laugh. Rachel winces. "Too soon?"

I nod, still grinning. "Too soon."

* * *

After the tour, we have an hour to chill around the Lincoln Memorial before heading back to the hotel. Rachel and I grab a soft pretzel and lemonade to share from a nearby stand, and then we head over to the stairs in front of the memorial, scanning them for the blue Charleston shirts.

"There," I say, nodding toward Zeke and his friends.

Rachel nods. "Right. Cool. So we should go over." She takes another bite of the pretzel. "Okay, so let's go."

My stomach tightens as we approach the group. I count them quickly. Eleven new people, all engrossed in conversations, all comfortable and laughing with each other. Well, except ukulele guy, who is busy strumming and humming.

I don't get it. How do people have these giant groups of close friends? Was there an orientation I missed out on where people were assigned to their packs?

Rachel is my only ride-or-die friend, not a sit in the cafeteria and complain about homework friend, not an awkward small talk at JZY Shabbat dinner friend, a true I will watch ten hours of Netflix in silence with you but also help you bury a body if you need it friend.

"Hey, y'all," Rachel says as we stop before them.

A couple of people glance up; a few smile and even wave. But Zeke stands. He's tall and lean, and his T-shirt lifts a bit when he goes to hug Rachel, revealing a sliver of his skin and a line of dark hair.

It's a long hug.

When they finally release, Rachel's cheeks are flushed. "Flat Latke!" she says.

"Matzo Bowl!" he responds.

They both break out into hysterical laughter at their inside joke. Their inside joke I am obviously on the outside of. They high-five, and then their hands stay clasped. I plaster on a nervous smile.

Out of the corner of my eye, I notice ukulele guy. He's looking at me. Grinning at me. He glances at Zeke and Rachel and rolls his eyes.

I freeze. How do I respond? Do I nod? Also roll my eyes? Do I smile and—

He turns to the guy next to him, and our moment is lost.

My Hollywood meet-cute moment is over before it started.

Did he even roll his eyes, or was it just a twitch?

"Zeke, this is my best friend, Naomi."

"Hey, Naomi!" he says. "I'm a hugger. Can I give you a hug?"

"Sure." I nod. He wraps me in his arms. It's a full hug. A real hug. A hug that makes my body all warm. People talk about kissing like it's this intimate be-all thing, but I think a real, solid, two-arm, breathe-the-other-person-in hug is supremely underrated.

"C'mon," Zeke says, stepping back. "Pop a squat."

I snort. "Pop a squat?"

"Grab a seat, take a chair, lean on a ledge," Zeke says.

"Sit our asses down?" Rachel asks.

He nods. "Exactly."

Zeke sits back right in the circle of everyone, and Rachel scoots in next to him. There's not really enough room for me to also squeeze in on the step, and the girl on my other side is deep in conversation, and I don't want to ask her to move over, even though there's probably room, so instead I sit on the stair behind them, a bit to Rachel's right.

They immediately launch into conversation, and I try to laugh and nod along, but it's kind of hard to hear, and they keep talking about things and people from past conventions, and my skin is getting all tight and itchy as I pretend like I'm part of this.

Rachel, being the best friend that she is, does try to loop me in. "Naomi loves *The Good Place.*" She looks at me, eyes bright, waiting for me to pick up the gauntlet and run with it. "Don't you?"

Zeke looks over at me too. All eyes on Naomi. I clear my throat, then nod. "I do," I say. "It's great. You should watch it."

"Cool! I will!" Zeke says.

Go me, social interaction with new person accomplished.

But then he's off again on another tangent, and maybe I should've talked more about *The Good Place,* but that might have bored him. My fingers itch for my phone, but I don't want to be that person who stares at her phone because she can't make conversation. So instead, I twist my fingers together and glance down at the Mall.

It's warmed up a bit more, and one might even call this bright March afternoon gorgeous. And here I am sitting on the steps of a national monument, something people come from all over the world to see, and I get this kind of stomach-fluttering feeling that even though I'm not having the best time ever, I will remember this moment forever, because I'm never going to be a teenager sitting on the stairs of a national monument again.

Rachel laughs. No, Rachel giggles. She leans into Zeke,

knocking shoulders with him. I want to be happy for her, and I am, I guess, but it kind of feels like she invited me on this trip just to be her third wheel, which is kind of shitty, but I also kind of understand, because what are best friends for if not to be each other's third wheels when they need some extra support?

I stand and mumble "Be right back" to Rachel.

She glances up and squints. Best friend telepathy: *You okay?*

I nod: *All good.*

Before walking down the stairs, I glance to my right, but ukulele guy is again deep in song, eyes closed. He doesn't even look pretentious. It seems like he really is enjoying playing.

As I walk down the stairs, I spot a group of people gathered at the bottom. At first it looks like a group of JZY kids in red T-shirts, but they're definitely older than us. One guy has thick facial hair, and a woman has a baby tucked on her hip and a toddler tugging at her hand. They're handing out flyers, and people are actually taking them, which is weird.

The woman catches my eye and waves me over. She's petite with bright brown eyes and hair down to her waist. My heart skips a bit. Someone's waving me over. *Me.*

God, I'm not that lonely, am I?

I walk over, and before I have a chance to worry about what I'm going to say, she shoves her free hand in my direction and says, "Hey! I'm Brit."

I shake her hand. "Hi, Brit. I'm Naomi. Um, what's all this?"

She shifts her weight to her other leg. "There's a protest here tomorrow." She grabs a flyer from someone behind her and passes it to me. "There's a website with more information, but basically we're protesting a bill that would allow people easier access to semiautomatic guns." She rocks her baby a few times and glances down at her toddler. "These ones will be in school before long. I want them practicing the alphabet, not active-shooter drills."

The toddler blinks at me, his eyes bright brown like his mom's. I'm not really a political person. I know there's important stuff happening, but adults spend a lot of time yelling at each other on Facebook. And I can't vote yet, so what's the point of getting into that mess?

But the school shootings do freak me out. Last year, there was almost one at my cousin Rebecca's middle school. They found a gun in this kid's locker and all these messages on his computer about his plan to shoot up the school. It's scary knowing we could have lost her just like that. Off to school one morning and never coming home again.

"The protest is tomorrow, ten in the morning," Brit says. "Right here on the Mall."

"It's going to be a great crowd," a guy says, turning to us. He's wearing the same red T-shirt, which I now see reads GUN CONTROL NOW. "Can you make it?"

"Um . . . ," I say. "I'm here with a Jewish thing, and we're not supposed to leave the hotel on Shabbat."

"I'm Jewish too!" Brit says. "I actually got involved with fighting for gun reform after that horrible shooting at the Pittsburgh synagogue."

"Oh God," I respond. "That was horrible."

I remember Mom telling me about the shooting, hearing the names of all those victims, feeling the immense pain of losing so many Jewish people at once. I remember the fear that it could happen at my own synagogue and anger that people still hate us enough to murder us.

"So can you make it?" the guy asks. "Totally understand if not."

"Um . . . ," I say again.

I'm not exactly a rule breaker. If I'm caught leaving the hotel without permission, I could get kicked out of JZY. My local chapter events are important to me. They're some of the few social things I *almost* feel comfortable at.

Also there's no way Rachel will go with me. Shabbat is her favorite part of the convention. Supposedly you get to know people really well when you hang out with them for a full twenty-four hours, and I have a feeling she wants to get to know Zeke very, very well during this Shabbat. We should basically have an eleventh testament that reads *And on the seventh day thou shall rest, and thou shall also make out.*

So Rachel won't go with me, and there's no way I'm going to go to a super-crowded place on my own. It seems like a cool experience. It seems . . . important. But it's not going to happen.

"Maybe!" I say in a way that probably sounds like no.

"Well, keep the flyer just in case," Brit responds. "There's a script on the back, so even if you can't make it, you can give your local representative a call and ask them to support safe gun laws."

My phone buzzes in my pocket. I slip it out. Rachel. "Hey," I say, spinning toward the stairs.

In the distance, I see her waving at me. "Mary Todd," she says, her voice deep again. "The time hath come for our departure. We mustn't be late to the *the-a-ter.*"

* * *

Services are held in a giant convention center room, like we're at one of those megachurches they put on TV. We sit in a row of seats with Zeke and his friends. Rachel sits between Zeke and me. They keep playing with each other's hands during services. It's basically hand sex. It's gross, and I'm weirdly a bit jealous.

Ukulele guy is on my left, so of course I keep glancing to my left. He's not having hand sex. Instead, he's praying, actually praying. Siddur opened in front of him, doing the little daven knee bend and head bob.

It's weird to see him without his instrument. He seems younger or something. I spot a couple of pimples on his jaw, along with a few errant hairs he missed shaving. I bite back a smile. Somehow knowing he's just a teenage boy makes him even cuter.

After services end, we wait for the crowd to slowly pour out of the giant room and into a different giant room for dinner. The crowd seems even larger than this morning, as if more busloads of Jews have been arriving every half hour. Rachel finally drops Zeke's hand and slides my way, her cheeks flushed. "I'm starving," she says. "You starving?"

"Worked up an appetite, huh?" I ask.

She winces. "Sorry, I'm being obnoxious, aren't I?"

"Possibly yes."

"He's just so *cute*." She glances at him, unable to keep the smile off her face. "But I'm the worst. I'm sorry. How are you holding up? Want to grab some food and go eat just the two of us?"

The offer is tempting. Maybe we could even sneak up to

our room, eat in our hotel beds while watching people watch other people renovate their homes. But Zeke has already secured a table and is waving us over, and I know Rachel wants to spend more time with him. It'll be time for bed soon enough. And besides, maybe I'll finally learn the name of ukulele guy.

"Nah," I say. "We can sit with them. You can make it up to me by letting me pick our Netflix binge on the bus ride home."

"*The Good Place* again?"

I grin. "Obviously."

My stomach grumbles as we approach the buffet tables. Hot food. Thank God. We have to keep kosher on these trips, and since the far majority of road food isn't kosher, we can only eat cold dairy to be safe. But now I smell roast chicken and potatoes and veggies, and ooh, that's a lot of challah.

We pile our plates with food, then join Zeke at his already packed table. I end up between Rachel and ukulele guy again. This time he looks right at me. "Hey," he says, extending a hand, voice muffled by the piece of challah in his mouth. "Adam."

I steal a quick breath before shaking his hand. "Eve," I say.

He bites off a chunk of the challah and grins. "Funny."

"You've probably heard that before, haven't you?"

"Never with such quick timing. What's your actual name?"

"Naomi," I say, cheeks warm. "So still biblical."

"Nice to meet you, Naomi," Adam says. Then he picks up a fork to dig into his plate, all greens and potatoes. Maybe he's vegetarian. Or maybe he just doesn't like roast chicken. I have the sudden urge to know everything about him, discover his specific likes and dislikes so I can nod and smile and say *Same here, me too.*

"Adam, help me out?" a guy next to him asks. Adam spins away from me to untangle a necklace stuck in the guy's long hair.

Rachel nudges me. "Holy crap. Have you tried this chicken? It's delicious."

I take a bite, and she's right, but the food sits funny in my stomach. I'm still thinking about that protest tomorrow, about my little cousin and how she's scared to go to school now, about how she's not wrong to be scared.

"Um, Rachel," I say. Zeke is busy in conversation with someone else, and I have her attention. "So I know it's probably a no, and that's okay, but there's this protest tomorrow morning at the National Mall, for safe gun laws, and I was wondering if you would go with me."

A sad look passes over her face. "I would love to, really, but we can't leave tomorrow. It's Shabbat."

I bite back a comment about her paying more attention to Zeke than the service tonight. "It's okay," I say. At least I won't have to deal with another giant crowd.

"You could go alone?" Rachel asks. "I could help you make a sign tonight."

We both know I won't go alone.

"Sign for what?" Adam asks, spinning toward us.

Rachel's eyes brighten. "For a protest, for gun control," she says. "You should go with Naomi, you know, if you're a rule breaker."

"I'm *here* because I'm a rule breaker," Adam says.

"What kind of rule breaker?" Rachel asks.

Uh-oh. This is what I get for crushing on a guy without any prior knowledge. Is he a drug dealer? Does he run a teenage fight club?

"I got in trouble for drinking," Adam says. I steel myself. Here it comes. "I drank one of my mom's Skinnygirl margaritas. Okay, I drank three of them. Okay, I drank three of them and then streaked down the street and ran into our eighty-year-old neighbor walking her dog."

I snort, loudly, then blush hard and cover my face.

Adam shakes his head, smiling with embarrassment himself. "I know, I know. It was bad."

"Your poor neighbor." Rachel laughs.

"It was traumatizing for all parties involved," Adams says. "So anyways, my parents decided I had too much free time on my hands and could use more 'structure' and 'community,' so they said I needed to become an active member of JZY."

"Well, I'm glad it landed you here," Rachel says, but then Zeke whispers something in her ear, and she goes back to her conversation with him.

Adam and I stare at each other for a long, uncomfortable moment in which my brain forgets how to produce words. Finally, he raises an eyebrow. "So, the protest. Um, want some company?"

My palms grow clammy. If Adam and I go to the protest tomorrow, it will be just the two of us, alone among a massive crowd. I'll have to make conversation with him. All morning. What if he thinks I'm boring? What if he thinks—

Rachel and Zeke break into a fit of giggles. Adam rolls his eyes at them and smiles at me, a smile that warms me up from my toes to my cheeks.

"Okay," I say, smiling back at him. "Let's go to a protest."

* * *

My sign reads GUN REFORM NOW!

Last night Rachel helped me make it. We found an empty cardboard box and tore off one side, then begged a Sharpie off the hotel concierge, who looked like he was ready to quit his job at any moment.

But now the sign sits in the corner of the room while Rachel, wearing only a skirt and bra, curls her hair in the bathroom. I stand, staring at my closet. Shabbos dress or jeans and a red T-shirt?

Adam gave me his phone number last night. I could text him and cancel, tell him I don't want to get kicked out of JZY, tell him we should just go to services and oneg with everyone else. But last night, I crawled into bed and read over the flyer Brit had given me to double-check all the details, and there was this script on the back with statistics about school shootings and domestic abuse, and I thought about how if that awful man hadn't had access to an AR-15, maybe more people would have survived the synagogue attack, and I realized this is important, and I do care, and maybe I can't vote yet, but I can still make my voice heard.

I take a deep breath, then uncap the Sharpie and add a new line to the poster: 2020 VOTER.

"So you're really going?" Rachel asks. She peeks out of the bathroom, her hair wound around the curling iron. She looks surprised as I pull on my red T-shirt. It's from *The Good Place* and says FORKING BULLSHIRT. Maybe my sign should read *These gun laws are forking bullshirt.*

"I am," I say, pulse racing.

"Heck yes!" She pumps the air. "I'm proud of you, darling. Get that cute boy! And give Congress hell!" She pauses. "And text me if you need to, okay? I'll send puppy GIFs."

I grin. "Okay."

There's a knock on the door, and, stomach tightening, I open up to find Adam standing in the hallway, his back facing me. His ukulele is strung around his chest, and he's wearing a kippah with music notes on it. He spins around to me and strums the ukulele twice. "Morning."

His right cheek is flushed and has little imprints on it, like just moments ago it was pressed against his pillow. I smile, half looking down, and quietly say, "Morning."

Rachel pokes her head out of the bathroom. "Morning! Also, Adam, don't come in, because I'm not dressed yet. Also, have fun!"

Now both his cheeks flush. His fingers fiddle with the ukulele strings.

"Ready?" I ask, nerves officially kicking into overdrive. Part of me hopes we *do* get caught sneaking out of the hotel, because then at least I won't have to deal with massive throngs of people, not to mention figure out how to make one-on-one conversation with a cute boy I barely know. *Oh my God! What have I gotten myself into?*

He strums his ukulele again. "Ready!"

There are probably trip leaders all over the lobby, just waiting to catch derelict teenagers, so we take the elevator at the end of my hallway instead of the central glass one. We ride down in silence, then step out into the quiet first-floor hallway.

"Now what?" I ask Adam.

He raises an eyebrow. "Uhh, wasn't this your plan?"

I take a small step forward, looking up to meet his eyes, proud of myself for meeting his eyes. "Aren't *you* the rule breaker?"

Adam laughs, and it's a laugh as pure as a kitten snuggling in fresh laundry. He shakes his head. "We are not good at this, are we?"

I can't keep a smile off my face. "We are not." But then I spy something out of the corner of my eye. "Ooh!" I race forward and snag a newspaper sitting in front of room 110.

"Theft?" Adam asks.

"I'm only taking the classifieds. Hopefully he isn't looking for a missed connection."

Adam watches, curious as to what I'm up to. I pull out two full sheets of newspaper. Then I try to fold the rest up correctly, but it's all jumbled and not working, so I just clear my throat and place the mess back in front of the door.

Adam's eyes glint. "Deviant," he says.

"It's for a good cause," I respond. "Come on."

I hand him one of the newspaper sheets. "Now what?" he asks.

I open my sheet and hold it up in front of me so it obscures my entire face and then some.

Adam breaks into laughter. "Seriously?"

"It works in the movies!"

"*What* movies?"

"Do you have a better idea?"

He pauses for a moment. "I do not." Then he opens his newspaper and holds it in front of his face. I can't hold my sign and the newspaper, so I leave the sign behind. We hold back more laughter as we not-so-surreptitiously walk into the lobby with the newspapers blocking our faces. We keep to the edges of the wall, inching along closer and closer to the main lobby doors.

Hmm, this is actually kind of nice. I'm forced to look only at my feet instead of avoiding awkward eye contact with strangers. Maybe I should try this at home.

Right as we're about to hit the lobby doors, someone shouts a bit loudly, "Are those two—"

And then Adam is grabbing my hand and the newspapers are dropping and we're running out the doors and into the brisk March air and sprinting down the sidewalk. Three blocks later, we stop, panting. Our hands stay clasped a moment longer before Adam pulls away his hand to fiddle with the bobby pin holding his kippah in place. "You good?" he asks.

I look down. I'm wearing jeans and a red T-shirt. I'm in Washington, DC, about to go to a super-busy protest with a cute guy I met yesterday. I am a human manifestation of nerves and excitement.

"Yeah," I manage to say. Then more loudly: "I'm good."

"Good." He smiles and pulls a ziplock bag of cereal from his pocket as we continue down the street toward the Mall. "Apple Jacks?"

* * *

A few blocks later, we both stop short. The bustling streets have transformed into jam-packed, clogged city arteries, thousands of people cramming into every available space, swarming their way to the National Mall.

My heart races. Not good racing. Scary racing. And I grip my phone, ready to text Rachel or turn back altogether.

"That's a lot of people," Adam says. And when I look at him, I notice his white-knuckled hand is practically strangling the neck of his ukulele.

"*A lot* of people," I agree.

"I don't do great with crowds." He gives me a shy smile.

"I'm kind of a homebody," he admits. "My favorite place is my room. I know—that's pathetic."

"No!" I shout, then flush and lower my voice. "It's not pathetic. I like my room too. It has everything I like in it, and it's *quiet.* I don't know if I could ever face the world if I didn't have my room to come back to." I pause. "Now *I* sound pathetic."

"Not pathetic," Adam says firmly, eyes locking with mine. "Brave. It's brave to face the world in the first place."

He keeps looking at me, and I keep looking at him, and I get this really warm, nervous, amazing feeling in my stomach, and this time my heart does the good kind of racing.

The crowd starts chanting, and our gazes are drawn back to the throngs of people. "Should we . . . ," Adam starts.

"We could go back to the hotel." But the idea, first spurring relief, quickly deflates me. Is this the best I can do? Walk *to* the protest? It's not like I have any daydreams about becoming the world's best activist, but I think—I know—I can do better than this.

"Or we could keep going," I say. "Be brave and all."

He smiles. "Yeah, let's be brave and all."

I take a short breath as we move forward, walking until we've merged with the rest of the crowd and there's not an open piece of landscape in sight. All of my senses are on overload, but I manage to keep calm by recapping the pilot episode of *The Good Place* in my head. Eventually my nerves ease enough for me to look around.

There are all sorts of people here. Young adults in their twenties, people my parents' age and older, and a surprising number of little kids with them. I spot one girl who can't be older than ten holding a sign that says I'M SCARED TO GO TO SCHOOL.

"Whoa," Adam says. "This is whoa." The crowd jostles us closer to each other, and instinctively I reach out to grab his hand just like I would with Rachel. I'm embarrassed and go to drop it immediately, but he squeezes mine and tugs me closer. The pads of his fingers are the slightest bit rough, maybe from the ukulele strings.

We keep moving farther down the Mall. It's another cold day, but Adam's hand is warm, and the upside of people packed around us is that they block out the wind. The crowd kicks up a chant, "Gun reform now! Gun reform now!" And Adam and I join in. It feels a bit weird at first, silly, like *What am I even doing here? Do I even know enough about all of this to belong?*

But as the voices join around us, and as I think of my cousin and all the other kids out there scared to go to school, I feel this swell of emotion, pride, and hope, and I think it's not always about knowing the most but about showing up when it counts.

I chant louder: "Gun reform now! Gun reform now!"

We walk and chant for at least half an hour, and eventually the crowd thins a bit, everyone finding their own breathing room, and Adam's hand slips from mine as he draws both up to the ukulele and begins fiddling. "I'm glad we did this," he says, looking at the strings, not me. "It feels important . . . it feels right. Like I'm supposed to be here."

He then meets my eyes, and I get this swooping feeling in my stomach. "Same," I say.

He plucks the ukulele strings. "And it's nice to get away for a little. Yesterday was a lot, the convention, all these new faces. It's not that I don't like people, but I just never know if they like me, and so then I'm awkward."

"*You're* awkward?" I ask. "You've been with Zeke's group all weekend. I'm the awkward one hovering around it."

"I am . . . awkward. Yesterday I went to give Zeke a high five, but he didn't high-five me back. I don't know, maybe he just thought I was stretching or something? So I failed a high five. I'm fail-a-high-five awkward." Adam glances at me, grins, and shakes his head. "And I hover too. That's why I brought the ukulele. So it looks like I'm just too busy playing music to talk to anyone. Seriously, I can only play, like, three songs."

I snort.

"What?" Adam asks.

I shake my head. "Nothing, promise." My stomach twinges with hunger. I glance at my phone and realize we've already been out here for two hours. I catch Adam's eye.

"Should we . . . ," he starts.

I grin. "Yeah, let's head back."

We turn around and start threading back through the crowd. It's overwhelming at first, pushing against the people, but we keep going until we're off on a narrow and relatively open pathway closer to the street. I reach out both arms and touch nothing but open air, then give a deep sigh of relief.

Adam laughs. "Same," he says.

I look back at the mass of people we just came from, and I swell with pride, because I did that. I showed up and made this movement one person louder.

We're stepping off the grass onto the sidewalk when I spot a familiar face. "No freaking way," I say.

"What?" Adam asks.

"That's Senator Burnham." I squint my eyes. "Yeah, that's him. One of my Georgia senators." He's probably one of three politicians I could recognize. Hard to forget that giant mustache and those bushy eyebrows. "I wonder . . ." The flyer Brit handed me yesterday sits folded in my pocket.

"You wonder what?" Adam asks.

I take the flyer and show it to him. "There's a script here for talking to your representatives. We're supposed to use it to call their offices or write letters, but . . ."

"But he's *right there.*"

"He's *right there.*"

My thoughts had already wandered back to my hotel room, lounged out on the bed, watching HGTV, impressed with myself for sneaking back without notice. I did the thing, and now I get my reward of delicious introvert solitude.

But even though I did do the thing, here's a chance to take it a step further, a chance to talk face to face with a living, breathing politician who will actually vote on these laws.

"I can't believe he's just standing around like that," I say. He's waiting for an order from a food truck. We're a few blocks away from the protest now, but still, it seems risky. He could be open to conversation with a concerned citizen.

My heart races hard at just the thought of going up and talking to him. "What are you going to do?" Adam asks.

"I don't know," I say. He's paying for his order now and stepping off to the side to wait. I should talk to him, but what if he's angry? Or worse, what if he's an active listener and engages in the conversation and then realizes I'm awkward and bumbling.

"Go on, Naomi." Adam nudges me. "Be brave and all."

"Be brave and all." I grin at him. "Okay, here I go."

"Good luck!" Adam calls.

I stride toward Senator Burnham just as he's being handed

his food. "Excuse me!" The words squeak out. "Senator Burnham." He doesn't turn around, just picks up his food and begins to walk away. I raise my voice. "Excuse me, Senator Burnham. I live in Georgia!"

This time a few people on the street stop, including him. He turns around, face in a grimace, muttering something about ". . . aide was sick, and I just *had* to have my falafel. . . ." Then he plasters on a smile. "Always nice to meet a constituent. I'm sorry, but I'm in a bit of a hurry."

I rush the last few steps up to him and say, "Just one quick thing, um—" I look down at the flyer. My hands shake, but I force myself to read the full script. When I'm done, I look up at him, heart pounding.

He pulls his bag of falafel closer to him and says, "Thank you for voicing your concerns. Good day."

And then he turns and speed-walks so fast it's basically a run.

Good day? Really?

"Good day to you, sir!" I shout back.

Someone taps me from behind, and I almost yelp. It's Adam, hovering over me with a smile. "How'd it go?" he asks.

"A disaster." But I feel another swell of pride. "I did it, though!"

"Heck yeah you did!" Adam says. He lifts his hand for a high five, but the flyer is still in my right hand, and in the second I use to put it in my pocket, he starts lowering his hand, looking unsure and uncomfortable.

"Oh my God," I say.

I grab his hand with both of mine and lift it back into the air, and we high-five.

He smiles. "Brave and all."

I smile wider. "Totally freaking brave and all."

NEILAH

BY HANNAH MOSKOWITZ

My zipper's stuck.

No. It's not stuck. The dress is too small. I haven't worn this dress since my high school graduation, and I thought it fit then, but maybe I'm remembering wrong. Maybe it didn't zip then, either. I probably looked ridiculous in it. Probably everyone was looking at me and thinking that my dress was too small.

I don't know what else I can wear if this dress won't zip. Mira said I'm supposed to wear white. I pretended like I already knew that. I should have already known that, just like I should have known that at Kol Nidre last night, people weren't pronouncing "breakfast" strangely when they were talking about the *break fast* tonight.

Those are things that good Jews know.

And these are dresses that good girls are supposed to fit into.

I've lost weight since I last wore this dress. It should fit now. But it won't zip, and it's my fault, and I'm too big, and—

The zipper clicks, tilts, edges into place, and glides smoothly the rest of the way up.

The zipper was stuck.

* * *

My family, if you couldn't tell, never did Yom Kippur. It's kind of the antithesis of everything my family did do with Judaism: basically, food or nothing. We have Passover seders, where my dad makes sure to throw in asides that there's no historical evidence that the Jews were ever slaves. We fry latkes on Hanukkah. My aunts compare the calorie counts of applesauce versus sour cream, ignoring that either way, it's fried potatoes.

We talk and sing and yell over each other, and I blend in and breathe and feel a little safer than usual, and they shove plate after plate on me and compliment me on how thin I've gotten in a way that sounds like worry, but not enough for them to ever actually do anything.

My ex-boyfriend was the same way. It was about the only thing he had in common with my Jewish family. He'd run his hands over my body and say all the right things about how he was concerned and liked me at whatever weight and it didn't matter to him, and then he'd sink his fingers into the gaps of my hip bones like he wouldn't know how to hold on to me if they weren't there.

We dated for two years, and he was vibrant and sweet with me but awkward and unnatural with my family, uncomfortable with the noise and the jokes, telling me his ears were sore after a night with my cousins, and my dad would give me looks behind his back: *Seriously, this is the guy?*

I was hardly ever invited to his house, but whenever I was,

I dressed up and sat at his manicured dining room table in a room so quiet you could hear the ticking of their expensive, imported clock and ate small, organized portions with his small, organized parents.

* * *

There's a knock on my dorm room door, and Mira pokes her head in, curls spilling over her shoulders. She smiles at me. "You look nice," she says. She looks like a nymph with her white dress and button nose, without a straight line on her whole body. She crosses over to me and stands on her tiptoes to kiss me—on the cheek; you can't brush your teeth on Yom Kippur, I found out from Google three days ago.

"How are you holding up?" she asks.

Mira doesn't know that going without food for twenty-five hours is no more than a light stretch away from my usual routine. Normally I might have eaten a granola bar from the box under my bed for dinner last night, but that's about it. She doesn't know that. I try to eat in front of her.

We've been dating for two and a half weeks. I've never dated a girl before. We're going slow in a lot of ways, which has been my excuse for keeping the food thing to myself. By the time we're at a place where keeping something this big from her would count as a lie, I'll be finished, I decided last week, though I'm not exactly sure what "finished" means, and I try not to think about it. Any definition feels too big for me.

So I say, "Going without water is a bitch."

"Only ten more hours! The second day is always the easiest." She takes my hand and smiles at me. "Ready to go?"

"Yeah. Thank you for inviting me."

"Are you kidding? I'm so psyched you're coming."

My first morning Yom Kippur service ever.

* * *

"Do you really even count as Jewish?" my ex asked me once, in his car. "You don't keep kosher or anything. You didn't even have a bat mitzvah."

"It's not about that stuff," I said, trying to be casual, trying to act like there wasn't a voice inside me going *FAKE FAKE FAKE* every second I'd ever breathed. "Well, it's not all about that."

"I read that you're not even Jewish if your mom isn't Jewish," he said, and I felt all the *that's not true*s and *why is it your business*es and *who the fuck are you to tell me*s rolling around in my mouth, but I didn't let them out, because . . . because. He was a boy and I was a girl. He was a guy and I was a lady.

"I don't know. I don't even, like, think of you as Jewish," he said, which didn't explain why he found my uncles' personalities too big and my cousin's naming ceremony too long.

I spend a lot of days in front of the mirror, counting and pointing and touching and thinking, *Do you even really count as having an eating disorder? You're not even underweight. It's not like people know when they look at you.*

FAKE FAKE FAKE

* * *

Rhode Island is cold already, and campus is quiet this early on a Saturday as Mira and I walk to the other end toward the Hillel. She goes every Shabbat; I've only been for Rosh Hashanah and

Kol Nidre last night and a mixer near the beginning of the semester, where we met.

"When I was a kid, I always used to hope I'd get sick on Yom Kippur," Mira says.

"Why?"

She laughs. "It's a mitzvah to eat if you're sick, just like it's a mitzvah to fast if you're not. I was always looking for that loophole."

I smile at her.

"It's so weird," she says. "Doing the holidays without my family."

This is her holiday season. It's supposed to be mine, and I learned that from Jewish Tumblr, not from anything I actually experienced. "Holidays" for me means December, like some gentile.

Except it does mean Hebrew blessings, candle lighting, hot oil, my aunt's voice gliding over the "amen," pronounced our way.

Mira has never asked me to apologize for not being Jewish enough. She knows I didn't have a bat mitzvah. She knows I flip to the transliteration when we go to services together and still get lost.

"Do you miss your family?" she asks lightly.

"I do, yeah." I hadn't really realized until this moment.

I wish I knew how to read Hebrew. I wish I were Mira instead of me in more ways than I could possibly count.

But I don't want to have to forget my stupid, assimilated memories to be a good Jew. I really love our Christmas tree, and pretending I don't is getting so exhausting.

We walk through the doors of the Hillel. Weirdly, I feel hungry.

* * *

The Hillel lobby buzzes with people picking out prayer books and volunteers directing them down hallways for each service. Orthodox, Conservative, Reconstructionist. Mira and I go to Reform.

The cantor, a junior who's in one of my big lecture classes, is already singing, and the girl who's up front with her to lead the service looks nervous as she goes through her notes. The rabbi will be in later to give a talk after the prayers—to be honest, that's the only part that means much to me, since Hebrew is just sounds as far as I'm concerned—but the lead-up is all student-led. I don't know if that's all the branches or just a Reform thing. It doesn't seem like I'm supposed to ask.

I don't know if Mira and I as a couple would be welcome in the other rooms, together. I don't think I'm supposed to ask that, either.

We sit near the back, and she takes my hand as we find our places in the prayer books. Her hair waterfalls over the back of her chair, free.

* * *

"At 'avinu malkeinu,' " the student leader says, "when we say it in English, you can say 'our father, our king,' or you can keep saying it in Hebrew, or you can say 'my mother,' or 'spirit,' or 'nature' . . . whatever feels right to you."

I like that, but I end up mumbling "our father, our king" because it's what everyone else does.

The Hebrew service doesn't mean much to me. It's just

sounds. I pray that I won't die this year, and I like the part where we hit ourselves.

* * *

I never would have guessed that I'd get involved with religious stuff in college. This is supposed to be where you pull away, isn't it? Where the kids who were raised religious start experimenting, breaking rules, not that I know much about religious people outside of reading books about falling in love with the preacher's son or something when I was a kid.

Mira. I know Mira. She doesn't come to mind when I think about religious people, because when people say it . . . they mean a preacher's son.

It actually still counts as religious when it's Jewish, too.

It counts.

I don't understand what all this Hebrew means, but I still feel a certain kind of floaty and dizzy. But maybe that's just because I'm hungry.

That wouldn't make sense.

* * *

My great-grandparents were religious. They were immigrants, and back then clinging to Judaism meant clinging to religion more than it does now, I think. Both sets of my grandparents raised their kids significantly less religious, and my father raised me with horror stories about how boring Hebrew school was, how he had to get up early on Saturdays, how lucky I was that they didn't make me do that.

I'm not saying I wish I had gone, necessarily, but it would be nice to not be told how I feel about it.

I just feel like I've been folded up for a long time, for a gentile boy with a nice smile, and secular parents with nice jobs, and a curvy body with a nice face. If you fold up small enough, you'll fit into all of it. And I'm just wondering when I stopped feeling hungry.

And why I feel hungry today.

* * *

I didn't ever really care about being *skinny*.

I just wanted to be categorically, unarguably, definitely *something*.

* * *

The rabbi comes in with his little girl balanced on his hip. She has a juice box, and we're all trying very hard to look like we don't want to lunge at her. He walks up and down the aisle as he speaks, bouncing his daughter slightly.

"G'mar chatimah tovah," he says, and we repeat it back to him. "I have a story for you." His steps are steady, slow, like a metronome. "In 1718, a boy named Zusha was born into a Jewish family."

"This is a good one," Mira whispers to me.

"From an early age, Zusha was invested," the rabbi says. "In his family, in his own sense of self, in Judaism, in passion. He used to sit and read the Torah, and if he didn't understand a portion, he would sit and cry and wouldn't stop until someone came and explained it to him."

Everyone laughs a little. I wonder if they already know this story, like Mira does.

"As a child in Hebrew school, Zusha heard the passage from Exodus 'And God spoke to Moses.' Zusha was so overtaken by this, so overwhelmed by the idea of God reaching someone so closely, that he repeated 'God spoke, God spoke, God spoke' over and over, and he was removed from his class for causing a disturbance."

Another laugh.

"Zusha grew up to be one of the greatest rabbis Jewish history has ever known," our rabbi says. "As he grew older, he never lost his emotional connection to prayer, and to Judaism, and he passed it on to his many students."

"Daddy, I want a yogurt," the rabbi's daughter says.

"Me too," he says. Again, we laugh.

He sets her down, and she runs to her mom, sitting in the front row. I don't know why I'm surprised the rabbi's wife is here. I guess I thought she wouldn't be here, in the Reform service, like we wouldn't be good enough for her.

"Deuteronomy 34:10," the rabbi says, abruptly. "'No one will ever be as great as Moses.' Pretty straightforward. But then the Talmud says—what?—'Everyone is responsible to be as great as Moses.' So what do we do? How do we engage in a world that tells us we have to be something that is categorically impossible for us to be? What does God want from us? What did he want from Zusha?"

I twist my hands in my lap.

"When Zusha was on his deathbed, after a long, beautiful life, his students came to visit him. They expected to see a man at peace. Someone who had been captivated by God his whole life, someone driven to tears with the marvel of the universe and the idea that God could speak to him, was about to encounter everything he'd dreamed of face to face. But Zusha was not at peace," the rabbi says. "He was terrified, and his students couldn't understand why.

"They sat by him and held his hand and relayed back stories of everything he'd accomplished. Still Zusha wasn't satisfied. They told him how he'd inspired them, all the lessons he'd taught them. Still it wasn't enough.

"And his students told him, 'Rabbi, when you get to heaven, you're going to be rewarded beyond your wildest dreams. Think of all the good you've done for the world. Deuteronomy 34:10: "No one will ever be as great as Moses"—but God will look at you and say, "No one could have been more like Moses. No one could have been more like King David." '

"And Zusha said, between tears, 'I'm not worried that God will ask me why I wasn't more like Moses. Why I wasn't more like King David. I'm worried he'll ask me, "Why weren't you more like *Zusha*?" And what will I say?' "

I feel like I've forgotten how to breathe.

The rabbi pauses in his walking.

"What excuse do we have?" he says. "For why we were not the biggest, most obvious versions of ourselves we could possibly be?"

* * *

My ex "I don't know, just didn't think of me as Jewish," but he definitely thought of me as a lot of other things that even back then always felt . . . coded.

Too loud.

Too dramatic.

Too picky.

Taking

up

too

much

space.

Get smaller and smaller until my nose straightens, my hair uncurls, my last name drops some clusters of consonants, my cultural baggage fits into a perfectly leveled teaspoon.

Get smaller and smaller until my stomach touches my back and I can finally pull my chair all the way in at a WASPy dinner party.

How long does something like that take?

How long ago did we start?

* * *

I wait for Mira outside the bathroom after the service, watching people hug and chat in the Hillel lobby. I wrap my arms around my waist and feel something like longing.

"Tina?" a voice says. It's the cantor, that junior I know.

"Hi," I say. "You, um. You did a really beautiful job."

She smiles. "Thank you. I don't think I've seen you here before."

"Yeah, my girlfriend's more observant, so I'm . . ."

She nods encouragingly, and somehow words just fall out of my mouth.

"My mom's not Jewish," I say. "We have a Christmas tree at home."

She nods thoughtfully, then says, "Christmas trees are beautiful."

I swallow. Breathe. "Yeah. They are."

"I hope you come back," she says.

Mira comes out of the bathroom, exchanges some small talk with the junior, wraps an arm around my waist. "Have a meaningful fast," we all tell each other, and Mira says, "Ready to go?" to me.

I fit my hand into hers, easily. "Yeah."

We kiss gently outside my dorm. I forget about my unbrushed teeth, don't think about my breath until afterward. It doesn't matter.

* * *

Services have been over for two hours, and I'm just sitting here. Mira went back to her room to take a nap before evening services and break fast. It's still three hours before sundown, when we're allowed to eat.

But I feel electric.

I feel big, and I could be bigger, and maybe I am also big enough.

It's wild.

It's a mitzvah to eat on Yom Kippur if you're sick, Mira had said, so I roll my desk chair to my bed. I dig around underneath, and I grab a granola bar and take a huge bite.

My chewing sounds like applause.

FIND THE RIVER

BY MATTHUE ROTH

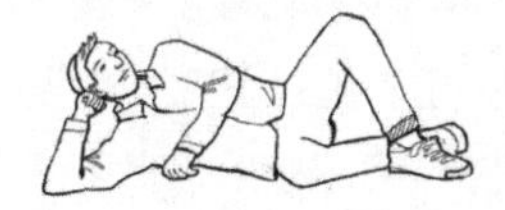

We used to swim naked together. Four years old, then six, then seven, all of us, boys and girls together. Other instances of public nudity made me feel shame, but in the lake alongside everybody else it made me feel better about myself, saggy and underdeveloped, a boy with the perfect girl's body. Across from me, Alix Blitman, who in school always wore blue jeans and plaid button-down shirts that looked like she should be going to a job, not class, who was tough and beautiful and untalkable-to, now was just another kid, just like me, only her head and birdlike shoulders visible, vulnerable and splashable.

And then Henry Bagelman, who everyone called Challah and who was my best friend, cannonballing between us, his face like a puppy's, asking, "Hey, Alex, I finally got here. Did you miss me?"

And neither Alix nor I knew which one of us he was talking to, since we'd sat next to each other in class all year, and we had somehow never realized that our names—the boy version, the girl version—when shortened, came out sounding like the same thing.

Challah was bigger than any of us. With his shirt off he was like a round rubber snowman, his belly a perfect sphere, shiny skin reflecting the yellow summer sun. This was Tookany Creek, a river running straight through the row houses and factories of Northeast Philadelphia, and was probably toxic, but we weren't thinking about that. When Challah jumped in, he covered us all in waves, but we didn't mind. That was what we came for.

Later we lost track of the river. We went away for summers, to camp or school programs or family trips, or the ones of us who had to get jobs. And we were still friends, most of us, but we became different types of friends to each other. I'm not sure there's anyone I would've let see me with my shirt off.

By ninth grade, Henry Bagelman was twice as tall and three times as wide as anyone else in our grade. We still stuck together, because there wasn't really anyone else for either of us to stick with. We weren't nerds—neither of us was that smart—but we kept to ourselves for the most part. We liked the same music, read the same comic books.

A few months into the year, he started disappearing some nights. I'd send him a text and not hear back for a few hours. In our language, that was weeks. *What wormhole are you disappearing down?* I asked him.

Synagogue, he wrote back.

I thought he was kidding. But a few days later, when we were playing Ms. Pac-Man at the local pizza place and a bunch of kids I didn't know walked up to us and started talking to him, three guys and two girls—the guys with their heads covered, the girls in skirts, and all of them a little more prim and well dressed than anybody we knew—I said, without looking away from the screen, "What gives, Challah? Are these your rabbis?" He got a little shy and a little embarrassed. "Please don't call me that anymore, Alex," he said. "My name is Hillel now."

We all got pizza. Challah took off his baseball cap, and there was a yarmulke under it. It'd been hiding there the whole time.

He said a blessing before he took a bite. He whispered it quick and quiet, but I heard. Of course I heard.

I was a little furious at Challah for his ambush, but the others seemed pretty okay. One of the guys knew a ton about X-Men—the comic version, not the movies—and one was in the middle of the same game I was. Mostly, though, they were just cool. When you talked, they really listened.

One of them looked really familiar, and I guess I was staring too hard, and he started laughing, at first a little bit, then harder and harder till no one could ignore it, and he said, "What's wrong, you don't recognize me with my shirt on?"

His name was Effie Spiegelman, and he was the rabbi's son. To Challah's astonishment as well as my own, he used to sneak away from his yeshiva, which ran all summer as well as the year, to join us on our swimming expeditions. He was always coy and nonchalant about it, as though showing up when we did was no big deal, but there was something about his attitude, the way he held his body and the way his gaze lingered too long in certain places, that we could tell this was an alien experience to him, that he was out of his element. And yet, he was still more funny and charming and flirtatious than I could ever manage, even at that young age when none of us really knew how to be.

"But how did your father *let* you?" I asked, horrified.

Effie laughed again and said, "Oh, my father lets me do *any*thing."

"What he means," said Challah, and I hated him more for trying to explain it to me than I did for keeping all this a secret, "is that his father doesn't let him do anything, anything at all. So he does just about anything, and gets away with it."

None of the Orthodox kids questioned that, so I felt like I shouldn't either.

We finished eating and said goodbye, and unsurprisingly the other kids told me I should come to youth group with them. I said I'd think about it. Then they left, and it was just Challah and me alone. "You really should come sometime," he said. "Just to check it out."

"Challah," I said. "They brainwashed you. Don't you realize? Can't you even see it?"

"You mean Hillel," he said.

"And anyway, what were they doing here? Were they stalking us?"

"I'm sure they weren't stalking us," Challah said, and his face turned red, and I knew he had sent them to us.

* * *

The youth group was all-consuming. You couldn't just go to one event. You had to go to them all. They had a way of getting under your skin, scheduling events at exactly the right times: Friday nights, Saturday afternoons, Sunday days. Half days at school became half school, half youth group.

The problem was, I liked them. Not the events but the kids.

I didn't care one way or the other about roller-skating nights or cold-cut lunches, but the people were cool, fun, these low-impact and low-pressure friendships where we could just hang out and do whatever and say anything that was on our minds. I didn't know what we had in common with each other, except I guess we were all Jewish. It didn't even really matter that much to me. Maybe it made them easier to talk to, knowing there was some part of my genetic makeup, something invisible inside me that, whatever made me different from everybody else, all the people at school I feared and resented and avoided, it was different about them, too. Did we have anything in common? Did they understand me, truly understand me? No way. Neither did Challah, though, for years. That was it, I realized one day. Hanging out at youth group was like hanging out with a roomful of Challahs.

But casual hang-outtage had been enough to seal our friendship. Maybe that was all I needed from life.

Well, that . . . and girls.

I didn't remember when girls had gone from invisible (they were like guys, only not) to weird (they're *really* not like guys, and that's gross) to awkward/exciting/dangerous (they're *really* not like guys, and I want to know more). Sometime between the days of swimming naked in the river and now, we had stopped talking to them entirely; they were an alien species, with their own language, culture, rules, and desires. The thing about youth group was it was coed. And along with all my new guy friends—who I didn't trust absolutely with my life, but I trusted for a good night—it was a way to meet girls, to see them and study them up close, but within a socially appropriate setting where you didn't have to approach them on your own.

Which is why it was so weird when, at one of the first Sunday-afternoon youth group roller-skating parties, I staked out a bench on the sidelines, right next to the bowl of potato chips, and found I was sitting directly next to Alix Blitman.

"Alex?" she said, doubling over and gaping at my face in what, if she was wrong about who I was, would've been the most explosive social blunder ever.

"Alix!" I squeaked in joyous bewilderment—then cleared my throat, lowered my voice into whatever it was becoming these days, and said once again, "Alix. What are you doing here?" I leaned in for a hug, which we never did as ten-year-olds, but that's what everyone seemed to do these days when a guy and girl saw each other, then froze up when I saw she wasn't moving to comply. Then I noticed she was wearing long sleeves and a skirt, which might not've been weird or noticeable on its own, but within the context of youth group it meant something completely different.

"Skating. Only, not. I'm part of this youth group, and today is skating day, only I—"

"Absolutely hate the idea of putting yourself on wheels and throwing yourself into a vortex of a cold white rink," I finished for her. I was smiling so hard my cheeks were throbbing.

"Alex, are you spying on my brain?"

She was smiling hard too.

I didn't give in completely. I wasn't not interested in G-d, or becoming Orthodox, or following all the rules and doing whatever the youth group rabbis wanted us to do, but it just didn't seem that important to me right now. G-d created us, right? So at this point, G-d probably just wanted me to try to figure out the operative points of Creation.

One day, Rabbi Yakov, the director of the youth group, told us that he wasn't satisfied. By now, our numbers had grown to include almost half the Jewish kids in our public school class. Some were devoutly interested; others, I sensed, were just there to meet girls. But we all watched the propaganda films, ate the potato chips, drank the kosher Kool-Aid. We didn't all do a hundred percent of Shabbos things a hundred percent of the time, but at youth group, at least, we were good about being Jewish. We didn't bring our phones to the Shabbos events. We didn't wear short shorts. We didn't eat at McDonald's.

"Not good enough," said Rabbi Yakov. Being Orthodox, he said, wasn't about the things you didn't do. It was about what you did. What you were.

He announced a study day. Rabbi Yakov needed a catchy title, so he called it Torah-Rama instead. Rabbis came from all over the city to speak. So did kids, although most of them were already in religious day schools and didn't need the reinforcement and protection from evil that marked our youth group's Torah-Rama classes.

"I'm not going to that," snorted Effie Spiegelman, who didn't really count—he always said he wasn't going to anything, then showed up anyway. One time I'd really cornered him, asked him why he put up with the rest of us Bible thumpers, and he admitted that this was the only place his father permitted him to hang out with secular kids. "So maybe I'll be there," he admitted stonily. "But I'm not letting those rabbis into my head."

The truth was, I wasn't so sold on Torah-Rama either. My motives for being here were purely non-Orthodox. I wanted earthly friends, things to do because I was bored, not because I thought G-d needed me to do them. Afterward, in the hall, I confided as much to Alix.

"Just because you show up, it doesn't mean you're never going to turn on the TV on Shabbos in your life," she said. "But who knows? Maybe it will change you. We aren't supposed to be the same people our whole lives."

"Do you think you'll change from Torah-Rama?" I asked.

She blushed a little and shrugged and said in a quiet voice, "I don't know," and I realized that maybe she already had.

Torah-Rama was on a Sunday. They held it at the Jewish Community Center, on the edge of town, a bus or a car trip away, since there was no synagogue in the neighborhood large enough to hold us. We'd scheduled ourselves into what was eight hours of solid learning, in both small groups and larger lectures.

The building looked like a giant Rubik's Cube, fluorescent and huge and crumbling with disrepair. The classes were held in classrooms that smelled like old people.

Most of the speakers were rabbis. They were insightful and inspirational and hard to listen to. It wasn't that they were boring, or that they weren't good speakers, but they kept tossing around words in Hebrew and Yiddish, which we might have understood in isolation, but they spoke hundreds of them a minute, and we were lost.

We glanced at each other helplessly, wondering what we'd committed ourselves to, what we were going to do for the next eight hours.

But nobody moved. No one wanted to be the first one out of their seat, the first to hit the eject button. A vague consent swept the crowd: we're here all day; eventually lunch will come; in the meantime we might as well just listen.

So we did. And instead of getting more and more bored, we found the little things to latch on to—moments, or thoughts, really, that didn't sound so crazy—and they started taking up space in our minds, growing. When Rabbi Yakov started telling us about eating kosher, and how it wasn't about which restaurants you went to or what brand of salami you ate, but what it was about was the kind of food you put in your body, what kind of stuff you wanted to become part of your skin and your flesh and your soul, it didn't seem like such an insane notion. And when I looked around the room and saw everyone else from my school—Rocky Kuzari, Challah Bagelman, even Alix Blitman—listening attentively and nodding furiously, I found myself listening too.

Love for G-d, I think, is the only love you actually have to learn instead of just being thrown into a hormone-knotted mess of it. The thing is that although hormone-infested teenage love is reckless and badly planned and inevitably destructive, it's actually fun to go through. G-d love usually involves reading a lot of esoteric theological texts or, like a bad audiobook version, listening to speeches.

Lecture followed lecture, rabbi followed rabbi, and at the end of the day, a young guy named Shmuly spoke. He wasn't more than a few years older than us, in a sharp suit and a black hat with the rim tipped down like a private detective. He leaned against the podium with one elbow, and when he talked, he sounded like an older brother giving us advice. No, not an older brother—an older cousin, just back from college for the first time, telling us about life in the big city and what it was like to be the only frum Jew in his New York City film agency and informing us, tantalizing us, that there was a world out there bigger than Northeast Philadelphia, that things happened beyond our understanding, and, most of all, that we had a destiny.

"Listen, guys," he said, abandoning his podium and hopping up to sit on the desk at the front of the classroom. "Being Orthodox isn't—*wooo*—some hard-to-reach mystical plane. It's not some secret code. I mean, look at me. I lead a normal life. I just remember, you know, who's in the driver's seat."

We nodded. By that point in the day, we knew who was in the driver's seat.

"Those people who think they can make up their own religion and tell G-d what they want from Him say, 'This is what I think you are,' and expect it to be true—they're lost. Clueless. Living in their own heads. They don't want G-d; they want an imaginary friend. What do you think Judgment Day's gonna be like for them? What are they going to say to their Creator? 'Hey, G-d, sorry I ignored what You wanted me to do and spent my life not following Your commandments and wasted it completely, and now it's all over . . . but that's okay, right? 'Cause we're friends?' "

The speeches ended. The first kids were out of their seats, making a run for the exit. Somehow, getting up seemed wrong. Moving in this world seemed wrong. Were we going to go back to hanging out and telling jokes, to the Challah and Alex Show? Everything felt meaningless—except that, really, it felt the opposite of meaningless. Every moment was a gift, a box of kinesthesis, empty and glowing with promise. We could fill it with whatever we wanted. We could fill it with stupid after-school stuff, the stuff I never cared much for in the first place—or we could fill it with commandments. What use did we have for this world of flesh and sweat, full of non-kosher food and temptations and distractions and girls?

I reached in my pocket, counting out exact change for the bus—we were still too young to drive, but I had just started discovering the city's bus system, which was scrappy and underdeveloped but functioned remarkably well in making me independent from my parents.

I met Challah in front of the building. Everyone else was hanging out in the parking lot out back, huddled in a circle, waiting for their rides. He waved to me.

"Hi there, Alex!" he said, and he sounded to me just then like a kid, like someone I'd have no more in common with than a cartoon. "Headed home? We could catch the bus together."

"No," I found myself saying before I'd thought about it at all, some instinct that arose in my chest, "I think I'm gonna stick around."

"Really?"

He followed where I was looking, toward the side alley. Guys and girls gathered together, talking, buzzing, laughing. The streetlights cast them in black blotches, and whatever those blotches were doing felt mysterious, indecent, an echo of today's warnings.

It also felt like the conclusion to a question I'd never thought I'd hear answered. Something that had started a long time ago, something about when the girls started splashing with us in the river.

He watched me doubtfully as I pulled away.

"Just be careful," he said. "Remember what Shmuly said."

Outside, the world felt wild around the edges. Like in movies, when someone's a superhero and then shows up at their crummy apartment at the end of the day: welcome to reality. We might have had a shared religious experience—hey, we might even have seen G-d together—but life moves on, everything crashes, and you remember that you still live in a working-class dump on the edge of town.

I turned the corner, slinking away from him, moving toward the kids who were still hanging out in the parking lot. I gravitated in the direction of a familiar-looking silhouette on the edge, part of the crowd, but not so close that our every word would be overheard.

The silhouette gravitated right back toward me.

"Hey, Alex," she said.

"Hey, Alix," I said back.

Our call-and-response chorus, a wry and dorky in-joke. Our banter was new and tentative, just like we were, and although we weren't totally in sync yet, our relationship felt curiously settled, as much as anything could in these strange lives of ours.

"There's nothing on this side of the building but the fire doors and the highway. You aren't taking off yet, are you?"

"Man, I don't know." I brushed my bangs out of my eyes, then let the wind blow them back again. "I don't want to hang out with those guys . . . and I've got a lot on my mind, and there's all this stuff I still need to absorb . . ."

"Alexander Gellar," she said sternly, like a teacher.

"Alixandra Blitman," I imitated her, not as well.

"Don't tell me my name—I already know it."

My stupid grin got loose. Outsmarting me was her favorite game to play. Being outsmarted by her was mine.

"Don't tell me what to think—I've already got a brain."

It was feeble, but she didn't mind.

"What you have is too many brains," she said. "Stop thinking so much. Give it a rest. Listen, everyone's going to Friendly's now. You should come along."

"Friendly's?" I made a face. "Didn't we just get done hearing why non-kosher food is going to burn your insides?"

"They have kosher ice cream, but whatever. We'll get tea. We'll sit at the far end of the table, apart from everyone else, and only talk to each other." Neither of us drank coffee. It was one of the things that made us understand each other more. "Come on. It'll be good for you. We're meeting up with a bunch of kids from Hebrew Academy; we can see how the other half lives."

"But I don't want to hang out with a million people," I said. "Or a million strangers, at least. I'd rather be alone."

"'It is not good for man to be alone,'" she said, and it sounded suspiciously like the Bible.

"Where'd you learn that one from?" I said.

She grew a little pale and looked at the ground.

"From this dating workshop," she said. "They had a special program for all the girls. It was about a week and a half ago."

"They did?" I said. "But they always call me when there's a program! How come nobody—"

She shot me a look. And I guess I was too busy acting interested to wonder why she hadn't told me about it before, and I was trying too hard not to be an awkward teenage boy to notice how much she was looking like an awkward teenage girl.

But all that came to a stop with the sound of a huge, resonant whack, and Alix pitched forward.

Someone had just fallen into Alix—or body-slammed her from behind.

She twisted around. She yanked her assailant backward

and away from her, so hard that his body literally flipped over. He landed on the ground on his back.

The guy gave a good-natured but stomachy laugh, rising back up on his elbows. The dark played off his face, making his grotesque smile seem even more deranged and more severe.

Alix gave a dry, throaty laugh, condescendingly humorless. She gave him that charity, but her eyes stayed wary.

"Don't you even try feeling me up, Effie Spiegelman," she said. "I don't touch boys. Some of us are good religious kids, or have you forgotten?"

I felt electric, a mixture of alarm and concern and a sprinkle of jealousy. Feeling her up? I tried remembering where his hands had been the moment before. Last week in school, Dan Price had said *I felt her up* when he was talking about a girl, about a full-on sexual experience. Or did that just mean skin-on-skin contact? Was he touching her breasts?

"Don't give me that." Effie offered up a sympathetic smile, as if the facts of human evolution had just possessed him, and he was an involuntary witness to what had transpired. "If I make a move on you, Alix Blitman, you'll be the first to know. I just wanted to keep you on your toes. Get the blood moving after that snooze-fest. Baby, remind me again why you guys are choosing this lifestyle?"

"My G-d, Effie," she huffed, pulling her windbreaker tight around her head. "Flesh and blood was wasted on creating you."

"Don't take the L-rd's name in vain," he shot back. "Right there, that's one of the ten big ones. Touching guys doesn't even make the top fifty."

Headlights beckoned at the end of the highway. I counted three or four cars and, behind them, a double-tiered row of lights, the telltale sign of the public bus. Little things like this reassured me of the divine order of the universe: I could not have prayed for a more auspicious time to make an exit.

"It's been good having this theological conversation," I broke in. "But my flight is departing. I've gotta split."

They stopped their conversation and turned to look at me in horror. "Where are you going?" said Alix. "You can't cut out now. Listen, Brett's older brother has the minivan; he's giving us all rides. It'll be a fun time."

"Come out with us, Alex," said Effie, although G-d knows why he was trying to get me to stay. He stepped close to us, slipped one arm around each of our shoulders. "The night won't be the same without you."

Maybe it was that particular moment, those particular words—calling it "the night," like in a movie the moment before everything changes—but those words seized me. Why would he even care? Alix was trying to squirm out of Effie's grasp. I had prepared a hundred ways to tell the other fifteen-year-olds of the universe about my newfound proficiency in public buses—everything from *It's like a car, only bigger* to *Oh sure, I've taken it across the city . . . haven't you?*—but, at this moment, all my excuses seemed feeble and flimsy and like that was what they really were: excuses.

My mouth emptied. My saliva dried up. The bus swung past, not even slowing down, not even suspecting that anybody would want to board at this particular stop. After evening rush hour, the buses were largely a formality in this part of town anyway.

The bus got smaller and smaller on the road. From behind, it looked like any other car.

I snapped out of it. Effie was in the middle of telling Alix some story. Doubtlessly, it involved dirty ways to say things in the Talmud.

"Fine," I said, startling them both out of the story. "I'm in. I'll go."

Effie Spiegelman was every charming villain in every movie ever. He was dashing and flirtatious and socially adept to an almost frightening degree, able to say all the right things to all the right people. Which was especially nefarious, considering that he ostensibly grew up without movies *or* girls. And yet he knew how to make it so the girls were all over him. But how did everyone buy his act when, as soon as someone tried to quote a Torah verse, he would correct them in note-perfect Galician Hebrew?

When we got to Brett's brother's van, the motor was running and the door was open and the only two seats left were in different rows. Alix sat next to Romy Vogosan, Brett's on-again, off-again girlfriend, who was asking him why he was sitting with the guys and not with her, did it *mean* something, what had that rabbi's talk done to him? I sat in back, half-heartedly eavesdropping, feeling the glow of Alix on my arm. Our skin close together, the secrets we shared. Why would anyone want to sit with the guys? I wondered.

At the restaurant, Romy yanked Alix into the seat next to her, and, smiling at me—as if I was Alix's special friend, and that was our special secret—she nodded for me to take the seat across from them. Which I did.

They were talking. I couldn't even talk. It was unbelievable to me how, after everything we'd heard and everything we'd talked about today, people could relapse to the same old things—talking about school and guys and the latest nighttime television dramas. *Help me,* I prayed, right then, in my seat. *I am fifteen years old, G-d was hanging out with me in my head, and physically I am still stuck with morons.*

We ordered. Most people did only get ice cream—it was almost ten p.m., after all—but some of them ventured into other desserts, and a few of those ordered the ones with marshmallows and the ones that were freshly baked, which were not kosher. At the far end of the table, Effie Spiegelman was actually ordering a burger and fries. I thought of my soul: we are what we eat. I felt physically ill.

I turned back to Alix, tried to immerse myself in her conversation. The other girls were talking about weddings.

I let my head fall into my hands. I was trapped in some parallel dimension where brains had been replaced by stale breakfast cereal and dryer lint. I had to be. I stared at the glow of light through my fingers, tried to seal it off completely.

Just then, I felt hands closing on my shoulders, my chair as it was yanked away from the table. My butt got pushed three-quarters off the chair, my finger mask fell away, and suddenly I was face to face with Effie Spiegelman.

How did he get here? It wasn't even a question. Hitchhiking and black magic were equally likely answers.

"Dude," he said. "Are you after Alix?"

"What?" I exploded. "No, are you crazy! And keep your voice down, she's right over—"

"Who cares?" he said. "Stop acting like a caffeinated lab monkey if you don't want her to notice. If you speak real low, every person at this table is going to notice."

I swallowed. I could be calm. "Fine."

"Good. Now, what's your scene with her?"

"Why do you want to know, Effie? What are you even doing here?"

He pulled back. He gazed at me levelly, and if I hadn't already known he was a total asshole, then he would've looked hurt. "What do you *think* of me, Gellar? I'm not completely inhuman."

"Stop it." I stared him down. "Do you *like* her, Effie?"

Now he really did look insulted.

"No!" he said, and then: "No way." And, after a minute, he added, in a tone so honest I didn't think he was capable of it, "I mean, I thought you did.

"You seem like a good kid, Gellar," he was saying, calling me by my last name as if he were my baseball coach, "and, honestly, I hate to see anyone get suckered into this whole thing. I can tell you what the next ten years of your life are going to be like. Religiously, socially, whatever. 'Cause they are about to put you through the wringer, and they've been putting me through the wringer since I was born.

"First, they're going to tell you to forget everything you've learned. That the only valuable learning is Torah learning, and everything else is crap. Don't listen to them. Okay, the Torah is a great book, maybe the greatest book that's ever been written—don't look so surprised; just 'cause I don't believe it happened doesn't mean I don't think it's true—but there's a lot of other true stuff in the world too. Don't swallow anything without digesting it all. These kids, they're like a herd. You feel it too. I've seen the way you look at them. But the thing you haven't accepted yet is it's completely fine. People like being in a herd. Just don't let them brainwash you, and don't let them take over your thoughts, and eventually you will rise to the top of them. They will let you walk all over them, and they'll thank you for it. So, what do you think?"

What did I think? What I thought was changing every minute, every moment. I could no more tell him what I thought than I could tell him the exact number of cells in my body, or the stars in the sky. I didn't want to think. I just wanted to believe and to trust the greater powers of the universe with making the call on what was right and what was true, and I would just go along with that.

Effie was wide-eyed and honest, looking every bit like a ghost, or maybe like a fortune-teller.

"Are you talking about the rabbis, or are you talking about girls?"

At that, he let out a laugh so huge that he couldn't control it, that knocked him off the three-quarters of my chair that he was occupying, and that centered everyone's attention on him. "Both," he gasped breathlessly. "I'm talking about every-fricking-thing in the world," he said. He shot me a grin, and I could see it was a real grin, and it was a grin that left me satisfied that I knew what he was talking about.

Later that night, the Friendly's manager told us we had to order full meals or leave, and then he kicked us out. We hung out in the parking lot, crowded around Brett's brother's minivan while he blasted songs out of the rear speakers. Romy sat in the front seat, long legs out the window, bare to her knees, twiddling the dial when she didn't like what came on. I craned my neck, looking for Alix and trying not to be too obvious. I spotted her in the middle of a crowd, close to Effie, who was stumbling into various members of the crowd, bouncing off their shoulders and sides, pinball-like. He kept reaching his arms out at Alix as he passed, as though he was trying to hold on to her, or maybe just to paw her.

"Watch out for Effie," Brett told me. He laid a stiff hand on my shoulder. "I think he's been drinking. He isn't acting normal, even for Effie."

Brett and I weren't close. He wasn't much to reckon with mentally, but he was a solid guy, and I knew he was saying this out of honest concern. Effie, I knew even less about. Had he been drinking? Is this what people were like once they drank? And did that mean that Effie wasn't always this way, and that his usual shade of weirdness came from somewhere that was completely different?

"All right." I nodded, looking back to Effie. Alix was scoffing at him now, pushing him away with the free neighborhood newspaper from the Friendly's. She could take care of herself.

"No problem." Brett eyed me, not convinced that I'd heard.

"Thanks for the warning, though." I rolled my shoulders, then set my jaw so that I looked tougher than I actually was.

I headed for Effie and Alix. Brett was right; Effie was being rougher. He bounced hard on the concrete, letting out war whoops, crashing into Alix with his whole body in a way that reminded me uncomfortably of Things We Should Not Do. She looked seriously pissed off now, so I went up to her and whispered in her ear that I was over this place, that we should leave.

"Relax," she whispered back at me. "We can't yet. Effie's out of control. We have to put him down."

I guess we weren't whispering softly enough, though, because Effie stopped, directly behind Alix now, and glared at me over her shoulder.

"One second, man," I said, extending the camaraderie that he'd shown me earlier that night. "We were just talking."

"What's wrong? Is she your girl or something? You don't want me messing with that?" He took a step back, flung out his arms as if to welcome the challenge. "Come on, Gellar. Show me what you got. You want to make a big deal out of it?"

"She's not my girl," I muttered into my own shoulder, backing away from him.

At the same time, Alix was gaping at him, mouth askew, going, "What's wrong with you, Effie? Are you crazy?"

He barked a dry laugh. "Come on, Gellar," he said. "What's your damage? You afraid to think about my hands all over her body, getting her nice and hot? You think you can take me?"

In the space of a second, he grabbed something out of his pocket and tossed it to me. I caught it in my hands, hard and black and cold, silver showing.

It was a knife.

Everyone shut up. Somebody ran behind a car. Brett let out a high, prepubescent gasp of fear.

"Come on. You can have first swing," Effie said, offering his torso to me. "Here—I won't even block you."

He raised his shirt. An antlike trickle of black hair trailed up his stomach from his belly button to the muscly protuberances of his chest.

I recoiled, tasting bile. I didn't even know how to say no to this. This was insane. I didn't know how we had arrived at this level. I didn't know how Effie had gotten hold of a knife, and now it was glued to my hand, which trembled uncontrollably. My hand felt as though it had been completely detached from my body. I didn't want to throw the knife down. Then he'd pick it up, and G-d only knew what would happen. Everyone watched me, baited, unsure what was going to happen next.

"Effie," said Alix, completely cool. "You are completely insane. I'm out of here." She turned around and waltzed off down an alley of cars.

Effie's eyes never left me. "Come on, Gellar," he said. "Whatcha gonna do? Should we fight? Do you want to run after her, comfort her, wrap your arms all over her and then try to get her to make out with you? Or do you still think you're one of the religious kids?"

For a moment I felt the temptation. I was actually stuck in his world, actually about to argue with him. Then I realized how stupid he was being, and how stupid I was being, and I threw the knife to the ground and ran after her.

Behind the Friendly's was a small forest. When we had come here as kids, it felt like the end of the world, like the forest kept going back forever. Turns out it was only three or four trees thick.

Behind that was a pond. The pond opened up to one side and the other, carving the forest in two. My brain did leapfrogs of geometry, and I realized it was a creek—the same hidden water that flowed through the little gatherings of trees beside the roads, the scant river that ran throughout the neighborhood.

Alix was at the bank. I lowered myself to the edge of the river, plopping my feet in the mud. She was a few feet over, lying belly-up, staring at the stars.

"Man, Alix," I said.

"Don't start," she said.

"What do you mean?"

"You know what I mean. You're going to say how everyone

else is so basic and they don't really understand and they're not worthy and they have no soul. Everyone has a soul, Alex—it's just that around here, people are a little rough around the edges. They're up front about what they're thinking."

"They have no class," I echoed, staring at the horizon of stars.

"You can put it that way if you want to," she said. "The fact is, they're honest. Even Effie Spiegelman. Maybe especially him."

"You're defending him?"

"No way. There is no defense for what he did. He's an asshole. But you know that and I know that and everybody else down there knows that, and you know they'd all take care of him if he did anything that was *too* assholey."

"He pulled out a knife!"

"And if he did anything with it, Challah and Brett and them would be there to take him down. Come on. He's just a teenager. He'll grow up."

"But we're teenagers, and we don't act like that."

"Yeah. We're just a little farther up the evolutionary ladder than Effie. The rest of them, they're getting there. But we're all in it. We're all stuck in this world together."

"For now," I said darkly.

She sighed. This was the subject that always shut us up, the one thing about me that she could never understand: how I dreamed, harder than anything, of leaving this place.

"I can't believe Effie," I said, lost in my thoughts.

"It wasn't his fault," said Alix. "Not totally, anyway. He was drunk. People turn into different people when they're drunk. He'll like you again in the morning."

"Yeah, but what about me?" I grumbled, still feeling the heat in my chest.

"You'll forgive him," she said softly, evenly. I didn't challenge it.

We were silent. Finally, when she spoke, it was with a jolt of disbelief. "You don't have a crush on me, do you?"

"No!" I said fast.

"Really?" Her eyes narrowed, giving me that *Are you sure?* look like she did when I got carried away with a story and started lying halfway through.

"No way," I said again, quieter this time.

"I know," she said, even quieter.

"Really?" My eyes popped open. "How do you know that?"

Her eyes were fixed on me now, totally riveted.

"Because," she said, staring straight at me. "Because I know that we could."

"We could what?" My body shot up higher. My eyes grew a little wider.

"Eat a hamburger. Break Shabbos. Have sex with each other. We can do anything, Alex. But we don't. We aren't totally Orthodox yet, but you know in ten years we're both going to be totally hardcore. We're going to be living these whole other lives. Having different things be important. We might not even know each other anymore."

"We'll know each other."

"How do you know that, though? We could be dead. Or one of us could be." She licked her lips. "It's like, the whole secular world is telling us that this moment right now is the important one. And G-d is telling us to wait."

"Not just wait," I said. "G-d is telling us that everything that's remotely good we should sit out from and pray instead."

"Because there are more important things. Because all the usual teenage things aren't things at all. Eating at Friendly's and going out on Friday nights, and even hooking up—they're just illusions. It's like cocaine; only your nose and your veins don't get all shrivelly and cracked—your soul does. That's what we're waiting for, Alex. We're waiting for something bigger than these people. We're waiting for something bigger than our lives."

We were both sitting up now, facing each other straight on. And without knowing why, without thinking about anything, really, we launched into a hug. Not a sexual hug, or an *I want you* hug, or anything that connoted any crush, unspoken or otherwise. Just a hug to let each other know that we were there for each other, that we could lean on each other. Not that there was a place for that in G-d's law, but maybe, just maybe, there was a place for that in G-d.

AJSHARA

BY ADI ALSAID

For the duration of his flight, Tzvi had respite from his ghosts. He was terrified of how many would be there waiting for him when they landed. A country always in the midst of war, or at least surrounded by the prospect of it.

But on his flight, there was the calmness of the jet engines humming everyone to sleep. There were dozens of movies at his disposal, a book to read, the flight attendant who had smiled at him a few times, the magic of her eye contact. There were also his friends scattered around the plane. They were loud and disruptive, and Tzvi was thankful for their volume, for the excitement about the trip that they had bubbling within them.

Back in Mexico City, Tzvi had bid farewell first to his family—Mom had cried while firing off a list of demands about how often to keep in touch—and then to friends who would have normal summers and then go off to college—a surprising amount of tears involved in these goodbyes, both from his longtime crush and, with different people, from Tzvi himself.

Finally he said goodbye to the ghosts in his neighborhood. They'd become accustomed to having someone who could talk to them, and in turn he'd grown used to this odd facet of his life. The trauma of his gift had faded partially with time, mostly because he'd become familiar with the ghosts and their stories. Linda, the girl who'd died from leukemia at sixteen. Sergio, who'd been struck by a car. Two men named Josue, who'd each died when their buildings had collapsed in separate earthquakes thirty-two years apart. He rarely saw other ghosts, since, like the living, they didn't often stray from their neighborhoods and comfort zones. They haunted familiar places. Even these that he knew, he ignored most of the time. Sure, they talked to him, but it was rare that he ever spoke back. He knew where they liked to spend time and avoided those spots, even steered his thoughts away from them whenever he could. Still, he felt he owed them an explanation as to his upcoming absence. They had so little else.

"An ajshara," he said.

The older Josue raised an eyebrow and looked at the younger Josue, who was just as confused. They were over fifty years apart in age at their deaths, and had grown up during vastly different decades, but how they died had brought them close together, or maybe that was death itself. Every time Tzvi saw them, they were roaming the streets, or sitting at Plaza Cibeles, their backs to the fountain, watching the living go about their days.

"It's a tradition," Tzvi explained. "We take a year to travel before going to school. Usually Israel and Europe."

The Josues had follow-up questions, but Tzvi didn't have the heart to continue the conversation past that notice. Every detail he added would have been rubbing salt in their wounds. It was hard to step away from the guilt that he was the only person they could talk to, aside from each other. But it was harder to stay and talk.

The pilot announced the final approach. Tzvi's friends, who'd settled into sleep over the last few hours of the flight, now resumed their too-loud chatter. Tzvi glanced out his window as if afraid that the ghosts would be visible from there, but he saw only the dark blue expanse of the Mediterranean. The flight attendant came by, collecting trash, and when she smiled at him again, Tzvi thought that he could be happy staying on the plane forever.

Wheels touched down in Tel Aviv, and Tzvi allowed himself to be swept up in the energy of the others. They were eighteen and free of their parents for the first time (though still tied to their bank accounts, thank God), a year of travel ahead of them. It promised to be a year of adventure and food, Israeli girls and European girls and South American boys; boys with guitars at hostels and girls dancing carefree at bars and boys with their bodies at beaches. A fantasy in more ways than one, since Tzvi and his friends were all shy and awkward, and their independence wouldn't magically change them. The boys assumed the girls would have it easier, but the girls were shyer and treated these fantasies as more far-removed than the boys did, so their opportunities advanced more slowly. Regardless, Tzvi was happy to think of them as sudden Casanovas, since it was more fun to think of girls than ghosts. That's all he wanted from the year, he realized: time without his ghosts.

The five adrenaline-fueled boys and two equally excited girls took two taxis to the city, checking in to a hostel a ten-minute walk from the beach. They ate shawarma from a small stand, fighting off jet lag by telling each other of all the glee they'd experience in the coming months. They commented on the abundance of beautiful Israeli girls, gorgeous Israeli men. Tzvi ate with his eye on the wrap, not wanting to look around and see the dead.

He'd noticed them already. Not what he'd apparently been expecting, victims of bombs and violence, all carnage. Here, too, people died of old age. They died of overdoses, died peacefully in their sleep, died happy. The ghosts looked like the living people, just a slight glow to their skin, wearing their deaths on their faces. Not in any obvious way that Tzvi could point at, but obvious enough that he always knew how they had died, even from afar. No matter how hard he tried, he could not hide from that knowledge. At least here he could hide in anonymity. He could pretend to be just like his friends.

Down the street from the shawarma stand, on the corner of the intersection, Tzvi spotted a dead man in a tank top, his hands in his pockets, a slight smile on his lips, taking in the sun. The man looked Tzvi's way, and before he could be recognized, Tzvi reached for the bottle of tahini and added another squirt to his shawarma, taking a bite and trying to tune in to what his friends were saying.

Boys, the beach, girls, the joys ahead.

Gabriel wiped the corner of his mouth with a napkin, which he crumpled up and tossed into a nearby bin. "We're finally here," he said to Tzvi. The rest of the group was chatting excitedly, giddy with exhaustion and the change of scenery.

"Yeah," Tzvi said, and looked around to take stock of their surroundings, avoiding looking in the direction of the man in the tank top. The sun was glaring, and everyone nearby looked beautiful in their sunglasses, basking in the heat. Could he do this for the whole year? Look to the light?

"It's going to be a great year."

"You think so?"

Gabriel laughed boisterously and then smacked Tzvi's knee, as if the mere possibility of a different outcome was preposterous.

They ended up going to their hostel and lying down, jet lag taking away all their plans and knocking them out until two a.m. At six they finally crawled out of bed and watched the sunrise, ready to explore the city, ready to start the adventure for real. They ate sabich and then shawarma again, dipped into a mall when the heat had them sweating everywhere. They saw girls in military gear and, in their boisterous Spanish, discussed how to start a conversation, but the girls walked by before any of them could act. At night they talked about going to nightclubs but ended up at a dive bar next to the hostel. It was full of travelers like them, and though Tzvi and his friends had all been able to drink as eighteen-year-olds in Mexico, there was something freeing about drinking without their parents anywhere near, something less intimidating about doing it in this friendly, dark place compared to a nightclub with twenty-five-year-olds. Tzvi saw a dead soldier at the end of the bar, playing with a pack of cigarettes. The soldier was in his forties, dead from heart failure, not bullets. He made eye contact with Tzvi and smiled, a look so desperate crossing his face that Tzvi couldn't bear to maintain eye contact with him. Tzvi ordered another beer and escaped to the patio with Ariela and Daniela, who were talking to two Belgian girls while the others hung around too closely and giggled too obviously.

Then they all overdid it and puked on the sidewalk on the

short traipse back to the hostel, passing out in their clothes and sandals. In the morning they emerged hungover into the blazing humidity, seeking something that would soak up last night's mistakes. But it was Saturday and everything was closed, so they ended up lying out on the beach on their too-small travel towels, moaning in discomfort and pain.

All of their mothers called at some point that day, each of the kids taking turns trying to fake pep and cheer while omitting the binge drinking and all the hope for sex and companionship. "Yeah, I'm having fun," Tzvi said to his mother in Hebrew. A dead girl walked by as he said this, and she glanced down, her jaw dropping slightly when she realized he could see her and he could speak her language. In response, Tzvi rushed off the phone call and then sprinted past her into the water, not ready to return to his ghosts. He was tired of collecting their names in his mind, collecting all the ways in which life could be cut short.

The girl followed. She had long, dark hair and dark eyes that bore into Tzvi's even from the shore. Her long skirt soaking didn't stop her approach, and though Tzvi wanted to swim away, he was pretty sure he would tire from escaping before she would tire from chasing.

"You can see me," she said. The waves lapped at her chest, sharp angle of her clavicle poking out from her off-the-shoulder blouse.

Tzvi nodded, unable to make eye contact.

"Why did you run from me?"

"My Hebrew's not great," he said, though he didn't strain to find the words, and his accent, which had been perfected by his mom's modeling, gave him away. "I'm on vacation," he added.

"Good for you." A large wave made them both rise up, their feet leaving the safety of the sand. Tzvi loved that feeling, which was closer to flying than anyone ever recognized. "Have you always been able to talk to us?"

"I think so."

"But you don't like it."

Tzvi didn't say anything. He looked past the girl, who was maybe a little older than him, toward the beach. His friends were buying Popsicles from a guy on the beach yelling out "Artik!" loud enough that his voice carried over the crashing waves. Two black women played paddleball on the beach, the thwack loud and satisfying.

Tzvi sank his head beneath the waves, letting the water wash over him. When he resurfaced, the girl was still there, looking out at the horizon. "You can go if you want," she said tersely, but not unkind. So he did.

Two full weeks in Tel Aviv, shawarma for most meals so they could spend more money on evening drinks and a little bit of hash bought from the Canadian who hung out all the time at the dive bar. They kept meaning to go to nightclubs, but the bar was comforting, and there were enough girls around there, or at least the potential of girls. Plus, here they could speak to each other in Spanish and hear each other's laughter.

It was Tzvi and Gabriel again, on the patio now. Inside, Victor and Ariela were playing pool against Eitan and Roni. There was a thin haze of smoke, though it was hard to tell if the smoke from outside was making its way into the bar or vice versa. Gabriel lit a cigarette, a habit that only a few of them had had before arriving in Israel. But so many more people smoked that it was hard not to get wrapped in it. Tzvi himself almost craved one now, the beer coursing through him making him forget how much he hated the feeling of inhaling smoke.

"I can't believe I haven't even made out with anyone yet," Gabriel said, resting his arm over the patio's banister. "We should be going to nightclubs."

"What's stopping you?"

Gabriel exhaled, a billow of smoke joining the haze from the bar. "I hate nightclubs." He laughed. "But I think I hate not making out with people less." Neither one made a move to get up, their eyes on all the people around them. Aside from the soldier the first time in the bar, Tzvi hadn't seen a single dead person enter, and it made the place feel like exactly the kind of refuge he had wanted from the trip. He wasn't worried about making out; life would be long enough for sex. "You don't?" Gabriel asked.

"I don't what?"

"Hate not making out."

Just then, two American girls walked up the steps to the bar, passing by their table. Gabriel said hello, but not loudly enough to be noticed, apparently. Tzvi laughed, feeling good. Then the quirky owner came by with a couple of whiskey shots for them, saying that your first time in the bar you got a free drink. He'd forgotten how many times he'd given them free drinks already. Tzvi and Gabriel groaned, then laughed together, their conversation fading. Tzvi felt a confession building on his tongue.

He had never told anyone about his ability to interact with the dead, had never particularly wanted to. Even if he were believed, what good could possibly come of it? But now, here on this warm night in Tel Aviv, in the company of one of his best friends, the alcohol coursing through his veins made him feel like it would be freeing to share, to open up. What else were nights like these—trips like these—for if not late-night confessions?

Just as he was about to speak, the American girls came back out onto the patio holding beers, looking for empty seats. The only two available were at the boys' table, and they came over and asked if it was okay to sit down, causing Gabriel's face to light up like the sun and the moment for the confession to pass by.

Nothing came of the encounter, and though Tzvi felt more disappointment about keeping his secret, he told himself that he needed nothing more from his trip than nights like those, Gabriel's face lighting up.

They went to Jerusalem to please their parents. They sent all the appropriate photos from the Western Wall. Jerusalem was full of the saddest ghosts. The ones he'd feared seeing on the plane. Little Arab boys from decades ago, dirt still on their cheeks, the kind of innocent dirt of boyhood that was not dealt out by life's shitty hand but rather earned by the bravery to still live with joy in terrible circumstances. These boys were at least not alone, cared for by women in wigs and ankle-length skirts. Death took away all distinctions between Muslim and Jewish, between people; the ghosts banded together. This was cold comfort, and Tzvi was happy to leave Jerusalem behind.

They canceled their remaining days at the hostel there and took a bus to Eilat, where they were sure sex would finally enter the story of their trip. But then they signed up for scuba diving certifications, which meant no drinking for a few days, a development they all half-heartedly complained about, though each one of them was ready for a break from that particular vice. Tzvi made a habit of waking up early and going to get iced coffee, people-watching on the boardwalk. The dead would always spot him, and though he still didn't encourage conversation, he could no longer bring himself to flee. Anyway, there was nowhere *to* flee. They were everywhere. The joys of the trip made him comfortable with this lack of escape, and he settled into the knowledge that he'd be moving on soon, and though the ghosts would follow, it wouldn't be these same ones.

When the scuba course was over, Ariela and Victor hooked up in the bunk bed below Tzvi, thinking he was asleep. The soft noises of sex and the bed straining against their weight felt at once too intimate and somehow wonderful. He didn't want to ruin the moment for them, though, so he remained perfectly still, not wanting to impose, not wanting to be present, and yet curious about what every single noise might have meant, trying to picture each little alien act. He was mortified and thrilled for his friends, the two contrasting emotions nestling comfortably within each other.

Two weeks later, on the last night in the kibbutz in Degania, two Argentinian girls traveling together took an interest in him and Gabriel and insisted on spending time with them after their shifts cleaning the chicken coops. The girls poured the boys more cheap wine, and they played a game that was basically just a string of confessions. They started off with innocuous, silly facts (broken bones in childhood, a hidden talent for hula-hooping), and then, because they were teens let loose on the world, hungry for others, the confessions became more intimate and more sexual (a clichéd fantasy to have sex on a beach, an admission to masturbating quietly in airplane bathrooms). Tzvi again felt a building desire to admit how he saw the world. He thought for a moment that in this setting, he would not be laughed at or thought of as crazy. That they would take the confession as simply as they would if he admitted to being a virgin.

Then Sofia grabbed Gabriel by the hand and led him away to privacy, leaving Tzvi alone with Mona. Before he left, Gabriel turned back to look at Tzvi again, such a cheesy smile plastered on his face that Tzvi was sure of life's goodness. Ghosts existed but so did that kind of joy, so what was so scary about the dead?

Mona looked a little like the ghost girl who'd followed him into the ocean in Tel Aviv, her eyes intense and intimidating. A pang of regret hit Tzvi, wishing he had asked the girl a few questions or let her talk longer. Then he refocused on Mona sitting next to him. They small-talked for a little while on the back patio, surrounded by night and silence, just enough laughter to make them feel close to each other. Mona bit her lip and pulled herself onto Tzvi's lap, straddling him. They held eye contact for three seconds before bursting into giggles, and the next thing he knew they were kissing.

On the flight to Budapest the other boys wanted all the details. Gabriel went into the progression of the evening, whispering so that the girls couldn't hear, though they were just as eager to know. Tzvi was happy to be across the aisle and not have to provide his own account. The sex had been clumsy and uncomfortable and wonderful, a blur of sensations and awareness about the sensations. There had been no ghosts around, and Tzvi would hang on to the details of the memory for the rest of the trip, and for years after. Mona's nose ring, a simple golden stud, glinting in the moonlight. Her body against his, sticky with sweat, giving off these little jerks as she drifted off into sleep and he lay awake in the weak breeze. The way her Argentinian accent reshaped words he thought he was familiar with. He didn't know if he had objectified her, or if she had objectified him, or if sex was the object both had wanted, and they had simply used each other to get it.

Europe was a different kind of beast. Tzvi was surprised to find that he hadn't been sad to leave Israel. Parental connection and Mona notwithstanding, he had looked forward more to the cities of Europe from the start, its hostels and coffee shops, the fortunate fact that he wouldn't speak most of the languages.

The group had been traveling for nearly two months together and had started to get sick of each other. They spent a week in Budapest and then, unable to agree on what to do next, they split into smaller groups, promising to meet back up in Ibiza later. Eitan, Roni, and Daniela headed off to Amsterdam for that particular kind of debauchery. Ariela and Victor decided to go on a couple's trip to a lake in Switzerland. The group's interests were scattered, some of them happy to check off the tourist sites the books recommended, others focusing all their efforts on girls or boys.

So it was Tzvi and Gabriel for a few weeks on their own. They took trains to Prague and Berlin, hopped over to Stockholm, then back to Berlin. Gabriel had gotten the taste of sex and couldn't think about anything else. He brought Tzvi to nightclubs at midnight and stayed until seven in the morning, then slept until three p.m., at which point he'd open dating apps on his phone or go downstairs to the hostel lobby and wait to find girls to talk to.

"You're addicted," Tzvi joked.

They were at a beer garden at a park in Prague, overlooking the entire city. There were a ton of people gathered around, enjoying the cooling late-summer weather and cheap beer. A lot of ghosts here, but they had plenty of company too, and if their eyes met Tzvi's and recognized him for what he was, they didn't come rushing to him.

"What better thing to be addicted to than human connection?" Gabriel said. There was almost always a cigarette in his hands now.

"Is that what you're after, then?"

"Of course. The fact that it's fleeting or mostly physical doesn't make it less of a connection."

"I think by definition it does, but I'm not gonna judge."

"No?" Gabriel craned his neck to follow the trajectory of a group of Czech teens passing a joint between them. "How come?"

Tzvi tried to articulate his thoughts but settled on a shrug.

There were times when Gabriel went home with a girl or nights when Tzvi wasn't up for the whole cycle again, and as a result he found himself alone more than he had ever been. He thought a lot about Mona and the girl from the ocean. He joined hostel pub crawls and practiced how to say "excuse me" in whatever language they spoke where he was, in theory to break into conversations, but it never seemed to be that easy. The living were less receptive.

The sneakers he brought with him started falling apart from the walking, and for the first time in his life he sat for hours on end with no agenda and no itch to move on. The dead sought him out, his static solitude easier to approach now.

Maybe it was loneliness that made him not flee, maybe it

was the fact that the trip wasn't exactly what he'd thought it would be. Not worse, by any means. But not the version that had existed in his head in the months leading up to it, or even in the first few idealistic weeks at the start. Maybe it was sex that had changed things, or maybe nothing had changed, and he'd simply grown tired of fleeing from the ghosts all the time.

At a photography museum in Berlin, Tzvi struck up a conversation with a ghost who looked to be in her forties, silver strands standing out in her black hair. She smiled at Tzvi and pointed at the woman in the picture, then said something in German.

"Is that you?" he asked, in English.

The woman smiled, taking his ability to see her and talk to her in stride, as if there were nothing special about it. "I was in university here," she said. "A lot of life ahead of me there, but not as much as I thought there would be."

"Does it make you sad to look at this?"

The woman clicked her tongue. "Why be sad that I lived? I love this picture." She took a step closer, crossing her arms over her chest. "I come to look at it every day. I wish I'd been in more pictures in my life."

Tzvi stood with her for over an hour, listening to her make statements like these, getting a sense of her life through the details she unloaded, the stories she told about growing up in East Germany. "I died right before the wall came down," she said. "It was easy to cross that way."

Later that week, Gabriel found a girl he liked and decided to stay a little longer in Berlin rather than continue on to the Balkans, so Tzvi went on his own for the first time in his life. And suddenly the ghosts were all he had. He came to realize that all they needed were the same kinds of things the living needed, the same things he craved: to be seen, to be heard. He didn't learn much more about death, but he saw how much the dead needed these interactions and how easily he could provide them. For two weeks, Tzvi did the exact opposite of what he'd done all his life: he sought out the ghosts.

He stayed with the ghosts on park benches and corner cafés and the cemented shores surrounding the Bay of Kotor in Montenegro. They would communicate in their broken English, the cracks in each tongue following different fault lines. An old woman in Kosovo wept to him for an hour, then wiped her ghostly cheek and hugged him, thanking him in her Slavic tongue. Tzvi sat and watched her go, feeling like he'd found the purpose of his trip.

In Ibiza, all seven of them reunited to party. They checked into a loud and overpriced hostel, now well versed enough in euros to know they were getting ripped off. They were all starting to catch flak from their parents about spending, and though for Tzvi, Asia and its affordability was next on the agenda, it felt like the grown-up thing to do was to care about money. Not that they'd actually stop spending it. Victor and Ariela had broken up in Switzerland, and Victor had decided he'd had enough of traveling and was going back to Mexico to apply to schools and work for his dad, so this was to be his last hurrah.

The beach clubs were chaotic flurries of party flyers littering the air and shirtless men, some younger than Tzvi and the boys, some significantly older, all of them seemingly grabbing at women, either with their hands or with their words. The air was thick with music and people shouting. The floor was thick with discarded plastic cups and spilled mojitos, the sand swelling under the weight of the partyers.

They all bought drinks and were quickly separated, the party pulling them in different directions. Tzvi squeezed himself past bodies until he found room to breathe, near the shore. It was amazing to look out at these scores of people and see how many dead were among them, without anyone other than himself noticing. Even at a glance he could spot dozens of them in the crowd. Some dancing, some leaning back and watching, some just standing in the middle of it all as if they were waiting for someone to run into them, for someone to start a conversation with them, flirt with them.

Ghosts hung on to life. Tzvi had learned that long ago, but it hadn't quite sunk in like it had over the past four months.

The water lapped at his ankles. He was holding his flip-flops in one hand, his drink in the other. The sun beat down on his neck and shoulders, which had burned early on in the trip, then darkened to the point that he was sure he'd never lose the tan. Not far from him on the beach, he saw a ghost standing much like he was at the edge of the water.

He was young, dressed like so many of the people at the beach club, a tank top and swim trunks, cheap plastic sunglasses resting on top of his head. He didn't notice Tzvi's approach, his eyes glued on the thumping mass in front of him. He appeared to be deep in thought, so Tzvi stopped nearby, not wanting to disrupt. He watched girls throw their arms into the air, watched boys keep their elbows at an angle as they tried to keep up. Puffs of weed smoke rose up from the crowd and curled skyward. The DJ danced in her little booth, fiddling with the equipment in a purposeful way that did not seem to affect the music at all.

Tzvi was about to break his silence when he saw Gabriel

approach. They'd caught up briefly at the hostel but hadn't had one-on-one time. He was glad to see his friend but cast a furtive glance toward the ghost, as if an apology was necessary.

"I'm surprised you're not chasing girls," Tzvi said with a smile, raising his glass to cheers with Gabriel's beer.

"Right now, just chasing after you. I thought I'd gotten sick of you, but turns out traveling without you isn't quite as fun. All those moments between hookups really drag on."

Tzvi laughed. "Why do I get the feeling that that's all life is for you now: the moments between hookups." He noticed the ghost look their way, eavesdropping.

"I want to argue with that, because it makes me sound gross." Gabriel fiddled with the cigarette tucked over his ear. "But, at least for the duration of this trip, it's kind of true."

They looked on at the party for a while, feeling the thumping beats deep in their chests. "So what've the last few weeks been like for you? Any girls?"

"To tell you the truth, I haven't really been seeking it out all that much," Tzvi said. He stole another glance at the ghost, not wanting to give himself away but curious to see if he had picked up on the fact that he could be seen.

The ghost was chewing on his thumb, a far-off look in his eyes.

"What have you been seeking out, then?" Gabriel asked.

Tzvi paused for effect, then smirked. "Human connection."

A wave crashed behind them, coming up above their knees, splashing at the bottom of Tzvi's shirt. Gabriel rolled his eyes, then tucked his cigarette back over his ear and nudged Tzvi toward the party. Behind them, the ghost still chewed on his thumb.

"What are you looking at?" Gabriel asked.

"Just a ghost."

They disappeared into the folds of the party for the rest of their time in Ibiza, and Tzvi allowed himself to forget about ghosts for this last shared portion of his trip. Gabriel and Roni were returning to Israel, Ariela and Daniela off to Australia, Eitan getting a coat and sticking to Europe. Tzvi wanted to be present for his friends, and for the first time since he had discovered how he was different from others, Tzvi was truly able to put ghosts out of his mind. He drank like the rest of them, chased sex like the rest of them, lost himself in beats and sand and all the sensations his body could feel.

Three days later Tzvi was in Cambodia, at a bar called the Angkor What?

It was loud and brash and a gross exploitation of the place that surrounded it, but there Tzvi met Elena. Their meaningless midnight kissing turned into the most fun of Tzvi's trip, hushed laughter in the balcony of Elena's home, fingers interlocked. When the tuk-tuk driver she and her friends had arranged to take them to the ruins at sunrise arrived, Tzvi squeezed himself in, already changing the plans in his mind so he could follow her as long as she would let him.

In Koh Rong they dipped their toes into the Gulf of Thailand, the Milky Way overhead. They had nervous, fumbling sex on the beach, and even Elena would have laughed at the cheesy thought he had that holding her after was his favorite part. Their sex got better; their travels extended longer than either of them could have expected. He got to know her habits on planes, how she always waited to be the very last one to board, the little crinkle in her forehead that would form when she slept, her neck drooping an inch at a time until it finally plopped onto his shoulder. He'd watch her take notes about her travels so she could remember the details, and he'd feel a swell of love that he'd be too afraid to give a name to, except for when he spoke to his ghosts.

Some didn't want to hear about it; some wanted every single detail. He came to yearn for that combination—rare, he now understood—of a ghost that he could communicate with, one that would be just as happy to bear Tzvi's secrets as they were to unload their own. He took long walks wherever he and Elena went, wanting to give her time to breathe away from him, but also now finding comfort in this gift he had. In Tokyo, word somehow got out among the ghosts, and glowing crowds followed him around, waiting for him to sit and talk with them awhile. In Taipei, one woman talked to him every day at six a.m. about her favorite foods and nothing else.

There were times when Tzvi felt that same urge to confess. Late at night, nestled into the same narrow hostel bed, whispering things to each other. At coffee shops and restaurants and bars and, once, on a boat cruise around Ha Long Bay, he'd wanted to share himself fully with Elena. It had been colder than either of them had expected, but they'd stubbornly stayed out on the deck, huddled close against the wind's bite. Elena was tucked into the crook of his arm, her hair whipping the side of his face, her warmth seeping into him. "I like this," she said. "I like you." And he pulled her close and felt the truth come again. But in the end, he didn't fully understand why, he swallowed down the confession and kissed the spot below her ear instead.

Perhaps, he thought, it was a gift to be shared only with the dead.

Finally, a year had passed. Tzvi booked a ticket back to

Mexico City while Elena's feet were in his lap. "Of course I'll come visit," she said, though neither one really believed that what they had could extend beyond the confines of their travels. "We'll figure it out, you'll see. Give it a year, we'll be living together." They spent their last few days together wrapped up in each other, alternating sex and laughter and deep bouts of sadness that they didn't believe they would recover from. They couldn't stand not to touch, and then their touching became too much to bear.

Before boarding the train that would take him to the airport in Hong Kong, Tzvi kissed Elena on the forehead, brushed her tears away, whispered a few sweet nothings about how the things that lived in this world never really went away. Then he told her he loved her and returned to his life in Mexico City, where his regular ghosts were waiting eagerly to see him again, and he was happy to return to them.

TWELVE FRAMES

BY NOVA REN SUMA

It's Saturday morning, and I've successfully made myself into something to stare at. We're headed to the flea market, and the car ride is magnificent at first. It's everything I wanted and then some.

For anyone who happens to catch sight of our pollen-dotted and dented Toyota with the out-of-state plates and me in all my glory in the passenger seat, I'm the thing to be noticing. I inspire a raised eyebrow. A double take. My eye makeup looks like it took a hundred years, because it almost did—first time drawing wings with the liquid pen. Cars in the slow lane go crawling at the sight of me or else they speed up as if I'm a hallucinogenic fright. The *Did I just see what I thought I saw?* expressions mixed with a, I suspect, *Is she seriously wearing that enormous hat?* get me floating, and I stay that way for a solid ten minutes, which is how long it takes my mother to drive us from our new house to the road leading to the weekly flea market I saw advertised online. I adjust the black veil of the hat, parting it a couple of inches and giving myself a window to the window, my black lipstick in the mirror still intact and licorice-slick.

Then something shifts.

"What a *freak*," I hear from the next car. I can see out, and there's a finger pointing.

I sink low in my seat and let the wide brim of the hat create shade.

We're at a red light, and in the car beside us are some kids about my age, maybe ones I'll meet on my first day of the tenth grade at my new school. That's three days away.

Through a peephole in my veil, I can see they're adorned in such drab, sad colors. Off-white. Barely blue. Beige.

One of them laughs, and then they all follow, like their strings have been pulled. I cover the peephole with my hand (really, it's the spot where the fabric ripped, but I was trying to make it seem intentional, like a periscope, or a camera lens).

That's when it all comes into focus. I've never dressed like this outside my bedroom (door sealed, knob lock secured, blinds squeezed fully shut). Safe inside my dim room in our new house, I didn't consider how funny I'd feel in direct sunlight. Or people looking, people being able to *see*. Or my physical comfort or, worse, my mother's *I told you so*. All that's hitting me, way too late, in the car, with an intense shot of sun straight to the face.

Green light, and the car filled with my future classmates speeds off. I try to strike their sounds and colors from my memory. Here I am in a moving vehicle, trying not to crush my spectacular skirt, which is deliciously black and encased in spiraling layers of tulle, the edges nice and crinkly. I made it, dyed it in the washer, and safety-pinned it together. I'm not sure I know how to sit in it yet. Or, I'll admit, how to detach it from my body when it's time to get it off.

My mother's driving, politely edging the skirt's netting over to my side of the car. She's noticed the dark cocoon I've made for myself, and the finger-pointing. She's an observant woman, not to mention a willing chauffeur.

"Second thoughts, Simone?" she says. "I'm not bringing you all the way back so you can change, FYI."

I had ten solid minutes of feeling good about being different. Feeling perfectly content and at peace and mostly all right in my own skin, knowing my inside self was expressed in such exquisite detail on the outside, for the first time ever beyond the confines of the house. Ten lone (perfect, precious, gorgeous) minutes.

But it's not over yet.

My mother makes a hard turn and stops the car. The flea market, there in the distance across the gravel lot, is a couple of tents flapping in the wind and a line of rickety tables. Maybe half a dozen people are milling around. It was so much bigger in my imagination.

My mother turns to me, only halfway. I swear she's shielding her eyes as if my jewelry spikes could scratch her corneas.

"You're the one who refused to bring a change of clothes," she points out.

"I'm not even hot or anything," I say as I peel the bare patches of my thighs off the seat. The complex knots in my knee socks keep rolling down, so I have to curl them back up. So much black lace will trap the heat, and if the veil attached to the hat is down over my face, the hat will create a vaporous compartment, like a steam room. I'd planned the outfit from the safety of an air-conditioned studio (my bedroom) without regard for seasonal weather patterns like sticky, slimy summer heat. What was I even thinking?

I tell myself to suck it up. There's a reason I'm headed to the flea market. A purpose.

I lift the contraption I've come to sell onto my lap, and the weight of it makes me sit there longer, keeping me in place. That's the only reason I don't get out of the car. It's not the anxious burnt-rubber taste in my mouth, not the way the collar of my dress smolders in a ring of fire around my neck.

"I can really keep the money?" I keep checking to be sure. "If I sell Pop Pop's camera? You mean it?"

She nods. "It's depressing to even have it around. He was such an unhappy man. I told you: do what you want with it."

She knows what I want to do with her grandfather's camera: sell it so I can buy more clothes. I never knew the man. My new look can't be fully expressed by what I scrounged from the attic when we were packing up the old house. I can't conjure a closet full of clothes with safety pins and old tablecloths. My wardrobe needs expanding. Enhancing. Experimenting—if only I could leave the car.

"You'll make friends," my mother says, completely unbidden. "It'll be easier this time. Just don't wear that costume to school on Tuesday, and you'll be fine."

"It's not a *costume,*" I snap. The contraption in my lap feels like a rock, but maybe something about that steadies me, as if my great-grandfather, a man who understood discomfort and that itchy, squirmy feeling of never fitting in, is right near the car, listening.

"I know, I know," she says, though that's the third time she's used the C-word this morning.

"It's who I am," I say weakly, fiddling with the fingerless lace gloves that probably *were* a part of some 1980s Madonna costume and not meant for actual daily wear out in the world.

"Moving to a new place is the perfect time to reinvent yourself," my mother says. "But you know, my pop pop reinvented himself when he changed his name, *our* name—"

"I know," I say, cutting her off.

"And none of it made him happier," she says.

"You told me all that already."

"Maybe you'll be happier here, even if you dress like you did back home. You don't have to try so hard, Simone."

"Stop talking," I say. Then, because she's a human being with feelings, and is also my ride home, I add, "Please?"

My mother thinks she's got me nailed down, but it has nothing to do with the way things were back home. Not entirely.

I used to carry around this fantasy, this cold, hard ball of wax in my chest. I used to *not* want people looking at me. I didn't want people talking about me or to me. I didn't want to be different. I wanted to be the same.

But I never was, really, was I?

I could be sitting in a chair, say in the food court at the mall where I worked my job at the juice bar, and a whole table of girls from school could sit with me, unaware or uncaring that one chair was already taken. Sometimes, when this happened in actual life, I waited to see if someone from the group would speak to me, to ask for a napkin or suggest I move to another table. When no one did, when they ignored me completely, it was the strangest thing. I tried so hard to fit in with them that I blended in to the wall.

I make myself busy so I don't think about how things were

where we used to live. My great-grandfather's camera is ancient and weighs as much as a small child. It says Rolleiflex on the front and has two closed bug eyes, one on top of the other, a few random knobs, and a winding crank on the side. If you pop off the lens caps and peer into the hood on the top, you see a blurry square, like a windshield dirtied up with smashed gnats. That's what I see now when I look through—yet somehow it's even better than the hole in my veil. The photographs would come out square. The crystal-clear photos my phone takes would probably make these look like Civil War–era daguerreotypes.

The camera was left to my mother when her grandfather died, along with a lamp. He'd been a photographer, though not near the level he'd dreamed of reaching, and at some point he gave up the dream; he simply stopped. The camera was cursed with disappointment, my mother told me; when her grandfather retired, it sat on the shelf near his recliner, where he spent the last long decade of his life lording over the remotes and watching Turner Classics on TV. It watched him live out his last years. Then it went to our house, to watch his granddaughter, my mother. The lamp tipped over on the tile and shattered, but the camera stuck around, gathering dust. Now I have it in my lap, and I have the distinct feeling it's watching me.

When I try to wind the crank on the side—it's stuck, I've tried turning it every which way—I guess I'm thinking of this man I never met and never will, of how what one person does generations ago can ripple forward and catch the rest of us in its current. Something like that. In reality, he probably never even imagined me.

We have my great-grandfather's name. We've all got it, tacked on to our own names like it's a real last name from a real family. But in fact, our family name used to be Cohen. It was the name we had a century and an ocean ago, the name we carried with us on the boat to Ellis Island and spoke at the gate and settled with and had etched in our family books, before it was dropped, discarded, crossed out, written over. He chose to change it after the war. He wanted to be a photographer, in Hollywood. He wanted to assimilate, to blend in. He stopped paying his dues at the temple, and he went to the city clerk's office and reimagined himself as someone who didn't sound so Jewish. When he married, he gave his wife the last name Jonathan and his children the last name Jonathan, and my mother had it (lost it when she married, gained it back when she divorced), and now here I am, carrying the name like some kind of New World invention. Did he imagine that?

The man who used this camera wanted to hide. But I'm done hiding.

"Simone, are you getting out of the car or what?"

My mother doesn't wait for me to fully embrace my intention, which I am about to do and am in the process of making happen. She reaches over my body and shoves open the passenger-side door.

"You did this to yourself," she says. "Own it."

I step out of the car and stare out at the flea market. No resident of this town has ever laid eyes on me before this morning in traffic, since I slept straight through the arrival of the moving truck, then entered our new home flanked by cardboard boxes under cover of night. I spent the first series of days getting the lay of the land (aka the interior of our house—room lights, hallways, door creaks, window drafts). I ventured into the backyard, once. But now I've emerged. Even if my legs are a bit shaky.

"I'll pick you up in an hour," my mother says.

"Wait," I say, leaning back in. (Note: I have left the car, but I have not yet let go of the door, which is still open.) "Aren't you coming with me?"

She looks me up and down, makes some excuse about errands at the hardware store and the market, even though we're stocked up on almond milk and own three hammers, and then drives off with tires churning up gravel dust. My own mother is embarrassed to be seen with me. She peeled off so fast, she almost knocked me over.

With that, I gather myself together. I pull up my knee socks, arrange my veil, adjust my skirt, hitch up the camera on its worn leather strap, and imagine heading for the flea market as my newly minted, reinvented self.

* * *

I don't make it all the way. Not at first. Venturing out as a whole new person isn't so easy when you've got platform shoes on.

Before I reach the flea market (all I see are old antiques splayed out on tablecloths and a few people milling about—so ordinary), my new self has an uncomfortable itch she's got to take care of. She needs some privacy to do it. I'm behind a tree, safely shielded by the leaf covering, scratching at the folds of my skirt, when I catch sight of the table I want and home in on my destination. I lift the veil and steady the camera to scope it out. A tall black hood on the top of the camera's box offers a single eyehole out into the distance. I feel protected, looking through it, at ease in a way I haven't maybe ever felt. It's almost as if I'm supposed to take a photograph with it, as Pop Pop once did. My finger is on the shutter button. Right there. Where his was.

For a moment, a shadow gets in the way of the glass, and I think someone's stepped in front of me, purposefully blocking my way.

But when I wipe the lens, the shadow's gone. It was only a smudge.

The plan is simple: there are no pawnshops in this town my mother chose for us—there are touristy boutiques with fancy windows, and there are cozy shops with lots of decorative glassware, but there's nowhere to sell something used, and possibly cursed with disappointment. I'd done my research while I was letting the designs on my nails air-dry. Obviously I could just sell it online, but that could take too long. What if I got no bites? I found out there's a booth at the flea every Saturday, and time is ticking. School starts Tuesday. And maybe I needed the excuse to get out of the house. Maybe I know what's best for this sad, old camera as it knows for fresh, new me.

I spot the tables in the distance and start moving toward them. There's a big banner that says DEVINE BROTHERS USED PHOTOGRAPHIC (NO DIGITAL—THIS IS NOT AN APPLE STORE) EQUIPMENT.

"Hello, sirs," I say into my high collar, rehearsing my intro as I walk. "I'm new in town, and I've got something for you. What's your best offer?" I try the "hello, sirs" in different octaves, but each time it comes out tinny and artificial. My mother said I'm trying too hard. This whole thing sounded better in my head, the way my clothing concepts do before I open the jaws of the scissors. I'm almost there, and I'm tempted to turn back and hide behind the tree again, when I spot her on her island near the Devine Brothers' U-shaped bank of tables. I swear there was nothing there before. But now she is. Suddenly some random girl, completely out of place at the flea market. I have no worldly idea what she's doing here. She's not browsing. She's not haggling. She's out in the open under a yellow umbrella, not caring who sees her.

I check with my hand to be sure, but it's not raining.

Maybe she's one of the vendors, but she doesn't even have a table. She's on the ground on what looks to be a blue bedsheet. There are some white pieces of paper fluttering in the wind, sometimes coasting away, that she keeps trying to hold down without at the same time losing the umbrella. Is she selling something? Offering to tell fortunes? Is this some kind of performance?

No one at the flea market acknowledges she's even there, like she blends into the background.

But I see her. How could anyone mistake her for a piece of scenery or a pocket of air?

Back home I'd secured myself a group of a few friends. We dressed mostly alike, an unspoken uniform I kept to religiously. I'd go along with whatever they said, doing what they wanted to do, being where they wanted to be, but there were always moments when my real feelings and tastes leaked out. They'd turn to me all shocked when I admitted I didn't like the song they were playing on repeat, or wasn't following the sports team, or spent an entire weekend under the spell of a book. These weren't freakish things—I knew that, didn't I?—but sometimes they acted like I wanted to tattoo my face and join a coven.

I use the camera like a periscope. I turn the focus. Sharper, sharper, as sharp as I can get with this old thing. The girl is maybe my age, as far as I can tell. I hold the camera steady from where it hangs around my neck and over my heart. She's looking back. She's looking at where I am. She nods once, then returns to arranging her wares on her blanket. Now she's using rocks to hold everything down while the umbrella dangles in the gravel. There's still part of a field between us, and two portable toilets and a couple of trees, but she's found me. And she wants me to know it.

I go to the Devine Brothers' tables, ignoring her completely. The camera is straining my neck and knocking with the heft of a dumbbell against my rib cage. I saw on eBay that vintage cameras like this can go for three hundred dollars, but something tells me it's worth so much more. Thinking in a dollar amount feels wrong. Pop Pop died with this thing on his shelf, collecting dust. He never sold it.

The tables are spread with every kind of camera body, lens, filter, wire, and other nameless items to the point of pure chaos. Nothing is new, and nothing has a price on it. I'm their only customer, and you'd think they'd be more welcoming, but instead, one of the Devine Brothers flinches at the sight of me. I forgot for a moment that I'm wearing this outfit.

"It's one of them," he says out of the side of his mouth. "Looks like she's got lots of pockets."

"Go play with the rest of your weird friends," the other brother says, waving off into the distance. "If we see you even think of shoplifting, we'll call security." He has a beard, which makes me decide he cannot be trusted.

"I think she's going to stun us or decapitate us with that hat." The other, beardless brother has an odd-shaped grin.

It takes a moment to comprehend that they were serious at first, and a whole bunch of signs decry shoplifting and promise prosecution, which I guess is meant for the teenagers of this town, but now they're making fun of me. Don't they see the camera in my hands? Then I realize my veil had it concealed, trying to swallow it up. I part the netting to allow the camera's double-snouted nose to come out. I hold it up.

"Aha," says one of the brothers.

Now they're interested. *Now* they want me to stay.

I clench the camera in my two hands, and it warms to the exact temperature of my body, as if it's gotten used to me already. There's something about it that feels exceptionally right, a familiarity in my fingers that makes me forget for a moment why I've come here. I'm remembering a photograph of Pop Pop—my mother had it in a frame. He had dark eyes and dark hair, like mine, but that's not the thing I'm remembering. I'm remembering that he had a certain set to his face, an expressive scowl, which was something people always pointed out on me.

Why don't you smile more, Simone?

You look like hell froze over, Simone.

She can't help it. She always looks like that.

Why was I only now realizing that this man I'd never met—but whose name I carried—and I shared the same scowl, as if a photograph of him was pressed flat over my face? And that no matter how hard I tried, I always stood out, always looked different, never fit in, not ever, not there, and not here?

I wish I could've met him.

"Is there a reason you're pointing that Rollei at us or what?" one of the brothers asks.

I segue awkwardly. "I'm wondering how much you'd pay for this, if I wanted to sell it. . . ."

"Speak up." That's another thing people say about me: I always talk too soft. My mother used to say that Pop Pop didn't talk much. He'd sit on his recliner with his three different remotes on the table beside him whenever she visited. He barely left the TV room.

I repeat myself, a cloud of self-consciousness descending.

"*Do* you want to sell it?"

I mean to say I do, yes, that's why I'm here, but instead I go, "I possibly maybe might." The lines I practiced drop into the dust.

"Give it here. Is the lens scratched? We're not paying for a dud." The beardless brother has his hands out, and so does the other brother. They both want to inspect it, and yet here I am, with the leather strap still wedged in place on my neck. The strap cuts a deep groove into the skin above my shoulders, and it would be easy to let the camera go, easy to let them take it. I'd feel lighter. My mother wants it gone. She said get rid of it. And yet.

I shouldn't be doing this—I shouldn't. But who here will stop me?

Here is a story I heard about my great-grandfather, who was once named Jonathan Cohen: He bought his first camera at the age of sixteen (the age I'm weeks from turning in this new town), and he bought it used, with money that he was supposed to save for books at school. When his father found out, he was told to return it immediately, and instead Jonathan left home and rode the bus. It was a double-decker, and he sat up top. He rode the bus up Fifth Avenue and down, and to prove to his father the camera was worth something, and his future could be of his own making, he took pictures all the way, carefully composing each one, since there were only a precious twelve frames on the roll of film. It was only when they were developed, months later, that he saw they were blobs and streaks and blurs. This would have been the 1930s, the years leading up to the war. My family was safe in New York City then, arguing over cameras and art school. And still he came to think he needed to hide, that in order to get a job, he needed a new name, one that sounded more American, safer, less weird, and washed away who he really was. Is that even a story worth telling? Could it be the same camera? Why does it matter so much that I could have another name?

The camera's heavy bottom is growing warm. It brims with heated electricity inside like a motor revving. Probably it's from being out in the sun, just like my whole body is close to overheating inside the dark getup, under the knee socks, under the hat, inside the lace gloves.

From the corner of my eye, a flash of yellow. I get a sense that someone in particular is observing me and listening to every word. I feel sure, the way my great-grandfather may have felt so sure he was taking beautiful, memorable photographs of the moving city beneath his feet, and he came away with nothing.

It's here that someone comes up to browse the telephoto lenses and the brothers give up on me, distracted by a possible sale. I could lift the strap over my neck and plop the contraption down on the folding table and call them back over. But something's pulling my attention.

The girl. She's waving her yellow umbrella at me.

She's surrounded by a circle of black-and-white photographs that she's successfully kept from the wind with well-placed rocks, some still muddy from the nearby creek bed. I try not to look at the singular white line of her part, because it's crooked, I suspect on purpose, and I also suspect she's the kind of person who *wants* you to notice and *wants* you to comment on it and I would not.

Still, I step closer.

"You can sit," she says. "I'm Goldie, by the way. You can visit for as long as you like."

"I'm Simone," I mumble. There's nowhere to sit, and I shuffle on my feet for a moment, fiddling with one drooping sock.

"Just move Molly Picon. Or let Anna Sokolow and Gertrude Weil snuggle up, though I usually like to keep the Gertrudes together. No, no, don't move Emma Goldman—she's my favorite, and I always want her up front, in the middle."

I sit in her circle, taking the place of one of the black-and-white faces from her collection. The names are all handwritten on the photographs as well as a year and what each woman—they're all women, I notice—offered up to the world.

Dancer/choreographer. Actress/entertainer. Activist. Anarchist/writer. Athlete. Biochemist. I've never heard of any of them.

Besides, who's she? I give her the once-over my mother gave me, and I come back with a waterfall of colors—bright ones, worthy ones, rainbows from here to the clouds and nothing bland. She's got rosy cheeks, long hair that doesn't care it needs a comb, long limbs that take up space, and an air of confidence I wish I could bottle and take sips from on Tuesday. Instead, I focus on her photographs. I pretend she's not as impressive as she is and that I want to compliment her on her choice of expression.

"Are these for sale?" I ask.

"Do you want one?" She lifts up Bobbie Rosenfeld and Gertrude Elion, one in each hand. "Five cents or free, depending on if you've got five cents. I don't make change."

"You sell pictures of random people for five cents each?"

"Not exactly. I've never sold one, not all summer. I come to the flea every Saturday, but I guess I'm just sitting here while my parents keep an eye on things over there." She points, vaguely, in the direction of a gaggle of adults.

"And they're not random," she adds. "These are Jewish heroines. I like to think of our history. What we were known for—the good things. The great things. What we've done."

"So these aren't people you know?" I ask. I figured they were family members. Great-aunts. Second and third cousins. Great-great-grandmothers, maybe.

She laughs. "Not all Jews know each other, you know."

I peer at Molly Picon.

"The great comedienne of Yiddish theater," Goldie tells me. "Molly was world-famous, I mean all over the globe. Did you know she made the very last movie in Yiddish in Poland before the Holocaust?"

I didn't know that. In her photo she wears a jaunty beret and has big dark eyes. My own eyes drift to Goldie's expressed favorite, Emma Goldman, anarchist and writer, who wears glasses perched on the bridge of her nose and a thoughtful expression.

"Emma! Oh, Emma used to speak to giant crowds—everyone, and I mean everyone, would come out to hear her—a true feminist who believed in equality for all people; that's what anarchism is. Emma once said, 'I'd rather have roses on my table than diamonds on my neck.' Isn't that beautiful, and important, too?"

I nod. It made me think of what was important—truly important—to me. I was so focused on the outside, I wasn't yet sure what my inside self wanted.

"You're new in town," Goldie says, not in the form of a question. "I'd remember if I saw you before. How could anyone forget?"

This is the best compliment I've had all morning. "Do you mind?" I lift the heavy, hot camera off my neck. I have to remove the hat to get the camera off, and there's a bit of a wrestling match with the veil, but finally I'm able to set it all on the ground.

Goldie makes no comment about my awkwardness. "Who's that man you were with?" she says. "He was just here. Where'd he go?"

"Who, them?" The Devine brothers are studiously ignoring me now. "I don't know either of them."

Suddenly I lean forward over her photos (Ruth Westheimer, sex therapist; Birdie Amsterdam, state supreme court justice), and I offer something I haven't offered before. "I'm Jewish too," I say. Then I add, self-consciously, "Kinda."

I look down. The camera has gone quiet, as if there's a recording device inside or an actual listening ear.

"What do you mean, kinda?"

"My mother is. I'm half."

"Then you just are," she says with a shrug. "It's not that complicated." Here is another thing in my old school, my old life: I wasn't much of anything there. Maybe that was part of what made me so uncertain, so malleable and able to disappear into the walls. Maybe I need to choose the things I want to be, and only then can I come into the light.

"You can't sell that, you know," Goldie says, indicating the camera. "I don't even need to know where it's from, but obviously you need to keep it."

"Miss," one of the brothers is calling. "Miss."

"They don't mean me," Goldie says.

I look up, but the sun's in my eyes, and it's the way it felt when I couldn't see who I was anymore when I looked in a mirror. When I was trying too hard to be someone I was not. When I went along with what everyone else said. I may have the same name, but I'm turning different now, outside and in. These guys who might want to actually buy my great-grandfather's camera don't know a thing about it, and it's not for me to explain.

"I changed my mind," I tell them.

"Let's take a look," one of the brothers says.

"I *said*"—and that comes out in my new loud voice—"I changed my mind."

Goldie clucks her tongue, I think in appreciation. The brothers shrug—they didn't care anyway. I'm the one who cares. I should have cared from the beginning.

"There's film in here," Goldie says. She shakes it, but it doesn't rattle. Still, she puts her ear to it and closes her eyes. Then she nods. "There's room on the roll."

"You can't tell just by listening," I say.

She guffaws. Her teeth are crooked, I notice for the first time, and she doesn't even bother to hide them. "Of course not. Film doesn't tick. If I open the back, the sun'll destroy the last pictures your pop ever took."

"Pop Pop," I correct her. "That's what my mom called him. I never met him."

She's putting her eye to the hole in the hood when it occurs to me. She's seeing through it, finger poised on the shutter button, as I think it.

Did I even tell her about Pop Pop? Did the words "pop" or "pop pop" ever cross my lips?

She winds the crank and then says, "It's ready. Look just like you're looking. You're perfect."

"Wait!" I say. I lift the hat with the hanging veil and position it back on my head. It may be hot out, stifling even, and I may look like something out of a monster movie, but there's also this cool, tingly sensation as I don it and embrace being fully myself. Or at least the self I am here and now, this moment, in time for Tuesday.

I smile, wide. The hole in the veil shows I'm smiling with all I've got.

When she clicks the shutter button, I see the spiral of the eye close. It takes a few seconds. But also it takes a year. It takes a hundred years. It takes me back to where I came from, and it tells me who I might have been or at least who I was. I don't want to blend in. I want to be bright.

The shutter snaps, and Goldie replaces the caps on the lenses and offers the camera back to me. "He was right there watching," she says in a low voice, "but I guess he went off to the car or something. I think he wanted me to tell you that."

She's squinting into the distance, using her hand to shield her face from the sun, instead of the umbrella.

Something comes over me, a cold streak up my spine even under all the dark fabric I'm wearing.

He who?

He wanted to tell me . . . what?

Quickly I turn and look off into the distance, toward the portable toilets and the stretch of field and the trees.

"He waved," Goldie says. "I dunno. Maybe that means he'll come back to get you later? Was he your ride home?"

I shake my head. I don't really have words for it, only questions. "I have a ride," I tell her.

"Great," she says, and then proceeds to tell me about every one of the heroines on her blue blanket. She's only getting started with her collection. While she talks, I hold the camera close and wonder about the twelve frames inside. If any are of him, and if the film hasn't been destroyed by the years; if I might see something there, something recognizable of my family, of my future self. For me, it's so easy. I can be myself out in the world, I can say who I am, and I can use my whole name when I do. I have to remember there was a time when not everyone in my family felt they could.

Fear is such a funny thing. When it flies away into the sky over the flea market, it looks like a blurry smudge on glass for a moment. Then I blink, and it's gone.

I don't remove my outrageous hat that'll make me stand out in any crowd. I keep it on for the whole rest of the day. I keep it on until the sun goes down and the veil shimmers and gleams in the moonlight.

* * *

Weeks later, on another Saturday, held down on the blue blanket (really and actually a bedsheet meant for Goldie's bed) and kept in place with two fresh, smooth river stones, lovingly arranged, is a new photo to take its place among Goldie's collection of Jewish heroines. Written at the bottom of the photo, it says:

Simone Jonathan (Cohen), 2019

She says it counts as a part of her collection, even if I'm "kinda" Jewish and even if I haven't done the thing that makes me a heroine to the world yet, or figured myself out by now, or talked to more than a few people at my new school, apart from her. She says my face and name are enough for now—and besides, we've both got time.

ACKNOWLEDGMENTS

We are incredibly grateful to bring this anthology into the world, to bring fourteen different stories about Jewish life into the mainstream, and to bring together fifteen contributors (including ourselves) from varying backgrounds. But we couldn't have done it alone. Thank you to Karen Greenberg and the entire Knopf team for believing in this anthology and pulling it all together behind the scenes. Thank you to our agents, Jim McCarthy and Louise Fury, for making this dream happen.

We are also grateful to have such an incredible list of contributors. Our authors worked on tight deadlines, answered what felt like a million emails, and, most importantly, shared their experiences and stories with us. We had a vision of what this anthology would be, but the end result surpassed even our greatest hope. These stories make us laugh and cry, and we hope our readers will experience the same wonderful emotions.

Laura would like to acknowledge her parents, who brought her up in a supportive and vibrant Jewish community. She is immensely grateful for every b'nai mitzvah party drop-off and pickup, for every Jewish youth group traveling fee, and especially for every bowl of matzo ball soup. She would also like to thank Congregation Etz Chaim and her rabbis, from both past and present: Rabbi Shalom Lewis, Rabbi Paul Kerbel, and Rabbi Dan Dorsch.

Katherine would like to acknowledge her family and all their support, not just for this book but always. She'd especially like to thank her mom for all the schlepping she did back and forth from synagogue—the super-supportive, kind mom in *Some Days You're the Sidekick; Some Days You're the Hero* is for you. She'd also like to thank Rabbi Yair Robinson, Marisa Robinson, Rabbi Elisa Koppel, and Congregation Beth Emeth for their support, wisdom, and teaching. She'd like to thank Congregation Rodeph Shalom for being a welcoming new home.

And, most importantly, we are grateful to our readers. Thank you for picking up this book. Whether or not you are Jewish, we hope you connected to these stories; we hope you found something that brought you joy, or made you think, or made you believe.

Thank you for reading.

CONTRIBUTOR BIOS

Dahlia Adler is an associate editor of mathematics by day, a blogger for B&N Teens, *LGBTQ Reads,* and *Frolic* by night, and an author of young adult and new adult novels at every spare moment in between. Her books include the Daylight Falls duology, *Just Visiting,* and the Radleigh University trilogy. Her short stories can be found in the anthologies *The Radical Element, All Out,* and *His Hideous Heart,* the latter of which she also edited. Dahlia lives in New York with her husband, son, and an obscene amount of books. She can be found on Twitter and Instagram at @MissDahlELama or at dahliaadler.com.

Adi Alsaid is the author of several young adult novels, including *Let's Get Lost, Never Always Sometimes,* and *North of Happy.* He was born and raised in Mexico City. He can be found online at AdiAlsaid.com.

Mayim Bialik is best known as Amy Farrah Fowler on America's #1 comedy, *The Big Bang Theory,* a role for which she has received four Emmy nominations and two Critics' Choice Award nominations, in addition to two Critics' Choice Awards. She also starred in the early-1990s sitcom *Blossom.* Mayim earned a BS from UCLA in neuroscience and Hebrew and Jewish studies, and she went on to earn a PhD from UCLA in neuroscience. She is the author of the #1 *New York Times* bestseller *Girling Up,* as well as *Boying Up, Beyond the Sling,* and *Mayim's Vegan Table.*

David Levithan is the author of numerous young adult novels. Some he writes by himself, like *Boy Meets Boy, Every Day, Two Boys Kissing,* and, most recently, *Someday.* He also writes books with other people, including five with Rachel Cohn (*Nick & Norah's Infinite Playlist* being the first), one with John Green (*Will Grayson, Will Grayson*), one with Andrea Cremer (*Invisibility*), and one with Nina LaCour (*You Know Me Well*). You can find more about him at davidlevithan.com.

Elie Lichtschein is a writer and producer based in New York City. His work has been published by PJ Library and can be found on *The Other Stories* podcast. He is currently developing a children's audio horror series with WGBH.

Katherine Locke is the author of *The Girl with the Red Balloon* (a Sydney Taylor Honor Book) and *The Spy with the Red Balloon.* They are a contributor to *Unbroken: 13 Stories Starring Disabled Teens.* They live and write in Philadelphia with their demanding feline overlords and secretly believe most stories are fairy tales in disguise. They can be found online at @Bibliogato and at katherinelockebooks.com.

Alex London, a 2009 finalist for the National Jewish Book Award, is the author of twenty-five books for adults, teens, and children. *Black Wings Beating,* his latest young adult novel, was an NBC *Today Show* Pick, a *Kirkus* Best YA Fantasy Book of the Year, and a We Need Diverse Books Must-Read. His young adult debut, *Proxy,* was an ALA Top Ten Quick Pick for Reluctant Young Adult Readers and a Best Fiction for Young Adults selection. He's been a journalist reporting from conflict zones and refugee camps, a young adult librarian, and a snorkel salesman. Alex lives with his husband, daughter, and dog in Philadelphia. You can find him online at calexanderlondon.com.

Goldy Moldavsky is the *New York Times* bestselling author of *Kill the Boy Band* and *No Good Deed.* She was born in Lima, Peru, and grew up in Brooklyn, where she still lives. Her perfect Shabbos includes family + friends + board games. She can be found online at goldymoldavsky.com.

Hannah Moskowitz is the author of over a dozen works for children and young adults, including 2013 Stonewall Honor Book *Gone, Gone, Gone* and 2013 Bisexual YA Book of the Year *Not Otherwise Specified.* Her first book, *Break,* was published when she was a senior in high school. She lives in Maryland. She hopes. She can be found on Twitter at @hannahmosk.

Matthue Roth is an editor at Hevria.com and a writer at Google. His work has appeared in *Tin House* and *Ploughshares,* where he was short-listed for the Best American Short Stories 2018. He also adapted the works of Franz Kafka into a picture book, which was called "eerie and imaginative" by the *New Yorker.* He keeps a secret diary at matthue.com.

Lance Rubin is the author of *Denton Little's Deathdate* and *Denton Little's Still Not Dead.* He's worked as an actor and written sketch comedy, including successful runs of *The Lance and Ray Show* at the Upright Citizens Brigade Theatre in New York City. He's also co-written a new musical called *Broadway Bounty Hunter.* Lance lives in Brooklyn with his wife and son. You can follow him online at lancerubin.com and on Twitter at @lancerubinparty.

Dana Schwartz is the author of the young adult novel *And We're Off* and the memoir *Choose Your Own Disaster.* She is currently based in Los Angeles. She can be found online at @DanaSchwartzzz on Twitter and at danaschwartzdotcom.com.

Laura Silverman earned her MFA in creative writing from the New School. She is the author of *Girl Out of Water* and *You Asked for Perfect*. She currently lives in Brooklyn. You can reach out on Twitter at @LJSilverman1 or through her website at laurasilvermanwrites.com.

Rachel Lynn Solomon writes, tap-dances, and collects red lipstick in Seattle. She is the author of the young adult novels *You'll Miss Me When I'm Gone* and *Our Year of Maybe.* You can find her online at rachelsolomonbooks.com and on Twitter at @rlynn_solomon.

Nova Ren Suma is the author of *A Room Away from the Wolves* and the #1 *New York Times* bestselling *The Walls Around Us*. She also wrote *Imaginary Girls* and *17 & Gone* and is co-creator of *FORESHADOW: A Serial YA Anthology*. She has an MFA in fiction from Columbia University and teaches at Vermont College of Fine Arts. She grew up in the Hudson Valley, spent most of her adult life in New York City, and now lives in Philadelphia. Find her online at novaren.com.